Ruins of
Civility

Also by James Bradberry

The Seventh Sacrament

Ruins of Civility

A Jamie Ramsgill Mystery

James Bradberry

St. Martin's Press New York

Library of Congress Cataloging-in-Publication Data

Bradberry, James.
    Ruins of civility / by James Bradberry.
      p.   cm.
    ISBN 0-312-14041-X
    1. Americans—Travel—England—Cambridge—Fiction. 2. College teachers—United States—Fiction. 3. Architects—United States—Fiction. I. Title.
PS3552.R2127R85   1996
813'.54—dc20   95-26252
                                                        CIP

First Edition: July 1996

10 9 8 7 6 5 4 3 2 1

For Butch and Buck

The author would like to thank the following for their assistance: DCI David Beck (formerly of the Cambridge Constabulary) for his tireless answers to my queries; Richard Muenow, forensics engineer, for advice on non-invasive structural testing; Mrs. Gill Hearvey-Murray for help with Queens' College; J. D. Salmon and Ashley Minihan for initial legwork in Cambridge; J. C. Rose for advice on computer minutiae; John Hunter for Anglotrivia; Bob Nissenbaum and David Braly for help with the manuscript; Dimitri Contostavalos for medical advice; Captain John Franklin and the Fulbright Commission, London, for supporting my study in England; Keith Kahla, Blanche Schlessinger, and my wife Nancy for unwavering support; and Guy Newsham, for more help than a friend has a right to expect.

Author's Note

Cambridge University as an institution, of course, exists. Queens', Darwin, and Trinity Colleges do also, though Trinity, to my knowledge has no plans for construction on the west bank of the River Cam. Smithson College is fictitious, as are all characters in the book. Any resemblance to actual people is coincidental.

At the sight of a ruin, reflections on change, the decay, and the desolation of before, naturally occur; and they introduce a long succession of others, all tinctured with that melancholy which these have inspired.

—THOMAS WHATELY, 1770

Queens' College

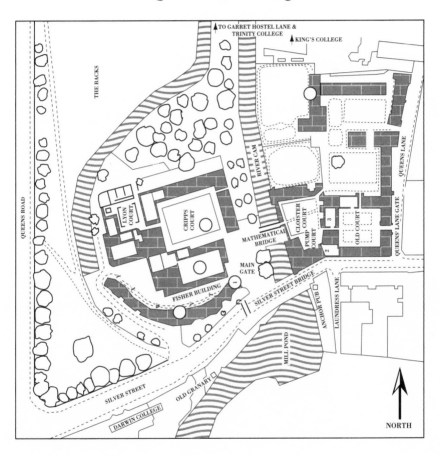

1. Porters' Lodge
2. Old Kitchens
3. Old Hall

Ruins of
Civility

Prologue

*I*t was the figure of a body lying in the bottom of the punt that first made Dennis Fortthompson think he was truly drunk.

Fortthompson had gotten off duty as night porter of Smithson College, Cambridge, forty-five minutes earlier and, as was his custom, had downed three Gold Star Barley wines at the college bar. He had then cycled the half mile to the bridge, before stopping at its base to dismount. At his age, sixty-three, Fortthompson knew it would be better to walk his bicycle up Garret Hostel Lane Bridge, than to be caught halfway when his left leg would certainly give out. It was a ritual he had performed many times before. Six nights a week for the past seventeen years he had followed this route. It offered a shortcut through the maze of colleges that made up the ancient University of Cambridge, a course that took him from Smithson over to the east edge of the university, where he would cycle down Mill Road to his tiny terraced house in the Romsey Town section of the city.

Pausing at the pedestrian bridge's base, he looked ahead of him to the lane on the other side of the narrow river. Crystals of frozen mist danced slowly under the street lamps, and he could see a glint of reflection as ice formed on the bridge's metal guardrails. To the right, beyond the bridge, he could just make out Trinity Hall, and next to it on the same side of the lane, Clare College. Clare, in silence, with its classical façade of Bath stone, pedimented windows (most of them dark, as it was a half hour past midnight), and a three-story order of soft Ionic pilasters. And Trinity Hall, not to be confused with the more famous Trinity on the other side of the lane, but one long and slender Gothic building that slinked its way right up to the riverbank, its dark, parapeted end gable a black geometrical silhouette against the sky. Across the lane on the left lay the vast stillness of Trinity itself, with its faintly lit windows peeking through the leafless willow boughs. The college stretched from the great shadowy quadrangle of New Court to the famous library by Christopher Wren at the bend in the river beyond.

He pushed the bicycle forward, his legs unsteady and his mind numb from cold and drink. At the top of the bridge he stopped again. Suddenly, upriver in the direction of King's College, he thought he saw something moving toward him. It appeared to be a punt, and surprised by its presence, he removed his wire-frame glasses to wipe them. Fortthompson had seen punts on the river at all hours, in all seasons, and in all manner of weather. It wouldn't have surprised him if some young lads, undergraduates perhaps, or the lager louts from town, had braved a bitter January evening for an hour of frolic in a flat-bottomed boat. But it wasn't young people he thought he saw. It was an elderly gentleman, spare of frame, lying faceup on the floorboards of the punt.

The boat disappeared beneath the bridge, and Fortthompson, slow to react, returned his glasses to his nose. Then, as if forgetting about the punt, he pulled a cigarette from his jacket pocket and fumbled to light it. He propped the bicycle against his wide waistline and reached down to massage his thigh. As always the cold brought a dull throb to his leg.

"Bugger," he groused at the pain.

He took a drag on his cigarette, then exhaled.

Now on the other side of the bridge, the boat reappeared. It had to be a boat, thought Fortthompson, certainly it was real. He dropped his bicycle to the pavement. A paper sack full of apples broke open in his wicker basket, and several bounced out and rolled down the incline of the bridge. Fortthompson hardly noticed, though, as he staggered for the north side of the span, looking down toward the dark water. The boat emerged from beneath the bridge in complete silence, skimming ahead in the calm water like a toy. He could see the man in the bottom of the boat from another angle, and for an instant he thought he recognized the face. He could also see a second person standing in the stern of the boat, propelling it silently with a long pole.

Fortthompson gripped the cold bridge railing and leaned forward to get a closer view. The man in the bottom of the boat was motionless, and appeared to be tied up at the waist and feet. For a brief moment, Fortthompson got a glimpse of him and could make out his features. He appeared slight, and was dressed only in shirtsleeves. He had exuberant white hair, teased up above his attenuated forehead. The jowls of his somewhat gaunt face sagged under their own weight. His eyes rested in deep pockets, and they were closed as if he were asleep. He gave no indication that the night's temperature caused him any concern.

For a moment Fortthompson thought of calling out to him, to see if he needed help. But he found himself paralyzed, unable to speak, unsure of what to say. He was confused and disoriented, and he wasn't sure the whole episode hadn't been a dream. He looked around him to see if anyone else had seen the boat. But the bridge was empty. So too was Garret Hostel Lane.

He stood upright, feeling not unlike a sailboat buffeted by wind. The swirling consciousness that in younger drinking days had felt like a violin sonata was now a protest, a portending threat to his body, a rejection that was sure to come. By the time he composed himself and again looked down to the water, the punt was gone.

He stood still for a moment, then turned his attention back to the bicycle. He could see the dispersion of apples strewn along the course of the bridge like an abandoned game of bowls. He wondered how they had gotten there. He tossed the butt of his cigarette over the side of the bridge and limped back to its center. When he had gathered enough of the apples to fill his hands, he raised the bicycle up by its handlebars, stuffing the fruit into the basket.

Pulling up the collar to his jacket, he mounted the bicycle and set off down the bridge, wobbling until he picked up speed. The whir of the generator lamp was the only sound to break the silence, and the light cast by the lamp peaked and dimmed with every push of the pedals. He weaved slowly down the lane. At its end, he turned right into Trinity Lane, wondering if Lillian would be waiting up for him. It suddenly occurred to him that his wife wouldn't tolerate bruised apples any more than she tolerated his drinking. If he was lucky, she would be asleep. That would allow him to avoid another one of their arguments.

It would also allow him to pluck a couple more Gold Stars from the refrigerator to finish off the night, and consider whether the punt he had seen on the river had been real.

One

Fiona Mallow made a bid to cross Trumpington Street, through a narrow gap in the thick Tuesday morning traffic, which at five minutes of ten posed a greater threat of being run over by an undergraduate's bicycle than by a car. As she ran, she balanced a large, white foam cup of cafe latte in her left hand and a cheese brioche in her right. She was a tall, middle-aged woman with thick, bobbed auburn hair, an attractive and energetic face, and a figure that even the students envied. She moved easily through the steady stream of traffic as if she had practiced the maneuver before, which she did almost every day.

She reached the west side of the street and hopped the granite curb to the sidewalk in front of Scroope Terrace, a collection of handsome and well-kept Georgian townhouses that served as the Faculty of Art and Architecture. She narrowly avoided a young Oscar Wilde look-alike in baggy umber trousers and a long wool overcoat, an undergraduate, who was wheeling his decrepit black three-speed up to the wrought-iron fence in front of the school, where scores of other bicycles were piled upon one another like jackstraws.

Fiona passed through an opening in the fence and made her way up to the front porch of the school.

"Fiona?" came a voice from behind her and to the right. "Not going to say hello? Or is the fact that you're out without a coat on this most bitter morning of an already dreadful winter simply a sign that you've taken leave of your senses?"

Fiona turned to see Cheverton Beggs in the small front yard of the school. He was hunched over his bicycle, on the opposite side of the wrought-iron fence, and was locking it to the fence. It was not a clunker like the others, but rather like Beggs's own attire: expensive and pristine. The bicycle looked as though it had never been ridden. Fiona watched as he struggled to secure the lock, bringing a most unnatural scowl to his face.

At forty-one, Beggs was ensconced in the Cantabrigian academic utopia, a Fellow at Pembroke College, Lecturer of Art and Architectural History, and son of the late Sir Seymour Beggs, author of the famous trilogy on the painters Piero della Francesca, Mantegna, and Uccello. He lived with his elderly mother on the family estate in nearby Grantchester, amid famous Renaissance paintings acquired by his great-grandfather and with 150 acres of gardens laid out in naturalized robustness by Gertrude Jekyll. Cheverton Beggs's rise to his current position was inevitable, if not completely deserved, as he had been trained at Harrow, and then briefly in computer sciences at Essex, before switching to history of art at Cambridge. He then did a stint at the Courtald and three years (which his father had arranged for him) at the Ufizzi in Florence before returning to Cambridge four years ago. Though Fiona found him pleasant, there were others in the school, particularly Rainer Gräss, who felt that Beggs's only attribute as an art historian was his famous last name.

Beggs finished locking his bicycle. The scowl left his face, replaced by a look of consternation, for in his fastidious world the thought of Fiona's being without a coat made him shudder. He had a patrician face, with sharp features and a prominent brow. He wore small tortoiseshell eyeglasses that enlarged his slate-gray eyes, above which eyebrows of rich coffee brown matched the tight brown curls of his hair. Though most of the cyclists rushing up to Scroope Terrace showed signs of fatigue, Beggs looked unwinded. He had, in fact, not cycled the three miles from Grantchester but, as was his custom, had driven his Bentley to Pembroke, where he kept his bicycle, and from there pedaled the quarter mile to Scroope Terrace, looking the part of the dowdy professor.

"Just popped over to Greenway's for a coffee," Fiona said, as Beggs followed her up the steps to the front door of the school. "No need for a coat, Chev."

"Right," he muttered, following her through a heavy walnut door into a tall whitewashed hall bustling with students. "I could do with a spot of coffee myself . . . after last evening's festivities."

Beggs referred to the retirement party held for Rainer Gräss, supervisor of the Ph.D. program in architectural history and theory, held the prior evening in the Old Hall of Queens' College. The party was a small affair, attended only by Gräss's students and a few of the faculty, a mere warm-up for the more elaborate parties that would surely come at the end of the term. It had lasted until well after one in the morning. Beggs, not much of a drinker and even less someone who lets caution fly to the wind, had, by the end of the evening, let himself go; three glasses of wine to silently celebrate Gräss's removal from the faculty and he was now paying for his sins.

"I've just made a fresh pot," Fiona said as the two entered the ground-floor offices of the Department of Architecture, where Fiona worked as administrator. She made her way behind a long oak counter and to a desk stacked high with photocopies, the Lent term course roster that she was in the midst of collating. She popped the lid to her coffee and went back to work, sorting papers with machinelike speed, while taking intermittent bites of her roll. It was generally accepted within the school that were it not for Fiona's energy (celebrated dons and chaired professors notwithstanding), the school would go down like the *Titanic*.

Beggs checked his pigeonhole for mail before making his way to the drip coffeemaker. Fiona kept the pot full but bought her own coffee across the street because she was unable to stomach the lesser blend from Sainsbury's that the department supplied.

"By the way," Fiona said, "you haven't seen Rainer this morning, have you? Jamie Ramsgill just rang me up. He's at Heathrow and Rainer was supposed to have picked him up . . . but he didn't show."

Beggs finished pouring and set down his cup.

"Who's Jamie Ramsgill?" he asked.

Fiona's gaze rose. Beggs was just now taking off his camel-hair overcoat, revealing his attire. Today he was wearing a well-tailored midnight blue double-breasted suit, the breast pocket of which was stuffed with a scarlet silk handkerchief that matched his necktie.

"What'd you say?" she asked, his dress having turned her attention away from the question.

"Who's this chap Ramsgill?" Beggs repeated.

Fiona looked at him in disbelief. She found it hard to believe that Beggs didn't know Ramsgill, who, besides being a well-known academic in Beggs's own field, was an alumnus of the department. She was sure they had met on one of Ramsgill's prior visits.

"You know," she said. "The American, from Princeton. He's going to be here for a fortnight."

"Oh. The chap that just published the translation of Vitruvius. Rather notable all of a sudden, isn't he?"

Fiona sensed a hint of jealousy. For someone in his position, Beggs possessed a publishing record that could only be described as minor. His work was predictable, and had never been taken seriously by the critics. His latest hopes were pinned on a soon-to-be-published book on the cult of ruins in eighteenth-century painting and architecture.

"Yes, him. But have you seen Rainer?" she pursued.

"No. Probably sleeping in. He was quite pissed last night."

"But his car's in the car park," she said.

"Someone drove him home, I imagine. He wouldn't have driven in his condition. In fact, he left his coat and briefcase at the party, which my man Cox will bring round later."

"I telephoned Rainer's cottage to check on him," she said. "But Ghislaine said that he'd not come home. You don't think . . . ?"

Beggs took a loud sip of coffee from a mug emblazoned with the Pembroke crest. His eyes moved across to Fiona's, and the two of them shared a corroborative look.

"Has *she* been in this morning?" asked Beggs.

Fiona stopped collating. Her gaze drifted out the window to a dull, blank winter sky, stagnant gray with the vestiges of an early-morning fog that hung about the eaves and parapets of the engineering school next door. The *she* referred to by Beggs was Amy Denster, a Ph.D. candidate and scholarship student in the department, with whom it was generally known that Rainer Gräss was having an affair. Fiona felt a tinge of embarrassment at even thinking about the affair. Embarrassed for Gräss, at least twice Amy's age. Embarrassed for Amy, a likable young girl but without a clue of what she was risking by involving herself with her tutor. But mostly embarrassed for the department itself, for which Fiona felt a personal responsibility that scandal was somehow festering beneath its institutional skin.

Just then the door to the office burst open and Iain Frontis hurried in, slamming the door behind him. Fiona winced as the door's translucent window rattled in its frame. She looked up just in time to see the Frontis glare staring down at her. He said nothing, but instead turned and made his way directly to the pigeonholes. He reached in and dug out the pile of papers that perpetually occupied his box. She knew that he would thumb through the first two or three pieces of new mail, but once he came upon those that had been in the box for weeks, if not months, he would stuff the whole lot back in.

He did.

"Good morning, Iain," said Beggs, now leaning against a windowsill and sipping his coffee.

Frontis gave Beggs a halfhearted grunt, then turned back to his pigeonhole to retrieve the papers. He would rather sort through his old mail than engage in conversation with Cheverton Beggs.

"Rough night, eh?"

Frontis said nothing.

"So Rainer's decided not to pack it in after all. Well, well."

Frontis's head rose and he turned to Beggs. He looked like a man who had been hit by a lorry.

"What are you talking about, Chev?" asked Fiona.

"Exactly as I said," Beggs replied. "Rainer's not retiring. Oh, that's right . . . you left the party early, didn't you, Fiona? Well, you missed the fireworks. After you left, Rainer announced with great fanfare that he had changed his mind, that he's decided to stay on for a few more years."

"He didn't. . . ." Fiona said.

Fiona looked to Frontis in disbelief. Although he was junior faculty and somewhat of an eccentric, she couldn't believe that Rainer would do this to him. Frontis had paid his dues with the department. She could still remember the first day he arrived at the school from Edinburgh on a research fellowship. Young and idealistic, he was willing to do anything to secure a teaching position. He just sort of hung around, soaking in the atmosphere, hanging on to Gräss's coattails long after his fellowship expired.

Not that he wasn't qualified. It was just that the department was small and prestigious, and not many positions came open. He eventually made instructor, teaching part time in the Diploma program, as well as helping Gräss with M.Phil. and Ph.D. supervisions. His star seemed to be on the rise until nine months ago, when, as a result of the government cutbacks in university funding, he found that his position was being eliminated, and he with it. The irony was that all of this had taken place during a period when Frontis had received unexpected renown. He had won an international design competition to be architect for the National Assembly in Singapore, a coup for an obscure forty-year-old professor. Suddenly the department was being flooded with applications from students who wanted to come to Cambridge to study with Frontis, whose bold and unique design philosophy had captured the imagination of an entire generation of young would-be architects. Thus Frontis was both a beneficiary and a victim of the great anachronistic gulch that exists between architectural academia and practice, but the ultrahot young turk was unable to hold on to his academic position because of events already set in motion. Given the circumstances, Gräss, who had been contemplating retirement anyway, had agreed to step aside and let Frontis take his position on the faculty. At least it had appeared that way.

Frontis looked at Fiona before his eyes dropped to the floor. A slight nod of his head acknowledged that Gräss indeed had changed his mind, and that he had announced it at the retirement party with (to Frontis's way of thinking) a certain sadistic pleasure.

Fiona rose and made her way to the coffeepot. She found Frontis's mug, an earthenware vessel with a cracked handle, and filled it to the top. She shoveled in two heaping tablespoons of sugar and stirred it for a moment before taking him the cup.

"I'm sorry," she said, handing the steaming mug to Frontis. He reached out and grasped it, and she noticed that his bony fingers were shaking. She also noticed that his usual disheveled appearance, in light of what she had just learned, was on the verge of complete chaos.

His face was savage to begin with. His eyes were intense, though it was hard to tell exactly what color the irises were because the whites were so often tinted red. Above his eyes were bushy orange eyebrows, well on their way toward gray. He had a high, shiny forehead and a bird's nest of hair, wavy and seldom combed, with thick sideburns that dropped well below his long earlobes. He looked as though he hadn't shaved for days.

"Iain, what'll you do now?"

Frontis found a filterless cigarette in the breast pocket of his rumpled shirt. He lit it with a gold lighter, even though he knew that Fiona had a distaste for tobacco smoke. As she watched him take a long drag, she said nothing, figuring that the cigarette might help to calm his nerves.

"Don't know," he said, exhaling in the direction of Beggs and the window. Beggs cringed at the thought of sucking smoke into one's lungs.

"I expect I'll search for a position in the States," Frontis continued. "There's no future here."

"America," said Beggs. "What a dreadful thought."

"Can't you find something in Britain?" said Fiona. "Rainer won't be around forever. You could come back when he's gone."

"I'd love to, Fiona, truly I would. But it's the same throughout England . . . and no better in Scotland. The money is in America. And the opportunity. Why, there're practically as many design schools in New York alone as there are in all of Britain."

Fiona couldn't picture Frontis in New York. He had a hard enough time pointing his bicycle in the direction of Scroope Terrace each morning. He'd never survive.

"But Rainer must be joking," she said. "We've got to talk to him."

"He's not going to change his mind," Beggs said. "Sorry, Iain, but you know how Rainer is."

"How'd he put it?" Fiona asked.

Frontis again cast his eyes toward the floor. He rarely looked at anyone anyway, a habit exacerbated by his agitation.

"As I said," Beggs stated. "With great fanfare. What time did you leave the party, Fiona?"

Fiona thought for a moment.

"Ten thirty . . . no, more like ten forty-five."

"Well, it must have been around eleven," said Beggs. "Yes. Yes. Because Rainer was out of his medicine, as he calls it, and Iain here, being the dutiful chap that he is, went to his college's cellar to retrieve a fresh bottle. Rainer can't live without his Fonseca, and he wouldn't dream of touching the wine we were drinking, though I'd have to say that I thought it was a rather adequate Côtes du Rhône."

"So he got a new bottle," Fiona said. "And then what?"

"I'm getting to that, my dear. Then, I believe, one of the students, the muscle-bound American, the rower, what's his name? Simpson?"

"Gaines Simpson," Fiona said.

"Yes, young Simpson. Well, he offered up a toast to our guest of honor, who at this point, I would have to say, was quite sloshed. Still, Gräss stood up in that overly controlled body manner of his, and announced with a certain Continental smugness that he, the great one, had reconsidered his decision to retire, and that for the sake of the department he was staying on."

" 'For the sake of the department'? What does that mean?" asked Fiona.

Frontis shrugged.

Fiona Mallow knew Rainer Gräss perhaps better than anyone at the school. Gräss, though somewhat of a curmudgeon and abrasive toward his colleagues and students, was the most dedicated teacher and academic she had ever known. He was also a very calculating person and, while he loosened up in social situations and even had a wry, if perverted, sense of humor, the one thing that he took very seriously, and about which she had never heard him joke, was the integrity of the school. He was fiercely proud of it. If he had said that he was staying on "for the sake of the department," then Fiona knew that, even in his drunken state, he had meant it.

" 'For the sake of the department.' Chev, what was he getting at?"

Beggs shifted his weight from one leg to the other and took a sip of coffee.

"I suppose he meant that he doesn't feel Iain here is up to snuff."

Frontis took a long draw of his cigarette and the orange glow raced closer to his fleshy lips.

"You sod," he muttered.

"Sorry, old boy."

Frontis then dropped the cigarette into his half-drained coffee mug, extinguishing it, creating an odd pungent smell. He looked down for his watch but realized he wasn't wearing one. Glancing up at the clock on the wall, he mumbled something to himself.

"I have a lecture," he said to Fiona. He attempted a smile and made for the door.

The door slammed, leaving an awkward silence in the office.

"That was cruel, Chev," she said, returning to her desk.

Beggs sighed and put down his mug.

"I only recounted what happened."

"Nevertheless."

"It's not my fault, Fiona. Rainer's made up his mind. Iain's being hung out to dry by Gräss, not me."

"Can't you talk to him, Chev? You two get along okay. He's proof-reading your book manuscript, isn't he?"

"Only because I helped him with his translation of Colonna's *Hypnertomachia*. He owes me one."

"But can't you talk to him about Iain?"

"He won't listen," Beggs said. "He's stubborn as an ass, more so with each passing year. Iain must have done something to make him reconsider the retirement."

Fiona took another bite of her brioche before tossing it half-eaten into the wastebasket.

"I just think," she said, returning her eyes and fingers to her collating, "that we have to do something to help him."

"Nothing's going to help Iain," Beggs said. "Unless Rainer changes his mind. Or unless by divine providence Rainer disappears from the face of the planet."

Just then, the phone on Fiona's desktop rang. On the second ring she picked it up, swinging her hair aside as she swept the receiver up and under her delicate ear.

"Hello," she said.

"Yes."

"He is, but he isn't in. Would you like to leave a message?"

"No, like I said, he isn't here."

"Yes, sure. Go ahead."

"You did?"

"Certainly, Sergeant. When I see him I'll let him know."

"Yes . . . yes . . . thank you very much."

"You too. Good-bye."

She slowly lowered the receiver to the cradle of the phone. Her eyes, rich green and full, rose to meet Beggs's, and her head tilted almost imperceptibly.

"Who was that?" Beggs asked.

She stared at him in silence.

"Fiona? Who was it?"

"Parkside Police," she said in an almost whisper. "Seems they've found Rainer's wallet. A cox from Trinity found it floating in the river near Jesus Green."

Two

*H*e reached the point in the river
that was his least favorite, the near-ninety-degree turn at Fen Ditton
that, when heading south, brought his twenty-five-foot single shell
into the beginning of Long Reach. As Gaines Simpson began his
blade adjustment to make the turn, he heard what he had hoped not
to hear at this narrow bend in the far too narrow River Cam: An eight,
almost three times the length of his own shell, was approaching, moving in the opposite direction. Although he couldn't see the other
boat, the incessant bark of the eight's coxswain pounded his throb-
bing head, a head still fogged by red wine and cigarette smoke from
last night's party.

Normally he would have been on the river at 6:15 A.M., which
would have assured some pinch of sanity. Instead, he had not been
able to drag himself out of bed until nine thirty, missing his Latin lecture for the third time in two weeks. Now, a good hour later, he found
himself rowing against an excess of late-morning river traffic.

Again he adjusted his oars' motions, bringing the tip of his port
blade to within inches of the riverbank, in order that the two shells
would have room to maneuver past one another. The northbound boat
came ever closer, moving with the lurching speed that eight rowers
provide, the coxswain's high-pitched voice imploring the crew, and
the slapping of blades echoing across the brown water. Suddenly,

Simpson sensed a problem. Years on Lake Washington in Seattle had honed his faculties, and he could tell when something was amiss. For a brief second he turned and peered over his shoulder, and in an instant he could see the dilemma. The eight was a novice boat from Pembroke College. It was moving at better than three-quarters speed, and the coxswain had let the shell drift too far to the west side of the river. Now, he (or she, Simpson couldn't tell) was desperately trying to steer her east. But while the shell should have been parallel to the riverbank as she moved into the tight left-hand turn, she was not, and unless Simpson stopped rowing altogether, he was certainly going to clip the stern of the Pembroke boat.

He dropped his blades and churned up water, coming to a rapid stop. He felt sweat building on his brow, even though the air temperature hovered at freezing. Beneath his Queens' College sweatshirt he felt the constriction of his lungs, a tightness around his muscular chest. He began to cough. He suddenly remembered he had forgotten to bring along his inhaler, which was in his gym bag back at the boathouse. As long as he was rowing, the asthma wouldn't affect him. But now, because of the Pembroke boat, he would have to hold his position in the water, and it would be minutes before he again reached a stroke count of forty.

The Pembroke boat, low in the water, kept coming. It was closing in on him fast, and he heard the coxswain yell a lame apology. Suddenly he felt a crack at his starboard blade; the first of the Pembroke crew's bow oarsman had clipped him. And then another. And so on, with the frigid water being showered across his lap. He watched stoically as the big boat barreled on, the groaning faces of the novice rowers each staring back at Simpson as they passed, flailing all the way, somehow making their pitiful boat move forward. The Pembroke boat was full of snotty little English boys, in their second term at Cambridge after finishing up at Eton, Harrow, or Cheltenham, most of them taking on rowing so they could "ring up Mummy at the weekend" and boast about their athletic prowess. Not a one of them would ever amount to anything in the sport. They reminded him of little frogs, the kind he used to torture on his grandfather's farm as a child.

The stern of the Pembroke shell crossed over his bow. His eyes then

"I sure did," he said. "And your"—he wanted to say boyfriend, but that was ridiculous—"your . . . well, Rainer . . . he was certainly smashed."

Amy's modest mouth worked into a frown.

"Did you ever find him?" Simpson asked. Rainer Gräss had disappeared just before the end of his retirement party and Amy had asked Gaines, the only person at the party who knew about her relationship with Rainer (or at least so she thought), if he knew his whereabouts.

"No," she said.

Simpson noticed Amy was about to cry. In fact, the redness around her eyelids was evidence that she had already been crying.

"Look," he said. "I'll walk you back to college. And we'll talk."

"I'm not going to college," she said. "I've got to go to the Financial Grants Office."

"Okay, so I'll walk with you."

He touched her shoulder and nudged her ahead. The two of them walked along the leaf-strewn quay and crossed the footbridge over to Midsummer Common. The air hung heavy with cold and damp, and a sharp wind from the west swept across the desolate green.

"So what happened between you two?" Simpson finally asked as they cut across the green in the direction of Jesus College.

"We had a row," Amy said.

"What about?"

A tear gathered on Amy's eyelash and dropped to her cheek. She was staring straight into the wind, which streaked the tear across her flushed face.

"About us," she said. "About our relationship. And where it's going."

"And where *is* it going?"

She stopped walking and turned to him.

"Nowhere," she said, wiping the tear away with her gloved hand. "It's over."

They began walking again.

Simpson didn't want to tell her that he knew this would happen all along. How could she have been so fucking stupid to believe that her professor, a sixty-six-year-old married man, would actually get him-

Three

The house at 24 Panton Street was a three-story Queen Anne of red Roman brick. The front façade had an anthropomorphic quality about it, especially at night, lit from within. The ground floor was fronted by tall leaded-glass windows set behind a continuous wrought-iron railing, the vertical balusters of which curved outward, so that the whole looked not unlike the lower lip of a mouth. Above this, and centered within the façade, were double French doors opening to a small balcony, capped by a Gothic transom in the form of an ogee arch, the effect being that of the nose. The second floor contained a pair of multipaned white sash windows, deeply set within heavy sandstone embrasures, the eyes of the face. And finally, capping the whole, a cornucopic Dutch gable with a variety of sculptural flora in terra cotta, like some eccentric hat worn by an old aunt.

Jamie Ramsgill dropped the heavy brass knocker against the door stile, then waited as he heard faint footsteps from within. A moment later the sound of a bolt being thrown was followed by a wedge of light spilling out onto the tile porch floor as the door was pulled back. Below him was a small boy with the face of a Hummel figurine, no taller than the height of the doorknob.

"Mummy, we've a visitor!" he cried.

He turned immediately and scampered off, not bothering to close the door or to get Ramsgill's name.

Ramsgill could see inside. A small foyer was lined with stenciled wainscoting and lit overhead by an ornate iron lamp. Beyond it was a darkened hallway, with a stair on the right side and two arched openings on the left. He could hear the low crackle of a fire from the archway closest to him, and could see the light of the fire reflecting on oak-paneled walls of what might be a front parlor. From the rear of the house came the aroma of dinner.

As the boy reached the end of the hall Ramsgill could now see the silhouette of a female coming out of the kitchen, her hands wiping a dishrag. She flipped on the hall's light switch, and Ramsgill could make her out more clearly, the long legs and thin waist, her pretty face framed by thick, red hair. When she recognized him her mouth formed a smile.

"Jamie. What a surprise."

"Hello, Fiona. I hope I'm not interrupting dinner."

"Oh, no no. Come in quickly. It's nasty out there."

Ramsgill stepped into the foyer and closed the door behind him. He turned to see Fiona Mallow standing close to him, almost as tall as he, looking radiant.

He leaned forward and kissed her on the cheek.

"Let me look at you," she said. "You've lost weight."

"I wish," he said. "You're the one who looks great."

From behind her, the boy came running up, wrapping his arms around her legs. She lifted him up and his arms naturally found their way around her neck.

"Robin, this is Mr. Ramsgill. He's from America."

The boy looked at Ramsgill in wide-eyed wonder, then blushed and buried his face in his mother's sleeve.

"Come into the parlor, Jamie," she said, mussing her son's hair. "Would you like some tea? Or dinner? We've just finished, but there's plenty left. And let me take your coat."

"No, thank you," he said, following her through the first arch. "I just ate. And I can't stay long."

She led him to a tuxedo-style sofa adjacent to the fireplace, placing his coat on a nearby chair. The room was small but well appointed, connected to the dining room beyond by a wide opening framed with Tuscan columns. He sat, and she took a chair across from him, placing Robin on an ottoman between them. She paused for a moment to look at his face.

There were shadowy circles under his eyes and a few crow's-feet at the eyes' extremities. But other than that, he had the same good looks as the last time she'd seen him. His eyes were the color of the Caribbean Sea at its most shallow points, an iridescent light blue, but gradated in hue and value toward aqua green. His wavy brown hair was parted in the middle, worn heavy on top and short on the sides. His face was boyish, honey-colored, and square, with smooth skin and pale pinkish cheeks. He had a cleft chin and prominent Adam's apple.

"Now tell me," she said, "how was your flight?"

"Fine, I suppose, considering the lack of sleep. Oh, and the airline lost my bicycle. They said I should have it by tomorrow."

"You're still riding, then," she said.

"A little. I used to ride thirty miles a day, if you remember. Now it's more like thirty a month. But I couldn't come to Cambridge without a bike. Hopefully I'll have a chance to get out into the country."

"Do you still have those expensive Italian bikes?"

"My worst vice," he said. "Three of them."

"And what does . . . what's her name . . . Elena?"

"Yes."

"What does she think about them?"

"Oh, she tolerates them, like she tolerates me."

"Rainer says she's *been* tolerating you. He says you've been together a year and a half. That's nice."

He gave her a smile. Robin turned his head toward his mother, a curious look in his big brown eyes.

"Mr. Ramsgill and I used to be good friends," she told him. "Before Mummy was married. Before you were born."

"Does he know Daddy?" the boy asked.

Fiona smiled, shaking her head. "No," she said. She looked up at Ramsgill. "He never met Daddy."

Just then a door off the dining room opened, and a girl and boy came through to the parlor. The girl was tall, like Fiona, and had the same thick auburn hair. The boy appeared to be twelve or so, and was dressed in a soccer uniform, with socks up to his knees. Both of them had Fiona's fine features.

"We've finished the dishes, Mum," said the girl. "Oh, I'm sorry." She looked to Ramsgill and her eyes came alive. They were the same sparkling eyes her mother had. Ramsgill stood and reached out his hand. He seemed to notice a little smile on Fiona's face as his hand met that of her daughter.

"Hello," she said. "I'm Margaret."

"I'm Jamie Ramsgill," he said. "You wouldn't remember me, but we've met before. When you were about his age." He nodded toward Robin.

"And this is Colin," said Fiona.

Ramsgill shook Colin's hand.

"Soccer player?" he asked.

"It's football to us," said Colin shyly. "But, yes."

"I'm five," Robin broke in.

"Well," said Ramsgill. "Then I'll bet that last year you were four."

Robin nodded, now warming up to the stranger. Margaret smiled, then looked down to her mother.

"Can we go up then, Mum?" she said. "I have a paper to work on."

Fiona looked at her watch. It was just after seven.

"Of course," she said. "But do me a favor. Take Robin with you and run him a bath."

"No," Robin protested, his lower lip jutting forward.

Fiona turned an admonishing eye toward him, and he immediately got the message. The lip retracted and he rose dutifully from the ottoman.

"Can't you come, Mum?" he said wistfully.

"I'll be up shortly."

She bent over and kissed him on the forehead. The children then left the room.

"Beautiful kids," Ramsgill said, once they were gone.

"Thank you," Fiona said. "It's tough, Jamie." She sighed softly.

"Raising them alone?"

She nodded, and Ramsgill noticed the tautness of her neck, as perfectly formed as any he had ever seen.

"Do they see their father much?"

"Not really," she said. "A week in the summer and one at Christmastime. Dick lives in Maidenhead now. But two weeks is all he needs. He manages to brainwash them adequately at each visit, such that I have to spend the next six months convincing them that life without a dad is okay. What I'd really like to tell them is that Dick walked out on us. Of course, I can't, and wouldn't ever."

"I was sorry to hear about that," Ramsgill said. "Rainer told me about it."

He reached across and touched her hand lightly. Her fingers were long and fingernails lacquered, but they were not the smooth hands of a young woman anymore. She looked up at him, and for the first time he could see her eyes as he used to see them. He thought of Elena back in Princeton, and how hard it was going to be to be away from her, if only for two weeks.

"Seems like I'm always getting walked out on," said Fiona, pulling her fingers into a fist.

Ramsgill looked away toward the fire, which had died to a low flame.

"I didn't walk out on you, Fiona. You left school to be with your father. You didn't return, remember?"

He looked back. Their eyes met again, but now it was pain that he saw.

"That's not fair, Jamie. Mother had just died and Father was lost. I *had* to be with him."

"And I told you to take as much time as you needed. But I was finishing up my thesis. I couldn't stay in Britain after that. I had to go home to get a job. To pay for five years of graduate school. I was thirty thousand dollars in debt."

"Rainer offered you a post-doc, Jamie. You could have stayed on."

"And have gone farther into debt? You don't remember how little money I had to begin with, Fi. I couldn't. Besides, Rainer also recommended me to the position at Princeton. If it hadn't been for Rainer I would never have gotten the job there."

She brushed a strand of hair away from her face, then stared at the bright orange embers of the fire, her thoughts floating back two decades. She knew that it wasn't Jamie's fault that their relationship had ended. They had come so close to making a commitment to one another, but after her mother died unexpectedly, she had left Cambridge for a year. By the time she returned to finish her degree, Jamie was already back in the States. They corresponded for a while, but one day Dick Mallow walked into her life and swept her off her feet.

She often wondered, especially now that she was divorced, how her life might have been different had she and Jamie stayed together.

She decided to change the subject.

"Rainer treated you well, Jamie. I don't know why, but he took you under his wing like nobody else."

"I wouldn't have come to Cambridge in the first place if it hadn't been for him," Ramsgill said. "He lectured at Virginia my senior year there, and I had the chance to meet him. I was all set to apply to graduate school in the U.S. He convinced me to come over and saw to it that I got the proper aid to make it possible. Plus the job at Princeton. I owe him more than I can ever repay. And it wasn't just school. He and Ghislaine always invited me out to Coton, especially on holidays when I couldn't go home. We even once celebrated an American Thanksgiving together."

Fiona laughed softly, shaking her head.

"What?" he said.

"I was just thinking. It was so different back then. Rainer and Ghislaine were *so* different."

"What do you mean?"

"They were civil to each other, for one thing."

"And they're not now?"

"They have serious problems now, Jamie. They have for several years. It's basically two people living separate lives under one roof. I think Ghislaine blames Rainer for Tal's death."

Ramsgill remembered that their son, Tal, had been killed in Northern Ireland as a member of the British forces.

"Why does she blame Rainer?"

"Because he was never around when Tal was growing up. Tal was sent to Leys for sixth form, but instead of going off to university like everyone expected, he joined the army. He was killed two years ago when a bomb went off in a laundrette in Loughinisland, a town near Belfast. At the time Rainer was lecturing in Vienna. Ghislaine had to go down to Duxford Air Base to identify the body. Alone. I don't think she ever forgave him for that."

"But Ghislaine is good for him. I never knew two people who cared more for one another."

"That was then, Jamie. Believe me, it's over now. In fact, Rainer's been having an affair with one of his students."

"You're kidding."

"I wish I were. She's a young girl from the north named Amy Denster. In some ways she reminds me of you. She came here on scholarship and Rainer saw to it she was taken care of. And they began a relationship. It's very odd. I think everyone in the department knows about it, and Rainer knows they know about it, but she doesn't have a clue. She's very naive in some ways."

"Like me," said Ramsgill.

"I didn't mean that."

Ramsgill leaned forward.

"Fiona? Why didn't Rainer come get me today? I mean, it's no big deal, but is something bothering him? I spoke with him by phone over the weekend and he seemed upset."

Fiona nodded.

"I know," she said. "But I don't know what about. We had that small retirement party for him last night. Among other things, he announced at the party that he had changed his mind, and that he's decided to not retire after all. And then at the end of the party he just disappeared. No one's seen him today."

"What do you mean?"

"He left the party without telling anyone. He left his things there, too. Today, the police rang me up and told me that they had found his wallet in the river."

"In the river? My God, that doesn't sound good."

"No. It doesn't. I rang Ghislaine up this morning and he hadn't come home. Amy claims she hasn't see him today either. And he missed two supervisions he was to have given."

"Fiona, this isn't funny. What if something happened to him? Why didn't you say something before?"

She shook her head, her lips parted.

"I don't know. I just keep expecting him to show up. With the way he's been acting, it just didn't seem that odd."

An ember from the fire broke off and slid forward in the hearth, popping and sending up orange sparks.

"Tell me about the party," Ramsgill said.

"It was held in the Old Hall at Queens' College. It was a potluck dinner with a lot of wine. You remember those parties. Iain Frontis is a Fellow at the college, so we often have our little get-togethers there. It went on until well after midnight, but I left early. I don't have the stamina for that sort of thing anymore, besides I've got the children. As the party was winding down, I guess they noticed he was missing. He didn't say anything about leaving to anyone, and as I said, he left his things in the hall. He'd had a lot to drink, too."

"And no one saw him leave the grounds? What about the porters?"

"At that time of night there's only one way out of college. The gates at Queens' Lane are locked at ten and the only open gate is next to the Porters' Lodge on Silver Street. The porter on duty says he didn't come that way."

"And there's no other way out?"

"Jamie, surely you remember. Cambridge colleges are fortresses, designed to keep students *in*. At least they were in the old days."

"And you're sure he didn't just wander off into one of the buildings? To sleep off a drunk?"

"I was thinking that. But if he did, he's still there. And what was his wallet doing in the river?"

Ramsgill sat up and his gaze froze. Fiona recognized the look, a specific kind of look that she had long since forgotten. It was an intense stare that seemed to bore through walls when he was thinking.

"The Porters' Lodge is on Silver Street," he said. "Isn't that across the river from the main part of the college?"

"Yes. The Mathematical Bridge crosses the river there. He could have fallen off. Or . . . have jumped."

Ramsgill's eyes returned to her.

"You don't think . . .?"

"Well, it would be hard to fall off, Jamie. The sides of the bridge must be a good six feet high."

Her words took a long moment to sink in.

"Was he depressed?"

"I wouldn't call him depressed. But as you say, something was bothering him."

"What did Ghislaine say when you asked her if he'd been home?"

"She was completely unmoved. She said this wasn't the first time he hadn't come home. Iain Frontis tells me Rainer sometimes sleeps in his office, just to avoid going home to Coton."

"And you say he missed some supervisions? I can't ever remember Rainer doing that."

Fiona shook her head.

"There must be a simple explanation," Ramsgill said. "Something we're missing. Who was at the party?"

"Iain Frontis, whom you know. He's the Scot who helps Rainer with the M.Phil.'s and Ph.D.'s. Cheverton Beggs, who does dual duty, teaching history for both the art and architecture faculties."

"I forgot he was back at Cambridge," said Ramsgill. "Following in his dad's footsteps, huh?"

Fiona nodded.

"Who else was there?"

"Amy Denster, the girl I told you about. And an American named Gaines Simpson. The interesting bit there is that he used to date Amy. There's some friction between him and Rainer. About Amy, I suppose."

"Who else?"

"Well, myself, of course, but I left early. And two more students. George Boye's a young Nigerian, I believe with Darwin College. And a German girl named Maria Lendtmayer. She's pretty good friends with Amy."

"And that's all?"

"That's all. There are as few Ph.D. candidates today as there were when you were around, Jamie. The university would like to see us open it up to more, but Rainer is adamant about keeping things small. Though that might change if he retires."

"Now tell me about *that*. How does a man go to his own retirement party and announce in the middle of it that he's not retiring? Everyone must have been shocked."

"Or outraged," said Fiona.

Ramsgill studied her face, trying to discern her meaning.

"He was supposed to retire to give Iain Frontis his position on the faculty," she continued. "Iain is being made redundant by government cutbacks, so to say that Rainer's announcement was a shock to him is an understatement. It's going to kill Iain's academic career, at least here in Britain."

"I see," said Ramsgill. "And how do Rainer and Beggs get along?"

"Not too badly. They tolerate one another, in fact even help each other with writing projects. But I don't think Beggs is enamored of the idea of Rainer staying on."

"And the students?" Ramsgill said.

"They abide Rainer. They have to. You know what it's like, Jamie. If you're an M.Phil. who wants to get into the Ph.D. program, you are controlled by Rainer. If you are a Ph.D. student who wants a good recommendation after graduating, again Rainer holds the cards. Junior faculty work in his shadow. He wields enormous power. You know that. Like you said, where would you be without him?"

It was true. Rainer had always gone out of his way for him, thought Ramsgill. He'd never considered what it would be like to be on the other side of his good graces.

"You get along with him, don't you, Fiona?"

"Yes. I guess he doesn't see me like he sees the others. I'm just an administrator."

Ramsgill paused, feeling momentarily seized by jet lag. And then something Rainer had said on the phone came to him.

"What is it?" said Fiona.

"I was just thinking of my phone conversation with him. I had apologized for being unable to attend the party. One of my Princeton students had his Ph.D. defense yesterday, which is why I couldn't fly to London until last night. Anyway, when I told him this, he said he was sorry too, because I was going to miss his surprise. I suppose he was referring to his announcement that he wasn't retiring, but he didn't tell me what it was."

"Did he say anything else?"

"No. He just said that it was important, and that it had to do with the department. Something about the department's reputation."

"That's interesting."

"Why?"

"Well, according to Beggs," said Fiona. "When Rainer announced that he was staying on, he added parenthetically that he was doing so 'for the sake of the department.' "

"You think he didn't want Iain Frontis taking his position?"

"That's what Beggs thought. But then why did he agree to retire in the first place? And why did he want to make a point of announcing his change of heart in front of everyone?"

"Maybe he'd found something out about Iain. Something embarrassing."

"Or maybe it had to do with one of the others," said Fiona.

"Like who?"

"George Boye, possibly."

"He's the Nigerian?"

"Yes. Rainer threatened to go to the Proctors last month because Boye had plagiarized part of a paper. Technically, a complaint can only be brought to the Proctors by an active faculty member, the professor for whom the illicit work was done. By stepping down, Rainer wouldn't be able to follow through."

"But that hardly seems reason to cause Frontis to lose his job. And how long does the process with the Proctors take?"

"A few months. And Frontis's contract runs out in June. If the complaint took longer, it wouldn't be finished before Frontis was forced to leave."

"Who else might the comment have been directed to?"

"Beggs, perhaps."

"You mean the fact that Beggs would like to see Rainer go?"

"More or less. Ever since Beggs learned of Rainer's planned departure, he's been lobbying Renny Heard-Matthews, head of the whole school, to take Rainer's place as head of the M.Phil. and Ph.D. programs. Stepping in front of Frontis's place in line, as it were. After all, he's been here longer than Frontis. As full faculty, that is."

"And you think that Rainer didn't want that to happen? But that's sort of a Catch-22, isn't it? If Rainer leaves, he risks Beggs getting his position. But if he stays, he *insures* that Frontis is let go."

"That's right," said Fiona.

Ramsgill stretched, inadvertently letting out a yawn. He had hardly slept in thirty-six hours, but his mind was now barreling along, trying to assimilate what he knew about Rainer Gräss's disappearance and to determine what he should do about it. Or whether it was even his place to do anything about it.

"Did you ask anyone what happened at the end of the night?" said Ramsgill.

"Yes," said Fiona. "I spoke with Amy. The group was all together until midnight. After that, different people left the hall at different times. Some went out to the loo. Frontis went out once or twice for more wine. Rainer himself had gone out at a little after midnight. At twelve forty-five they noticed he was missing."

"How can she be so sure on the time?"

"Because they had a present they wanted to give him. And they wanted to take a group picture, but he never showed. They took the picture anyway, and the present's in my office. Beggs took it and Rainer's other things home with him. His valet dropped them off today."

"Fiona?"

She looked up at him with eyes as bright as his own, but hers were green and not as weary.

"Do you think Rainer's disappearance mightn't have been accidental?" he said.

"You mean suicide?"

"No, I mean planned by someone."

"Absolutely not."

"Why?"

"Because this is Cambridge, Jamie. There's plenty of academic greed and Machiavellianism, but what you're talking about is another matter."

"It happens everywhere, Fiona. And there have been more murders in the British royal family than I'm sure you folks would like to admit."

"So what do we do?"

"We go to the police, for one thing. Tonight."

"But I have . . ."

"We owe it to Rainer, Fi."

She looked at the resolute set of his jaw, and the intensity in his eyes. She knew that Jamie Ramsgill wouldn't rest until the matter of Rainer Gräss's disappearance was resolved or he had exhausted every ounce of energy at his disposal. He was like that with everything he did, and especially with people he cared for. She thought of the many times she had needed Jamie in the last four years, but how she had never acted on it.

"I'll get my coat," she said. "And tell Margaret that we're leaving."

George Boye sat at a corner table in the Darwin College bar, at just past eight on Tuesday evening, nursing his second gin-and-tonic after dinner, though it was probably his last. He was a handsome young man, with skin the color and patina of finely oiled mahogany. He had a large round head with closely cropped black curls on top. His dark brown eyes were wide and friendly. His mouth was simple, straight, and small lipped.

His large frame was draped with an open academic gown, beneath which a dressy rayon shirt and black trousers could be seen. But what distinguished George Boye was not his clothes, but rather (and particularly in contrast to the black academic garb) his jewelry. It was all gold. Around his thick neck were three simple, yet elegant, gold choker chains. On his right wrist, a heavy Rolex watch. He wore a gold ring on each of his eight fingers—some simple, some elaborate, but the whole collection chosen with care. They were interesting in juxtaposition to one another, almost to the point of mitigating their ostentatiousness.

Between his fingers he toyed with a small rectangular piece of plastic bubble wrap, popping the bubbles insistently but in very slow fashion. Popping bubble wrap was for Boye a ridiculous but interminable habit, no more controllable than cracking knuckles or biting one's nails. He couldn't remember when he had first started it, or for that matter if he had even been aware of bubble wrap's existence prior to leaving Lagos to come to school in Britain. It was simply addicting. If you were in a room with George Boye, you would have to be aware of the noise, but it would be with such infrequency, and with such control, that unless you watched and listened intently you would never sense the source of the irritating sound.

"Stop it!" said Jaide Bjedaue, George's friend, who sat across the table from him and who was more than aware of George's habit. "For God's sake, George, stop it!"

"Can't help it," George muttered. He had a deep, soft voice.

George lifted his glass and drained his drink.

"I've changed my mind," he said, now sensing the click inside his head that told him that the gin was kicking in. "I'll have another. You boys?"

Tidiane Munier, a tall, thin Senegalese, followed George's lead and polished off his pint of ale.

"Yes. Yes, I think I will," Tidiane said. He reached into his pocket and pulled out a five-pound note.

"Are you *mad*, George?" said Jaide. "You have a paper due in the morning, man. You haven't even started."

George rocked his head back and smiled at Tidiane. It was one of those implicit smiles between the two friends that confirmed what the pair already knew about Jaide Bjedaue, that he was daft, and thoroughly too interested in his academic area of land economy for his own good. He rarely drank, tonight sipping an orange squash and trying to direct the conversation to academic matters. He studied too much, and George had never seen him without a book in his hand. Jaide no doubt would go back to Nigeria and take up a minor job with the government, accepting an extension post in some godforsaken village in a northern province like Kaduna or Sokoto.

George, on the other hand, was at Cambridge to have a good time, to enjoy the best years of his life in style. He had chosen architecture for the opposite reason that Jaide was studying agrarian economics. George had no intention of returning to Nigeria. He would work in London after taking his degree, perhaps with a flat in Docklands, and ultimately a BMW, or a Jaguar. He would find work with one of the many well-known London architects with ties to Cambridge, and he would visit Lagos once or twice a year to stay in touch, perhaps even to secure a commission or two in his native country. When he did, he knew that he wouldn't look up Bjedaue, whose university friendship was a matter of convenience, and a matter of a certain dependence George had on his countryman.

George considered carefully how he would bring up the bit about the car. But first he had to have another drink. He took Tidiane's money and headed for the bar.

"Another gin-and-tonic," he said to a lanky student who was bartender for the night. "And a pint of Newcastle."

While the bartender fixed the drinks, George discreetly smoothed out his bubble wrap on the bar and gave it a single short pop. And then another, and then two or three in succession.

He turned and looked around the room. The bar looked more like a living room than a collegiate rathskellar. With the exception of a decorating scheme that had a decidedly 1970s look about it, cane and chrome and mirror and glass, the room was really no more than a Victorian parlor, one of the many rooms of the former residence of Charles Darwin's family that had been turned into a college some thirty years ago. The bar crowd was growing, the swelling voices making it hard to hear. This was a place to party, George thought. How could he work on his paper with so many of his mates making a night of it?

When he'd first entered the bar, the only thing on his mind was the paper he was due to give on Robert Adam's Syon House the next day in Rainer Gräss's seminar. The paper was already three weeks overdue, and twice he had convinced classmates (who were due to deliver their papers in weeks subsequent to his) to take his slot and present early. All year Gräss had told him that his work for an M.Phil. degree was substandard, and that it was looking more and more like he wouldn't be able to enter the Ph.D. program.

And then the bombshell of his last paper hit. Boye had wanted to surprise Gräss, to pull a rabbit out of his hat. He had found what he thought was an obscure source for his analysis of Pietro da Cortona's Baroque church, SS. Luca e Martina, in Rome. A very good thesis in the faculty library from 1933. He cribbed most of his own paper from the thesis, thinking there was no way Gräss knew of it. But Gräss had a spiderweb of a mind when it came to sources. He knew of the work, and called Boye into his office immediately. He told him in no uncertain terms that he was going to report Boye to the university Proctors. Even if the Proctors didn't suspend Boye for plagiarism, he said, his chances of getting into the Ph.D. program were nil.

The bartender returned and set the pint of ale on the counter, then went after Boye's gin. Gräss was a smug bastard, Boye thought. When Gräss had presented him the option of either doing a year's worth of remedial work in the next seven months or of not graduating at all, he had told George that he would have to return to his country in shame, an embarrassment to his people. What the fuck did Gräss know about *his* people? George was from a family of rank and privilege in Nigeria, an oil family, not some tribe of wild natives that dressed in grass skirts and spent the day tattooing themselves. And who was Gräss, anyway? He was nothing, as far as George was concerned. He was as full of himself as anyone George had ever met. An aging near-alcoholic with nothing to show for his career but a couple of pompous books on subjects that nobody cared about. His wife had all but abandoned him, and he was having an affair with a woman practically young enough to be his granddaughter. He was a pathetic old bugger.

"Bastard," Boye said softly.

The bartender brought his gin and George gave him Tidiane's fiver. He thought momentarily about changing his drink order to a double, but instead he just waited for his change, before turning and walking back to the table.

"Thank you, my good man," said Tidiane, accepting his ale and working off the froth with his mouth.

George sat and pressed the cool glass to his lips. He then kissed the glass before tipping its contents into his mouth.

"Hey," Tidiane said. "You forgot my change."

"Did I?" George asked. "I'm a little light tonight, Tidiane, can I pay you tomorrow?"

Tidiane bellowed, slapping his friend on the shoulder blades.

"Okay," he said, though he knew it would be days before he would see the money again, if at all.

"I must be going," said Jaide Bjedaue as he rose. "Have to study, you know. As you should be doing, George."

"Wait," George said, placing his bejeweled hand on Jaide's shoulder. He pulled him back down to the table.

"I need to borrow your car, man."

Jaide might be one of the most boring people George knew, but he did have one very important asset, a ten-year-old Vauxhall that was nothing to look at, but which provided reliable transportation.

Jaide looked over to his countryman with distrustful eyes.

"No way, friend. You've been drinking."

"I've only had one," Boye lied. "I'm perfectly sober. Besides . . . I'll put some petrol in it." He thought of the two pounds and change that he still had from Tidiane's fiver.

Jaide started to rise again, but George wouldn't let him.

"No," said Jaide.

"Listen," said Boye, now putting his arm around Jaide. "Please, Jaide. I have a date. I really need to borrow it. I promise, no more after this. I'll even clean it out for you, if you wish."

"Clean it tomorrow?"

Boye nodded, though he had no intention of doing so.

"Okay," Jaide said. "But it's your funeral." He reached into his pockets and retrieved the keys. He slapped them on the table with enough force to register what was a genuine concern for George, and for his car.

"Thanks, man," George said. He stuffed the keys into his pocket quickly, before Jaide changed his mind.

"Where are you going?" asked Jaide. "In case I have to identify your body."

"Coton," George said.

With that, Jaide rose for a third time, this time unrestrained. He rolled his eyes up to the corniced ceiling and walked away.

George grinned and tilted his drink in Tidiane's direction.

"Drink up, Tid," he said.

"You're too much," Tidiane replied. "What about your paper?"

George took a long draw on the drink, licked his lips, and ratcheted up the grin into a full-blown smile.

"No worry," he said. "My paper may be due tomorrow, but the wanker isn't going to show up for class."

Four

*D*etective Chief Inspector Lyndsay Hill turned his aging Austin Maestro onto Warkworth Terrace then, ten yards up the lane, he turned again, this time maneuvering the small vehicle into the car park behind the Cambridge Police Station. It was quarter past eight, and the car park was all but empty. He parked in his reserved space, retrieved his gray Burberry from the front passenger's seat, and stepped out into a cold evening drizzle.

As he emerged into the dead-white illumination of the station's rear entry porch, he could see his reflection in the glass doors. DCI Hill was six two and walked with a long, assured stride. At forty-three, his body could hardly be described as middle-aged. It was the body of an athlete, due in no small measure to his unwavering commitment to weight lifting and rugby, the latter a minor passion, having once played at the first-class level for Cambridge City. His face was angular and bold. His bright red hair was cut short, and his hairline retreated up a high, rounded forehead. Narrow eyes the color of weathered bronze rested beneath a thick, protruding brow. A small, angular scar disrupted his left eyebrow.

"Evening, guv," said Sarah Fray as Hill stepped through the doors and into the police station's lobby. The lobby, like the rest of the building, was severely modern, with precast concrete walls and a hard terrazzo floor, all under a textured beige ceiling that looked as though it were made of dirty popcorn.

"Evening, Sarah."

"The Raj, tonight . . . was it, sir?"

"Yep."

"Tandoori, guv?" Sarah was a rotund woman, with an obvious interest in food. Since she worked the lobby desk as a civilian inquiry clerk most evenings and wasn't allowed off for dinner, she usually made do with a tin of fish or some cheese and chutney while on duty. To Hill, who heard Sarah inquire about his dinner habits all too often, the questions were a slight infringement of his privacy, though he knew in the back of his mind that Sarah didn't intend them that way.

"No," he responded in his congenial manner. "Chicken Lababda."

Her eyes brightened, and he patted her broad shoulder as he passed her for the stairs.

Hill climbed to the first floor and stepped out into the corridor. He walked quickly through the CID suite, toward his office in the far corner of the building. Typewriters clacked softly from behind open doors and the droll hum of fluorescent lamp ballasts weighed the corridor down from above. Passing through an outer vestibule, Hill entered his own office, a neat room fifteen feet square with once-white walls and an oak parquet floor stained the color of walnut.

He lay his coat on a chair and made his way behind his cluttered desk. His usual reason for coming back to the office in the evening was to get in a few concentrated hours of work, without the distractions that seemed to swarm about the station during the day. Tonight he wanted to finish up year-end performance evaluations, the ones that should have been completed in December, but they had taken a backseat to the CID's annual budget review. As he began the evaluations, it occurred to him that this type of bureaucratic paper-processing was exactly the kind of work he didn't want to be doing, but it was, unfortunately, what success had brought him. Each day he told himself that if he could just get caught up on the paperwork, then he could finally free himself to pitch in on a new case—something with meat to it, something important.

But it never happened. For one thing, he never got caught up. Also, there were very few serious crimes in Cambridge anyway. In the whole of last year he had been directly involved in only a couple of investigations, and even they had been of little intrigue.

He sat at the desk and began to plow through his papers. He had been at it for no more than five minutes when a light knock came at his open door.

"Excuse me, boss."

Hill looked up from his desk and his eyes came upon Detective Sergeant Chris Detler standing in the doorway to Hill's office. If one hadn't known that the two men were unrelated, the younger one, Detler, might have been mistaken for Hill's own son. He was twenty-three years old, had Hill's same muscular build and short brown hair with signs of impending hair loss. Behind Detler was a uniformed officer whom Hill recognized, but whose name he couldn't remember. In the officer's hand, Hill could see he was holding one of the department's official forms.

"Sorry to bother you, sir, but Turtonham here has a problem."

Hill set down the letter he was reading.

"What is it, Chris?"

"There's a gentleman and lady downstairs, sir, and Turtonham, he's taking this missing-person report from them."

He pointed to the document in Turtonham's hand.

"And?"

"Well, they don't think Turtonham, er . . . the uniformed division . . . is important enough for them, sir. They've asked to see someone higher up."

"You know procedure, gentlemen," Hill said, his eyes returning momentarily to his desk. "A missing-person report is for the uniformed branch. Unless there's cause to suspect."

"That's just it, guv," Turtonham piped in. He was a wiry man who looked as though his uniform was two sizes too large for him. "They do suspect."

"And who's missing?" Hill asked.

"A professor . . ."

Turtonham glanced down at the partially completed report.

"Sorry, sir. An architecture professor from the university. He went missing last night after a party what was being held for him at Queens' College. He didn't report to the school all day, missing a lecture he was to teach and several of his supervisions."

"Turtonham, what's your first name?"

"Clive, sir."

"Well, Clive, that's hardly a case for the CID. Take the report and assure these people that you'll have the uniformed branch look into it."

"I don't think that'll be good enough for them, sir."

Hill pushed himself back from the desk. Without thinking, he swiveled in his chair and retrieved the blue exercise ball that occupied the slate windowsill behind him, alongside a photograph of his daughter. He slowly squeezed the ball, rolling his eyes briefly toward the ceiling such that Detler could get the message that he was not thrilled by this intrusion.

"Boss," Detler said. "The man's been gone for almost twenty-four hours. This morning his wallet was found in the river."

Hill stopped squeezing for a second, then resumed his exercise, now shifting the ball from his right hand to his left.

"All right, then," he said, shaking his head at the two men in his doorway. "I'll be down in a minute."

The pair left, and Hill rose from his chair. He retrieved a dark blue splatterware coffee mug from a desk drawer and left the room. He walked down the hall and into a large room to the left of the corridor. It was empty with the exception of Chris Detler, now back at his desk, and two detectives examining a bulletin board on the far side of the room. On the wall nearest the corridor, Hill found the coffeepot with an inch or two of black tar festering above the warmer. He poured the thick liquid into his mug, topped it off with cream, then turned off the burner and made his way out the door.

When he entered the ground-floor interview room, he found Turtonham sitting across the table from an attractive middle-aged woman in a green Barbour jacket. Next to her was an equally handsome man of similar age, in a black wool sports jacket and chinos. His face immediately struck Hill as familiar.

"Evening," Hill said, standing behind an empty chair next to the uniformed officer. "I'm Detective Chief Inspector Lyndsay Hill."

"Good evening," the woman said. "My name is Fiona Mallow."

She reached out her hand. He shook it but Hill's eyes were still trained on the man.

"Do I know you?" he said to the man.

"I'm Jamie Ramsgill."

"American?"

"Yes."

"Have we met?"

"I don't see how. I've only set foot in this station once before, and that was over twenty years ago, when I filled out my alien registration application."

"You were at the university?"

"Graduate school."

"What college?"

"I was at Darwin."

"I thought so."

Hill smiled and Ramsgill could see the one imperfection to his mouth, the chip on his upper right incisor, left over from his rugby-playing days.

"You played on the college basketball team, right?"

"Yes . . ." Ramsgill suddenly remembered Hill. "You did too."

"I was a *member* of the team. You chaps didn't let me play much, though. There were four of you Americans and one Canadian who sided up. I seem to remember we did quite well."

"We won cuppers. And I'm sure you played as much as I did, when I went out for cricket."

They both laughed, and Hill sent a glance over to Fiona Mallow. He did a double take, her polite smile catching him off guard.

"So what brings you to Cambridge?" Hill asked Ramsgill.

"I'm researching a book. Using the faculty of architecture's library."

"And who's missing?"

Hill took the "Missing Person/Abscondee Report" from Turtonham and began to scan it.

"Rainer Gräss," said Ramsgill. "He's on the faculty where Fiona works as secretary. They had a party last night in the Old Hall of Queens' College . . . a retirement party for Dr. Gräss."

"The Old Hall?" Hill said. He raised his mug and took a sip of the bitter coffee. "That's the Gothic Room that was done up in the nineteenth century by what's his name . . . Bodley, with tiles by William Morris, right?"

"Yes."

"Well, that would be the perfect setting for an architectural party, wouldn't it?" said Hill.

"Quite," Fiona responded.

"And you were both there?"

"I was there," said Fiona.

"I didn't arrive in Cambridge until this afternoon," said Ramsgill.

"Well, tell me about this party."

"We often have our little soirees there," said Fiona. "Two of our professors are fellows at Queens'. The party went on until well after midnight, but I left early. I've got three children to get up and off to school in the morning."

Hill noticed that Fiona Mallow wasn't wearing a wedding ring.

"As the party was winding down," Fiona continued, "someone noticed that Dr. Gräss was missing."

"Yes?" said Hill.

"Well, no one seems to know where he went. He didn't say anything about leaving to anyone and there's only one way out of the college. The gates at Queens' Lane are locked at ten P.M., and the only open gate is next to the Porters' Lodge on Silver Street. If he had left that way, he would have come into contact with the porter. And today I was rung up and informed that his wallet had been found in the river."

"By us?"

"Yes, I received the call this morning. We're afraid something serious happened to him. He left all his belongings in the hall, his coat, for instance, and his briefcase, with lectures and slides. You'd have to know him, Inspector Hill, to know that the briefcase is not something he would leave behind. Also, according to the people who were there late, he was in bare shirtsleeves. Do you remember how cold it was last night? Not the kind of weather one goes out in, not in shirtsleeves, anyway."

"I dare say not."

"This morning he was to have picked me up at Heathrow," Ramsgill said. "He didn't show."

"And later today," added Fiona, "he was to have given a lecture and a couple of supervisions. Rainer is an extremely serious man about his academics. In the whole time I've known him, I can't recall his ever having missed a lecture, unless he were abroad, or lecturing somewhere else. It's just not like him."

"And you've checked to make sure that he's not at home? Nor that he stayed over with anyone . . . friends, perhaps?"

"I've done some checking. No one seems to know his whereabouts."

"What about Addenbrookes?"

"I rang up the hospital this afternoon. No patient under the name of Gräss. And no anonymous patients either."

"Right. Well, let's say that he is indeed missing. Has he ever gone off before?"

"No."

"How's his health?"

"He's fairly fit for a man his age. He smokes and drinks too much, but he's perfectly stable. No mental problems."

"Ms. Mallow, who else was at this party?"

"The two faculty members there were Iain Frontis, a Scot who teaches in the Ph.D. and M.Phil. programs with Dr. Gräss. He's a Fellow at Queens'. And Cheverton Beggs, a lecturer of architectural history. He's with Pembroke."

"Beggs? Should I know that name?"

"You might be familiar with Cheverton's father, Sir Seymour Beggs. He's dead now, but in his day he was one of the most renowned scholars at the university."

"And who else was there?"

"A few students. Amy Denster, a young Brit. She's at Newnham College, I believe. And Gaines Simpson. American. At Queens'. A Nigerian named George Boye, with Darwin. And Maria Lendtmayer, a German student. I'm not sure of her college affiliation. Smithson, possibly."

"Have you spoken to any of them about what happened after you left the party?"

"I did. I spoke with Amy. She can't remember when Rainer left. She did say, however, that the others were together until around one A.M. No one seems to remember when he was last seen. She had gone out into the courtyard with him around midnight, but she returned a short time later. She didn't see him after that. She went looking for him at around twelve forty-five because they wanted to present him with a gift, but couldn't find him."

"I see," said Hill, turning his gaze back to Ms. Mallow. "Now, did anyone else leave the hall toward the end of the night?"

"According to Amy, Frontis left about twelve fifteen to retrieve some more wine. He's the Queens' wine steward and has keys to the cellar. Also, Gaines Simpson left at some point to go to his room and change shirts. He'd spilled a drink."

"Anyone else?"

"I'm not sure."

"Do you happen to have a picture of Dr. Gräss?"

Fiona reached into her purse and pulled out a newspaper clipping. She passed it across the table to Hill.

It was a profile of Gräss from *The Guardian* from two years prior. At the top was a photograph of him sitting in what appeared to be a leather wing chair next to the edge of a table. On the table were a pair of horn-rimmed eyeglasses, a writing pad, and three stacks of books of varying heights. He was a small man with bad posture, and he crouched forward toward the camera. His hands were folded in his lap, and a burned-down cigarette emerged from his tight fists. He wore a dark sweater and the contrast between his clothes and his hair could hardly be more striking. The hair was longish and white, shooting up above his forehead in the manner of lion's mane. His face was dark and handsome and, though it was obvious he was not a young man, his features were sharp, his eyes captivating, and his smile infectious.

"That's a pretty good likeness," Fiona said. "But his hair's actually longer than that now."

"How old is he?" Hill asked.

"Sixty-six," Fiona responded.

"He doesn't look it. Does he have a family?"

"He has a wife, but no children . . . not living anyway."

"A wife?"

"Yes, Ghislaine. They live in Coton."

"Ms. Mallow, is . . . is there any reason that Ghislaine didn't report him missing? I mean . . ."

"I know what you're thinking. Yes, there's a problem with their marriage. Rainer could be missing a week before Ghislaine would notice anything. In fact, the only thing she'd miss would be his paycheck from the university."

"I see."

"I suppose I should tell you that Amy Denster and Rainer are having an affair."

Hill pushed himself back in his chair and looked over toward Turtonham. Turtonham's eyes were staring out to the lobby. He caught DCI Hill's glance and quickly returned his mind to the report form. He jotted down the comment about Professor Gräss and Amy Denster.

"There's something else," Ramsgill said, sitting forward, his hands folded on the table. "I spoke with Rainer by phone over the weekend. He seemed distraught. Something was bothering him about the department. At the party he announced that he had decided not to retire after all. He said that 'for the sake of the department' he was not going to resign."

"What does that mean?"

"You should know, Inspector, that Rainer had problems with some of the people at the party."

"Call me Lyndsay, Jamie."

"Okay. But one of the reasons he was retiring was to give Iain Frontis a place on the faculty. Otherwise, Frontis was being let go. His announcement puts Frontis in a bind. And George Boye, the African, was having plagiarism charges brought against him by Rainer, which threatens Boye's place at the university. Rainer didn't get along with Cheverton Beggs too well either."

"Nor Gaines Simpson, for that matter," said Fiona. "Simpson used to date Amy Denster. Perhaps he still holds something for her."

"Am I to understand that you think someone at the party was responsible for his disappearance?"

"I think so," said Ramsgill flatly.

Fiona nodded reluctantly.

Hill looked over to Turtonham, who was scribbling furiously on the report.

"Okay," Hill said. "We'll launch an investigation. I'll have Turtonham here ring up the college straightaway and tell them we're going to search the grounds in the morning. Also, we'll contact Mrs. Gräss and get permission to report the disappearance in tomorrow evening's paper. We'll ask that anyone with information come forward. And I want Gräss's things. Where are they, Ms. Mallow?"

"Cheverton Beggs took his things after the party. They're in my office."

"Right. Well, I'll be over in the morning. I would also very much like to speak with everyone who was at the party. Could you arrange that?"

"Actually," Fiona said, "the students and Frontis have Rainer's theory seminar together tomorrow afternoon at one. You could come to that."

"I will," said Hill. "And I want you to ask Cheverton Beggs to be there too."

She nodded.

"Then we'll see each other tomorrow," said Hill. He looked down at his watch. It was 8:45. "I think I've about had it for one night."

"Thank you," said Fiona. Hill looked at her and smiled.

"Yes, thanks," said Ramsgill.

"Can I give you a lift home?" asked Hill. "I'm afraid I've had enough work for one day."

"I have my car," said Fiona.

"Where are you staying, Jamie?"

"At Darwin," Ramsgill said.

"Look, ride with me. It's not out of my way. In fact, how about a pint? We can catch up on each others' lives."

"Sounds good."

"Ms. Mallow? Would you like to join us?"

"It's Fiona, Inspector. And no. Those kids, remember?"

"Very well. Another time, perhaps."

They rose and Hill shook Fiona's hand. She responded by giving him a smile.

Maria Lendtmayer exited the women's room on the second floor of Scroope Terrace, wearing only a pale pink terry-cloth bathrobe with a gold sash. Carrying her clothes to the south end of the hall, she entered a pair of double doors into a large studio. She noticed the immediate look of surprise from the circle of students surrounding the room, and the kind smile of the teacher. She placed her things carefully in a pile by the door. She then walked in her bare feet to a ladder-backed chair that was atop a large purple satin cloth, the cloth, in turn, draped artfully over a number of unseen stacked boxes.

She reached the chair and removed the bathrobe, revealing a stunning body, at once supple as well as muscular. She had a head of silky midlength blond hair and fleshy, pouting lips outlined in purple lip gloss. Her skin was smooth and fair, and her high cheekbones held enigmatic hazel eyes. Her eyebrows looked like they had been painted on by a calligrapher's brush.

Maria stood still until the teacher, an attractive brunette woman in jeans and a paisley waistcoat, came over to her. Gently, without speaking, she guided Maria into the chair, manipulating Maria's arms and legs into attitudes that she liked before stepping back and tilting her head as she studied her model. She then adjusted two hot white lamps that stood on metal light poles.

"Maria, are you comfortable?"

Maria nodded, her face whitewashed by the light. In truth, she was never comfortable in this undersized chair. But tonight, as on each Tuesday night when she acted as model for the life drawing class, she didn't complain. She appreciated the money, twenty pounds for two hours of work, and she liked the teacher, Christina Appleford. She had met her two years ago, and when she had learned that Appleford taught life drawing at the school, she offered her services as a model. Appleford had originally asked Maria to her own studio, where she did countless nude oil sketches of her, the bulk of which had been exhibited at Kettle's Yard Gallery this past August in an exhibit that had been a minor sensation in town. And then Appleford brought her to the Tuesday evening class, where she both surprised and fascinated the students. Like a full-figured Rubens model, Maria was a classic, from the wonderful proportions of her body to the refined Teutonic beauty of her face.

"This will be a quick one, students," said Appleford. "Just thirty seconds. Okay? Let's start."

Maria held her head stationary while her eyes wandered around the room. She watched as arms moved into full motion, the newsprint pads being inscribed with charcoal. Appleford instructed the students to do five of these quick studies, with Maria changing her position in the chair each time. After the fifth, Appleford walked over to Maria.

"Okay," she said. "Now let's do a longer pose. Five minutes. Is five okay with you?"

Maria nodded.

Appleford helped her rearrange herself into a position with her bare legs stretched out along the floor, toes pointed, her long arms hanging at her side. She then took Maria's head and gently tilted it backward, until her blond hair fell free of her neck. It was then that Appleford noticed several scratches on the rear of Maria's neck, just above the shoulder.

"What happened?" she whispered. "Cat fight?"

Maria looked up at her and smiled. "Tree branch," she said. "I was jogging along Grange Road, and a low branch caught me."

Appleford nodded. She then turned to the students.

"Okay, class, let's begin. And be loose, keeping your eyes on the model. Try to draw her without looking down at your paper. Ready, go."

Again, the arms swung into motion. Maria stared out beyond the lights, trying to sense who was here tonight. It was only the second class of the Lent term. She was sure that some who were here today hadn't been in attendance last week. It was always that way. The male freshers, mostly, who had told their friends to come and ogle the model. What would they think, she wondered, if they knew that the German girl was a lesbian?

She found her mind drifting back to the summer of her fourteenth year, the summer of the incident at Immenstadt. Her parents had taken a *häuschen* with two other couples and their children for a week's holiday on the shores of the Bodensee, near Friedrichshafen. A young Maria, already five foot four and beginning to blossom, spent every hour of every day by the water's side, on the small beach on the outskirts of town. Late in the afternoon her mother would send her father down for her in the car, in order to get her back to the cottage by sundown. On the fifth evening of their stay, her father didn't come, but instead Gunthar Krupps was sent to fetch her. She hardly knew Mr. Krupps, who was younger than her father but was one of his associates from the electric cooperative.

When he arrived at the beach, she was alone. The sun was low in the sky, and a brisk, cool breeze swept off the lake. Herr Krupps asked if she were ready to go, and she rose to walk with him to his car.

Halfway up the beach, he turned to her suddenly and mumbled something that she could not quite make out, an expletive that she had heard in school, but one that she didn't know the meaning of. He then slipped his hand beneath her hair and, touching the nape of her neck, he clumsily pulled her forward to him. He began to kiss her. His tongue was cold, and tinctured with the taste of schnapps. He then reached around her waist and lifted her, setting her back down on the sand. For half a minute he explored her body, and before she could protest, he had removed her bathing-suit bottom. The next thing she knew he was shoving his penis into her, and it was too tight—it hurt. It hurt very badly. She tried to fight him, but he had most of his weight upon her legs. He penetrated her vagina as her protests grew louder, but her own voice couldn't overcome his groans. She bit him on the shoulder, through the skin, but that only made him push harder. She felt extreme irritation, a friction, sand probably, inside her. He was then rocking, moving back and forth like a piston, like a machine for sex, but it wasn't sex, not that she knew then what sex was, but this was just pain and hurt, and embarrassment.

That was the way with men, she thought. Never gentle like her female lovers, always rough and heartless.

"Time's up," said Christina Appleford, shattering the silence of Maria's mind. "You can rest for a moment, Maria."

She loosened up, rotating her head to stretch her neck. While the students compared each other's work, she again thought of the summer at Immenstadt, and of a small pleasantness in the midst of an otherwise deplorable encounter. She now remembered how Krupps, when he was finishing with her, had finally looked her in the eyes and gave her a smile. Repulsed, she stared away, not crying, but impassive. She gazed out to the water and saw a sailboat, a long sloop with bright yellow sails. It was moving parallel to the shore, and it was only two hundred feet away. On the deck of the boat was a dog, a large tan retriever. Its paws were almost up to the boat's side rails and its warm, friendly eyes looked toward her longingly. The boat moved fast, keeled over stiffly in the afternoon wind. As the mainsail passed in front of the setting sun, she could see a woman in the stern of the boat, guiding it silently, peacefully, with one hand on the wheel. The woman was looking straight ahead, her other hand atop her head, trying to keep a wide-brimmed straw hat from blowing away. It was clear that she had not seen what had just transpired on the shore. For a moment Maria thought of calling out to the woman, to implore aid, to seek assistance in extricating herself from beneath Mr. Krupps. But instead she smiled. At the dog. She had always loved dogs.

Jamie Ramsgill stared out into the night, the broad plate glass of the Anchor Pub's windows enveloping faint white ripples on dark water. The pub was quayside on the River Cam, overlooking a wide eddy in the river known as Mill Pond. It was after nine on Tuesday evening, and the river and fens beyond were dark, a cold drizzle having laid a damp silence on the whole of the town. Straight ahead, across the river, he could see the lights of Darwin College, with the Old Granary at river's edge taking up most of his view. To his left was Scudamore's Boatyards, with most of its punts-for-hire turned upside down on the riverbank, where they would remain until spring. To his right was Silver Street Bridge. Traffic streamed steadily over the bridge, car lights flashing through the bridge's stone balusters like a giant Zoetrope that had been unwrapped and stretched across water.

Beneath the bridge, under the graceful catenary curve of its single arch, he could make out the tip of the Mathematical Bridge on the western river bank beyond. Closer to him, jostled up against Silver Street was the brown brick of Queens' Essex Building. Just beyond the Essex Building were the interior courtyards of the college, closed to outsiders, and within which was the Old Hall, scene of Rainer Gräss's retirement party.

"Here we are."

Ramsgill returned his gaze to the pub and saw Lyndsay Hill approaching their table, a tall pint of bitter in one hand and a glass of what Ramsgill hoped was bourbon in the other.

"Did they have it?" he asked Hill.

Hill set down the glasses and slipped into the bench seat across from Ramsgill.

"They did indeed," Hill said. "Jack Daniel's. A little light on ice though, I'm afraid."

Ramsgill took his drink and sipped from it.

"Thanks very much. Cheers."

"Cheers to you, Jamie. So tell me, what have you been doing for the past twenty years?"

"In a nutshell? Teaching at Princeton, mostly. Rainer Gräss helped me get a position right out of graduate school and I've been there ever since. I did take a year off in the late seventies. I had a Guggenheim Fellowship in Venice."

"Very nice," said Hill. Hill had also brought over a packet of Bombay mix, which he was now opening. He dipped in and took a handful, then offered some of the spicy snack to Ramsgill.

"Thank you," said Ramsgill. "It's nice enough, I guess. I sometimes wish I was practicing architecture, though. Academia can be a bit stifling."

"And this book you're working on. What's it about?"

"An analysis of a French Enlightment text. Marc Antoine Laugier's *Essai sur l'Architecture*. You'd find it terribly boring."

"Would I? Actually, Jamie, I matriculated in history and philosophy of science at Corpus Christi. It wasn't until graduate school that I studied criminology."

"Isn't that unusual?" said Ramsgill. "I mean, I doubt most of your colleagues came to the force that way."

"Quite unusual. We have very few college graduates, much less Ph.D.'s."

"What made you decide to join the force?"

Hill took a sip of his beer, leaving a thin foam on his upper lip.

"I don't quite know, really. But even with my degree I started as a uniformed PC. Of course, I moved up fairly quickly. The irony is that now I do very little of what I thought I'd be doing when I made the decision to become a policeman."

"Why's that?"

"Well, mostly I push paper. In fact last year I was involved in only two cases. And even they were less than sensational."

"Cut and dry?"

"Essentially. The first involved the suicide of an eighteen-year-old at Emmanuel College. The poor lad had come up to Cambridge to study history, because, as his father later told me, it was 'in the blood' for Jacobsons to read history at Cambridge. Never mind that the old man was a surgeon, nor that the boy wanted to study physics. Anyway, he killed himself just after Easter break, overdosing on secobarbital in his room at college. His parents refused to believe he would do such a thing. They thought it must have been murder. So the superintendent got me involved, because of the sensitivity of the matter."

"What happened?"

"Well, from the postmortem, there was no doubt how he died. I simply went to the parents' home in Salop where the boy had been for the holidays. In his mother's medicine cabinet I found an empty bottle of Seconal, which the mother admitted to having recently replenished."

"That's rather grim," Ramsgill said. He took another sip of his drink and looked to the next table, where a group of rowdy young men had broken into song.

"It's not usually that bad," said Hill loudly, trying to combat the noise. "I had another case over in Newnham, just this December, in fact. Rather funny, that one. The owner of a grocery store was found dead in his meat freezer in the early morning by one of his employees. He was wearing a bloodied apron and a neighbor, a spinster, reported having seen a suspicious-looking van parked behind the grocery the previous evening."

"And?"

"And as it turned out, there *had* been a suspicious van. Two brothers from Saffron Walden were delivering uninspected pork. Seems the grocer was buying the illegal meat and doing his own butchering, hence the blood on the apron."

"Then how did he die?"

"Heart attack. It was just a coincidence that he happened to be in the freezer at the time."

Hill began to laugh, and Ramsgill joined in.

"We really shouldn't be laughing," Hill said. "Poor man. But I have to tell you, that's the kind of cases we get. I'm hardly a real-life Inspector Morse."

Hill took another sip of bitter and set his glass back on the table.

"Then how about the case of Rainer Gräss?" asked Ramsgill.

Hill's bronze eyes drifted out the window, downriver toward Queens'.

"My guess is that the river holds the answer to that," he said.

"So you think he left Queens' by water?"

"Seems logical."

"How so?"

"Look at it this way, Jamie. Say we search the college tomorrow, and find, as I suspect, that neither he nor his body are there. That means he left the college grounds."

"Right."

"Then the question becomes when and how he left."

"The *when*," said Ramsgill, "is some time between midnight and twelve forty-five."

"And the *how?*"

"Well, certainly not through the Porters' Lodge just across the bridge here. And the buildings prevent any other way out."

"Within reason," said Hill. "A younger, more fit man might have climbed to the roof or scaled a fence or something. But it doesn't sound like Dr. Gräss would do that. Nor would he have the ability at his age."

"Agreed."

"Which leaves us with the river. Now you can't walk the riverbank. The college buildings come right up to the water on the eastern shore. The western bank is walkable, but without a public footpath. If he went north by foot, he would've run into the drain that separates Queens' from Kings'. If he came south here, he would have run into the Silver Street Bridge. The only other way up or down the river is by water. Perhaps we'll drag it tomorrow."

"Then you're considering the worst?"

"I didn't want to say so in front of Ms. Mallow, but death's probable. As is murder."

"Why?" Ramsgill didn't want to believe him. He had thought of murder himself, of course, but this was coming from a police inspector.

"Because a body hasn't turned up. Alive or dead. If it was an accident, if he just fell off the bridge, then surely the body would have surfaced. The river's only four or five feet deep."

"Fiona seems to believe that murder is just . . . just too unreal. That it couldn't happen within the department."

"Oh, it could happen," said Hill. "It's been a few years, but I remember a murder involving a member of the law faculty."

"If that's the case, do you think it was one of the people at the party who did it?"

"It would be hard to argue otherwise. Robbery as a motive or an attack by someone unknown to Gräss seem unlikely."

"Why's that?"

"Several reasons. First of all, the assailant would have to get into the college to commit the act. Second, he would have to get out. Third, why would a robber hide the body? Just off the chap, take his money, and flee. And though I haven't seen the wallet yet, no one's mentioned that any money or credit cards were missing."

"And the wallet leads us back to the river."

"It does."

"Okay," said Ramsgill. "I'm with you. But then someone from the party had to come upon Rainer outside the hall, kill him, get him away from the college . . . *and* get back . . . within forty-five minutes. Not to mention without being seen."

"Which would not be easy."

"I should say not," Ramsgill replied. "How'd they do it? By punt? Whoever it was certainly didn't get into the river themselves, otherwise they would have come back to the party soaking wet."

"You're beginning to think like an investigator, Jamie." Ramsgill smiled.

"It's also doubtful they would have come in this direction," he continued. "If they'd passed through Mill Pond here, they'd have been seen by everyone in this room."

Hill finished off his beer with a single long gulp.

"Right."

"So instead, they headed north. Downriver, through the Backs, the rear of each of the colleges that adjoin the river. It's dark and it's isolated. The only question is to where."

"You want another drink?" Hill asked.

"No. I'm tired enough as it is. But do you want me to get you a pint?"

"No thanks."

"So to where?" Ramsgill asked again. Hill dipped again into the bag of Bombay mix.

"That's what we'll have to find out. I think I'll get the dogs out tomorrow, too. See what they can find. Maybe the body is buried out there in one of the college gardens. Or in King's cow pasture."

Ramsgill stared down at his glass, wiping condensation from its side.

"It seems morbid to be talking about Rainer as a *body*," he said. "Two hours ago I was at Fiona's simply inquiring why he didn't pick me up from the airport."

"Sorry, Jamie. I don't mean to be insensitive."

"It's just going to take some time to sink in," said Ramsgill. "Rainer really was a good person. He had his faults, but I owe him a lot."

Ramsgill took in a long breath and realized he was speaking of Rainer in the past tense. He looked down to his watch.

"I should let you get some sleep," said Hill.

"Yeah," Ramsgill said. "I suppose I should go out to Rainer's cottage in the morning. Though I'm not sure what I can say to Ghislaine to comfort her."

"If she's estranged from him, she won't need much comforting," Hill said.

"Sounds like you've been there."

Hill nodded.

"I've been divorced eleven years now. It sounds cruel, but the primary reason I would mourn my ex-wife's death would be concern for our daughter. Lynn's the only decent legacy of our marriage."

"How old is Lynn?"

Hill produced his wallet, showing Ramsgill a picture of the girl.

"Nineteen. Wonderful girl. She's studying at the University of Edinburgh."

"She looks like you," Ramsgill said.

Hill returned the wallet to his pocket.

"I don't know if that's a compliment."

"Of course it is."

"How about you, Jamie? Married?"

"No. But I'm living with someone. I suppose we'll do it at some point. I'm not getting any younger."

"All-American girl?"

"Actually she's Italian," he said. "And she'd probably belt you if you called her a *girl*."

"Right. *Girl* connotes sexism now. What's her name?"

"Elena."

"Is she back in the States?"

"Yes. We met a year and a half ago at her father's villa on Lago di Garda. He's the famous furniture manufacturer, Piruzzi, SpA."

"Sure."

"Anyway, Elena came over to Princeton this past summer and has just taken a job in Philadelphia."

"And you're alone again?"

"It's only for two weeks. I'll survive."

"Jamie, how well do you know Fiona Mallow? I noticed earlier you called her by her first name."

The question surprised Ramsgill.

"Quite well."

"Attractive woman," said Hill.

Ramsgill noticed that Hill hadn't said "girl." His eyes seemed to communicate an interest, and for a second Ramsgill felt a tinge of jealousy. He still thought about Fiona, and about the pain he had suffered when she left Cambridge. He loved Elena—God, did he love Elena—but for some reason he felt that he still had a stake in Fiona.

"She's a *very* attractive woman," Ramsgill said. "In fact, Fiona and I lived together my last year here."

"I see. Is she married now?"

"No, divorced. Less than a year after I left Cambridge, she married a wealthy estate agent. But he walked out on her and her kids four years ago."

"That's terrible," said Hill.

"Yeah. She never deserved Dick Mallow."

Hill raised his eyebrows. Ramsgill finished the last of his drink.

"I guess we should go," said Ramsgill. "By the way, I usually sit in on Rainer's seminars when I'm here. If I do tomorrow, are you going to kick me out when you question the others?"

Hill looked over to Ramsgill, his face haggard yet warm.

"I doubt it, Jamie. Murder can be enlightening. And you've just begun your education."

Five

*R*amsgill woke the next morning to the muffled whine of a vacuum cleaner. As he rolled over, his eyes met bright white sunlight, streaming in low through the bay window of his small, but comfortable, room on the second floor of the Old Granary at Darwin College.

In actuality the Old Granary was neither old nor a granary, but rather a very pretty Victorian conceit that overlooked the Cam at Mill Pond. Away from the river it formed a small courtyard with the Darwins' former household, Newnham Grange. It had been built in 1890 by J. J. Stephenson, a pupil of Sir George Gilbert Scott and friend of William Morris. Rooms in the Old Granary were among the most romantic in college, discounted only by the fact that the rustic building had a dearth of heating in winter and drafty windows that rattled like wooden wind chimes each time a gust blew off the water.

Ramsgill hopped out of bed and put on a pair of sweatpants. Pulling on a T-shirt, he walked to a solitary French door adjacent to the bay window and stepped out to a balcony. The sky was a brilliant blue, with a few high, white, scudding clouds. The temperature was well above freezing. From his student days he knew how rapidly the weather could change in Cambridge; there were days when it alternated continuously between sun and rain. He remembered how, when the air was clear, the silver light of Cambridge made the landscape almost shimmer. He could also remember the short, dark days of winter, when an oppressive blanket of gray seemed to hover just above the city's Gothic spires and the sun went down at three thirty in the afternoon.

He returned inside, resolved to take advantage of one of the good days. He thought momentarily about calling Elena. He had missed her upon his return from the Anchor Pub the previous evening and he wanted to tell her about Rainer Gräss. It was the middle of the night in the United States, however, so the call would have to wait until afternoon.

He put on his cycling shorts and cleats, and the old Cambridge sweatshirt he planned to replace on this trip. His bicycle had been waiting for him when he got back from the pub, no worse for the wear, its hand-painted graphite frame as shiny as the day he had bought it. He went to the gyp room at the end of his hall and retrieved his water bottle from the communal refrigerator. Downstairs, he unlocked the bike and pedaled across the Fen Causeway toward town.

He set off in a southerly direction, down Trumpington Road, going against the traffic that clogged one of the main routes that led into the city. A mile south of town the traffic began to thin just as he turned west off of Trumpington onto Grantchester Road, a winding country lane that led past small farm cottages and hedgerows set close to the road.

Grantchester itself was a picture-perfect village, with a church, two pubs, a few shops, and numerous thatched-roof cottages along its High Street. Plumes of blue-gray smoke drew from daubed chimneys, and the pungent smell of burning leaves hung heavy in the winter air. Sharp-winged swallows did fast figure eights around the treetops, and a lone postman made his way in and out of gated front yards.

Ramsgill crested a hill and left the heart of the village. His breathing by now had accelerated into short, rapid breaths, and his calf muscles were beginning to burn. The long grade led past fallow fields that stretched all the way from Grantchester to the M11. He soon passed a mammoth estate on his left, larger than the whole village of Grantchester. It was a sprawling Elizabethan manor house set some fifteen hundred feet back from the road on a rolling site whose thick woods stood in marked contrast to the surrounding farmland. A high iron fence ringed the property, and in the distance he caught a glimpse of the house, a four-square block of brown brick and gray stone capped by what seemed to be a forest of chimneys atop the house's parapeted roof. It was then that he recalled that the manor house was Purdington End, the late Sir Seymour Beggs's family home and likely now that of Cheverton.

He hardly took it in, though, because he was past the estate in a near instant, now pedaling in his highest gear combination, crouched down to mitigate drag, looking up only periodically to ensure that no obstacles littered his path. He was approaching the M11 overpass, heading up an increasing grade. He downshifted his derailleur to the second sprocket of his rear wheel and crested the bridge with speed to spare. Another mile would take him into Coton. He could recall with clarity Short Reach Cottage, Ghislaine and Rainer's house, which they had renovated during his time at Cambridge. He could still picture the new thatched roof, with its scalloped lays and cuts, and the brilliant red door with its hand-forged wrought-iron hardware. He recalled the small front yard, with yews sculpted into near-perfect balls, and the pristine rectangle of lawn contained by low, dry-set stone walls.

He coasted down a long hill. The road made several sharp turns as it steepened again, coming into the village of Coton. Ramsgill pedaled straight on through without stopping. Just outside of town he could see the cottage beyond, its gray roof framed against the azure sky.

He slowed, trying to catch his breath. When he reached the house he unclipped his shoes from the pedals and came to a halt at the edge of the driveway. His eyes rose to take in the cottage. It was the same house, though it was in a considerable state of disrepair. The thatch roof, which had been put on anew some twenty years ago, was a grayish black, no doubt from fungus and two decades of exposure to windswept weather. The whitewash of the house's cob walls was all but faded, much of the paint having peeled. The front door was no longer scarlet red, but weathered to a near rust color. The yews had grown unpruned, with shoots of new growth protruding in all directions. In the yard, a formidable stump occupied the spot that had once held a large beech tree. A stack of newspapers was tucked beneath one of the yews near the front door. In the driveway was an old Vauxhall.

For a moment he wondered whether they still lived here. Then the front door opened, and a young black man hurried out. He was big-shouldered with a round face, and wore gold rings on virtually every finger of both hands. Just behind him came Ghislaine Gräss, a heavier, more weary-eyed Ghislaine than the one who existed in Ramsgill's memory. She followed the young man out to the car and watched as he got inside. The engine started, coughing twice before sputtering to a smooth idle. Ghislaine kissed the fingers of her right hand, then pressed them to the young man's cheek. The rear lights of the car came on, and it began to back up.

Ghislaine caught sight of Ramsgill, straddling his bicycle at the end of the drive, and brought her hand up to her mouth. Ramsgill pulled onto the grass as the Vauxhall rolled backwards past him. The young man looked at him briefly before turning ninety degrees into the road and within seconds, the sound and sight of the car were gone.

Ramsgill dismounted and walked it up the gravel drive.

"Ghislaine, it's me. Jamie Ramsgill."

He approached her slowly, and it would seem to him later that it took the better part of an hour to walk those few steps. She was dressed in a turquoise satin dressing gown, tied loosely around her waist. Her once blond hair was streaked with gray, and it stuck out in every direction, as if it had been permed in a wind tunnel. Her eyes were puffy and wet, and one side of her mouth curled inward, as if she had been the victim of a stroke. On her feet she wore light leather sandals.

"Jamie."

She attempted a smile, which accentuated the age lines in her face.

"I'm sorry, Ghislaine. I should have telephoned. I didn't mean to come upon you like this."

Ghislaine's eyes skirted off to the distance before returning to Ramsgill.

"Don't worry about it. Come in. Come inside."

He followed her into the house. The smell of decline met him immediately. It was the smell of rugs that needed beating, and of mold, and of rooms that had gone too long without being cleaned. The front hall was dark, and they walked through to a brighter living room, then to a dining area that overlooked the rear yard. The yard was lit brilliantly by the sun, but like the front yard, it was strewn with the detritus of Ghislaine and Rainer's lives. At the back of the yard, beyond a low stone wall, rose a broad crescent of fallow earth.

"Have a seat, Jamie. Could I get you some coffee?"

"No thanks."

He sat in a pine chair at a round table. The table was cluttered with mail and newspapers and stacked dishes waiting to be put into the sideboard. Ghislaine poured herself a cup of black coffee, then found a pack of cigarettes on the kitchen counter. She returned, and sat across from him.

"It's good to see you, Jamie. How long has it been?"

"Three years since I've been here, but I don't remember if I saw you on that trip."

She smiled at him.

"You know," she said, "you bring back memories of Tal."

Ramsgill tried to smile, but it seemed his face muscles wouldn't let him.

"Really?"

"Yes. I remember how you used to cycle out here when you were in school. In summer the fields would be ablaze with flowering rape. Rainer, of course, would have his nose buried in some book. I would be trying to tend the garden or prepare dinner and at the same time trying to keep Tal from getting into trouble. He crawled over everything. You used to keep him occupied."

"I enjoyed it," Ramsgill said. "He was a cute baby."

She lit a cigarette and pulled a glass ashtray toward her.

"Rainer used to say that if Tal ended up with my looks and his intellect, we would be very lucky indeed."

"And did he?" Ramsgill asked.

"Who's to say?" She exhaled, blowing a stream of smoke up toward the ceiling. "He didn't live long enough to know."

She flicked an ash into the ashtray, staring off to the field behind the house.

"I was very sorry to hear about his death," said Ramsgill.

She turned back to him. Even without makeup and despite the circles beneath her puffy eyes, he could distinguish her beauty, hidden beneath layers of pain and time.

"Yes, I know. You sent that beautiful letter. I still have it somewhere."

"Ghislaine? Have you heard anything from Rainer? Do you know about him?"

She nodded.

"I know what the police have told me. The chief inspector from Cambridge just telephoned. They're sending round a car to take me to the constabulary to answer some questions. And they came by last night to get a photograph for the newspaper."

"I see. But you haven't seen him since Monday night?"

"Jamie, I haven't seen him since last week. He came by to pick up some of his things on Thursday. Iain Frontis tells me he sleeps at school now. Or at Iain's flat. He comes here to check his mail, retrieve clothes, that sort of thing. Which is all right with me. The less he's here, the less friction between us."

"Fiona told me about your problems. I was so surprised. You couldn't reconcile?"

"What's the point?" she said. "Rainer hasn't loved me for a long time, Jamie. And I quit loving him the day I saw Tal laid out on that mortuary table, half of his face missing."

Tears welled up on her eyelids. She rubbed out her cigarette, then wiped the tears with her hand.

"It's possible Rainer's dead," said Ramsgill. "In fact, perhaps even murdered."

"What?" Her look of surprise was genuine, or so it seemed to Ramsgill.

"Yes. I'm sure the police will talk to you about that."

"But how? Why?"

"I don't know. But I do know that he was upset about something. Something related to the department. At the retirement party he announced that he had changed his mind, and that he wasn't going to retire."

"But what about Iain?" she asked. "Rainer was going to give up his place for him, otherwise Iain was being sacked."

"Exactly."

Ghislaine lit another cigarette, inhaling long and hard.

"Do you have any idea what he was upset about?" asked Ramsgill. "It was something to do with school, perhaps a scandal of some sort."

"No," she said. Her eyes followed the cigarette to the ashtray, where she tapped out an ash.

"Are you sure?"

"Well . . ."

"What is it, Ghislaine?"

"Well, he'd had it out last week with one of his students. He was going to take him to the university Proctors for disciplinary action. He told me he wasn't going to retire until that was taken care of."

"What student? What action?"

"George Boye," she said. Her voice had lowered to a near whisper.

"About Boye's alleged plagiarism?" asked Ramsgill.

She nodded.

"When did he tell you about that, Ghislaine?"

"Just last week. The day he came by here."

"But why did he tell you? In what context?"

She brought the cigarette to her lips but just held it there, tugging on her upper lip with her forefinger and thumb. She was looking at Ramsgill, but the blankness of the look made Ramsgill feel he wasn't even there.

"It was a threat, Jamie. He wanted to see me suffer."

"But I don't understand."

"The young man who just left here, Jamie. The one you saw . . ."

"That was George Boye?"

"It was."

The rare books room of the Art and Architecture Library was a small space off the main faculty library, dominated by a long Empire-style pedestal table of burled walnut over which hung a neoclassical chandelier. A plush floral carpet of deep green and burgundy covered the wood floor, and the walls were lined by glass-fronted bookcases, most of them locked, and all filled with a variety of old and valuable books. A few large folios lay on top of the bookcases, and framed etchings, most of them Roman scenes by Giambattista Piranesi, hung about the area of wall not taken up by the cases. The room smelled of leather, of old paper, and of dust.

Six people sat in uneasy silence around the table. They were here to attend Rainer Gräss's seminar on iconography and metaphor in post-Enlightenment architecture, yet no one in the room actually expected Gräss to show up.

Iain Frontis, as was his custom, had taken the chair next to the head of the table, where Rainer Gräss always sat. In front of him was a stack of books and a tattered white steno pad, on which he was currently scribbling what looked to be tree roots with a red felt-tip pen. As he drew, his torso rocked back and forth like an upside-down pendulum, a habit each of the others in the room was acutely familiar with. His gouged brow did little to conceal his inner feelings, the angst that had been present since Monday night when Rainer Gräss had announced he wasn't retiring.

To Frontis's right was Amy Denster, her pretty features marred by disheveled hair. Her eyes were pink with dark crescents beneath them, and her body seemed to quiver beneath her heavy overcoat, even though the room was quite warm. She stared at the table in silence, wondering what the future held for herself and, if she chose to keep it, for the baby. She wished she could talk to Rainer once again, but she didn't think she was going to have the chance. Instead she would suffer stoically and try to remember what had happened Monday night, when she had last seen Rainer in the courtyard outside Old Hall.

Next to Amy on her right was Cheverton Beggs, dressed in a Saville Row suit, sitting with such good posture as to appear inanimate. His manicured hands were clasped before him, their stillness representative of the patience Beggs had always considered one of his most admirable traits. His mind was comfortably blank, not thinking about Rainer Gräss—frankly, not giving one good goddamn about him. His thoughts were more on the inconvenience of being here in the first place, when he had two dozen exam papers to mark before tomorrow.

Across the table was Maria Lendtmayer, who could not be a greater contrast to the architectural historian. Whereas Beggs was thin and proper, Maria was robust, and she sat with an ease that bordered on slouching. Her body language contradicted her emotions, however. She was hardly enamored of the thought of being interrogated by a police inspector, or with what Amy might remember from the end of the party.

Gaines Simpson sat next to her. His arms were folded across a blue shirt with a designer crest on the breast pocket, and his sleeves rolled up. He stared at Amy Denster, who sat across the table, with detached concern. Though he considered her overly emotional and immature, he didn't like seeing her hurt, even if it was only over the disappearance of a man who deserved the worst that could befall anyone, a man who made it a habit to consume people and then spit them out.

George Boye sat next to Simpson, across from Frontis, in the chair nearest the window, through which the sun warmed white muslin drapes. His long right arm stretched out to the table and there, beneath his massive brown hand, a remnant of unpopped plastic bubble wrap waited to be spoiled. A confident smile was planted on his face. He knew with each passing moment that Gräss was not going to show, and that therefore he wouldn't have to present his paper. It was for this reason that, for the first time all year, he had perched himself next to where Gräss was to sit.

In the corner of the room, sitting in a comfortable club chair, Jamie Ramsgill sketched the faces of those before him, quickly, accurately, and with significant artistic flair. In but a few scrawling lines he captured each person's facial language: Frontis's angst, Amy Denster's despondency, Beggs's inquisitive eyes, Lendtmayer's casualness, Simpson's concern, and Boye's composure. Ramsgill had been at Scroope Terrace for little better than a half hour, but already he had heard the gossip that was spreading through the architecture school like wildfire. Not only was Rainer missing, but hearsay had it he was dead. Various rumors had him drowning in the Cam, freezing to death in the forecourt of King's College, drinking himself to death somewhere on the grounds of Queens', or being murdered by Iain Frontis. Ramsgill found it distasteful when people talked about death as if it were sport, as if there were not a human casualty involved, a real life being extinguished. Suddenly, he felt a twinge of guilt for his conversation with DCI Hill.

"I don't know why we have to just sit here," said Maria Lendtmayer, the first of those around the table to break the silence. "It's twenty past one as it is."

"We're sitting here, my dear," said Cheverton Beggs, "because a police inspector has asked us to. And I'm sure that none of us wants to be here any more than you do."

At that moment the tarnished brass door knob to the door turned, and Fiona Mallow stepped in. Behind her came a nice-looking gentleman with short red hair, followed by a thin, nervous-looking uniformed policeman.

"This is Detective Chief Inspector Hill," she said. "From the Cambridge constabulary. And PC Turtonham. As you know, the inspector wants to ask you a few questions about Rainer's disappearance."

Iain Frontis stopped rocking, and like the others he turned with interest toward the inspector.

"Good morning," said DCI Hill. "And thank you all for your patience. I hope not to take much of your time, but first I'd appreciate it if you would each introduce yourself."

The group went around the table, each giving his or her name and affiliation with the department while Turtonham scribbled the information onto a pad.

"Right," said Hill. "Now, this is a preliminary inquiry. I understand that each of you was at the party on Monday night."

There were nods around the table.

"I'm going to ask some rather direct questions. Some of which you might take offense at, but my job is to get to the bottom of Dr. Gräss's disappearance. So, to begin with, did Dr. Gräss tell any of you that he was leaving the party?"

The six people at the table responded in silence, shaking their heads.

"Did he ask any of you to watch over his briefcase, his coat . . . whatever?"

Again, six times no.

"I'd like to know who saw him last, and at what time."

Several pairs of eyes drifted to Amy Denster, who seemed to cower momentarily beneath her coat, but who then, almost as if to throw off the accusatory glares, leaned forward.

"I saw him in the courtyard outside the Old Hall just after midnight," she said.

"And you again are . . . Miss Denster?"

Amy nodded.

"Can you be precise about the time, Miss Denster?"

"Yes, five minutes past. I distinctly remember looking at my watch and thinking that he was leaving. I . . . we . . . didn't want him to leave. We were going to give him a present and we wanted to make sure that he stayed for that."

"Is that why you followed him out?"

"I didn't say I followed him out."

"Then how did you come to meet him in the courtyard?"

Amy reached up and unbuttoned the top button of her coat. She felt warm, and she wished the eyes would look away.

"Well, I . . . okay, I guess I did follow him out. Like I said, we wanted him to stay for the present."

Hill smiled gently.

"And what did you say to Dr. Gräss when you caught up with him?"

She hesitated for a moment.

"Just . . . could he please stay a bit longer," she said.

"And what was his response?"

"He said that I had it wrong. He wasn't leaving. He was just going to the WC."

"And what happened after that?"

She paused again.

"That was it. I returned to the hall."

"What time was this?"

"I don't know. A few minutes later, I think."

"Did anyone see Dr. Gräss after that?" asked Hill.

There was a short period of silence before Gaines Simpson spoke up.

"Maybe," he said, in his distinctly American accent.

"You're Simpson?"

"Yes. And I'm a student at Queens'. I'd spilled some wine on my shirt. It was red wine and would stain, so I went to my room for a new one. Crossing Cloister Court, I think I saw the old man standing near one of the planting beds, taking a whiz. He was bent over, facing the bed, at least I assumed that's what he was doing."

"Cloister Court? That's in the direction of the river, right?"

"Yes," said Simpson.

"Is your room in that direction?" asked Hill.

"Yes. It's in the Fisher Building. Across the footbridge."

"What time was it you went to your room?"

"I don't have any idea," he said.

"Before or after Amy returned to the hall?"

"I really don't know."

He paused, then spoke again.

"No, I take it back. It must have been after. I remember Amy coming back into the hall, and the look on her face . . . as if she'd been crying. I went to my room after that."

Hill looked momentarily to Amy, then back to Simpson.

"Did you see anyone else when you went to your room?"

"I don't know. I was pretty lit."

Turtonham made a note to follow up on this.

"Can you tell me how long you were gone?" asked Hill.

Simpson finally unfolded his arms and rested his palms on the table.

"I don't know," he said. "Twenty minutes, I suppose."

"Did anyone else see Dr. Gräss outside in the courtyard . . . after?" asked Inspector Hill.

Ramsgill noticed that George Boye almost said something, but restrained himself.

"Right. Then who was the first to notice him missing?"

"We all did, I suspect," said Cheverton Beggs, his head turning stiffly.

"And what time was that?"

"I suppose it was quarter to one."

"Are you sure?"

"Yes, that's the time we were preparing for the gift presentation. We were all in the hall. All of us except Rainer, that is."

"And you didn't think it odd that he was missing at this point?"

"We didn't consider him missing," said Iain Frontis. He spoke with a strong Scottish accent, and rocked to the rhythm of the words. "We waited for him, and Amy even went back out to look for him. Soon after the party just sort of broke up."

"Okay," said Hill. "Now, did anyone else leave the Old Hall between the time that Dr. Gräss went out of the hall at a little past midnight, and twelve forty-five, when it was discovered that he was missing?"

"I would imagine," said Maria Lendtmayer, "that several of us did."

"You are Miss Lendtmayer?" Hill asked.

"*Ms.* Lendtmayer," she replied.

"Did you leave the hall, *Ms.* Lendtmayer?"

Maria brushed a strand of her silky blond hair away from her face.

"Yes," she said. "I went to telephone a friend at about midnight."

"Did you see them?"

"Them?"

"Ms. Denster and Dr. Gräss."

"Not on the way to make my call. But on the way back I did."

Ramsgill noticed Amy adjusting herself in her chair.

"Can I inquire," asked Hill, "who you telephoned?"

"I thought this wasn't an official interrogation."

Hill stared at her a good five seconds, but she didn't yield.

"Okay," he said. "We'll find that out later . . . if we have to. Would you answer this, then? How long were you out of the hall?"

"Twenty-five, maybe thirty minutes."

"Seems like a long time. Where are the phones?"

"They're near the river, off the portal there."

Ramsgill and Hill exchanged gances before Hill turned his gaze away.

"Who else left the hall?" he asked, his eyes now panning the table.

"I went out to get some more wine," said Frontis. "At about a quarter past twelve."

"Did you see Gräss? Mr. Simpson here has told us that he saw him in Cloister Court at about the same time."

"No. The college's cellar is in the other direction. Across Old Court, toward Queens' Lane."

"Did you see anyone on your way?"

"Maria. She asked me where the loo was, and I showed her."

"And this was at quarter past twelve?"

"No. More like twelve twenty-five. I had already been to the cellar."

"Ms. Lendtmayer, did you see Professor Frontis?"

"Yes. I was just coming back from my phone call."

Hill brought his hand up to his temple and rubbed it, slowly making small circles. His brow tightened, and it was clear that something bothered him.

"Someone's mistaken," he said.

"What do you mean?" said Maria.

"Was Professor Frontis carrying wine when you saw him?"

Maria thought for a moment.

"I believe so."

"And you're sure it was after you had made your phone call that you met up with him?"

"Yes. Quite sure."

"But you also told us that you saw Ms. Denster and Dr. Gräss after making your call."

"That's correct."

"So you went to make your call at midnight."

"Right."

"What time did you see Amy and Dr. Gräss?"

Maria looked to Amy, whose face was flushed.

"I, uh . . . I suppose it was around twelve twenty."

"But Amy already told us that she was with Dr. Gräss just a few minutes."

"Then maybe it was earlier," said Maria. "Twelve ten, perhaps."

"Then what did you do for the next fifteen minutes, between the time you saw Amy and the time you saw Professor Frontis?"

"I . . . I uh . . ."

"Maybe Iain's wrong," Amy broke in. "Isn't that possible, Iain?"

Frontis shook his head. "No," he said.

Hill stared back at Amy, then to Lendtmayer.

"If Professor Frontis was wrong," Hill said, "and it *was* earlier, then Maria should have seen Gräss up at the loos, right? Because according to Amy, that's where he was heading also."

Maria didn't speak. The weariness on Amy's face seemed to deepen.

"I want to know the truth," said Hill.

"I'm just not sure," said Amy. "Maybe it was later. I don't know."

Hill turned back to Frontis.

"And how long were you out of the hall, Professor Frontis, when you went to get the wine?"

"I'd say ten minutes . . . fifteen at the most."

"Did anyone else leave the hall during this time?"

Again, Ramsgill thought he noticed Boye begin to speak. But there was silence around the table.

"Okay," Hill said. "What I'd like to know now is what each of you did after the party."

His eyes fell upon Iain Frontis first.

"I walked home," Frontis said.

"Where do you live?"

"In the Charrington Flats, at the intersection of the Fen Causeway and Newnham Road. I walked across the fens."

"Were you alone?"

"George walked with me as far as Laundress Lane. I cut down by the river at the Anchor Pub and he took the Silver Street Bridge to Darwin."

"Do you know what time you arrived home?"

"Quarter past, twenty past one, I suppose."

"Is there anyone who can vouch for you?"

"My cat."

A nervous laughter rose quickly and slowly died down.

"And you, Mr. Boye?"

Boye smiled.

"I went to Darwin, like the professor said," he replied. "I saw nobody. I spoke to nobody. And I was in bed by one thirty."

Hill turned to Gaines Simpson.

"Mr. Simpson, what did you do after the party?"

"I went straight to bed. I was supposed to row the next morning at six, and I knew that I was going to have a hell of a time getting up."

"And you, Professor Beggs?"

"My car was at Pembroke. I offered to give Amy a lift to Newnham, which she accepted. I dropped her off at twenty past or so, and I got to Grantchester by half past."

"Anyone to vouch for you?"

"I don't have a cat, if that's what you mean."

He looked around, but no one laughed.

He cleared his throat then said, "My man Cox was asleep, as was my mother. She's eighty-six years old."

"Amy?"

"The porters were off duty at my college," she said. "I slipped in with my key. I did see one student who was up late studying. I think she saw me."

"Ms. Lendtmayer?" Hill said.

"I cycled home," she said.

"And where do you live?"

"I share a house on Thompson's Lane, near Magdalene."

"That's next to the river, isn't it?"

"It is."

"Did you see anyone at your house?"

"I crawled into bed with my . . . my significant other. We had a brief snuggle, if that counts for anything."

Hill looked down toward the carpet, considering whether he had anything else to ask.

"Right," he said. "Well, I think that's all I have for now. There will be more questions undoubtedly, depending on what turns up."

"And what have you found, Inspector?" asked Beggs.

"Here? Nothing much."

"But you're certainly doing more than just interviewing *us*. Anything on other fronts?"

"No. But we've just turned over a few stones. We're searching the college, the river, and the Backs today."

"You're considering the worst," Amy said, looking as if she were about to cry. "Couldn't he be safe somewhere, away on his own?"

"Of course he could, miss. We'll just have to see. His picture will be in today's paper, describing the disappearance. And we've sent out a nationwide file via the Police Network Computer. If he's out on his own, someone will spot him and they'll contact us."

Amy tried to smile.

"Any more questions, then?" said Hill.

No one spoke up.

"I'd like to hear of any other information you might recall," he said. "I'll leave my card with Ms. Mallow. I'm at Parkside Station."

With that, Hill looked briefly at Ramsgill, then bolted from the room. Fiona followed him out and shut the door. The group at the table looked warily at one another, no one knowing exactly what to say, but each face clearly full of questions and the desire to talk further.

George Boye, who was still feeling invincible from not having to deliver his paper, spoke first.

"Amy," he said in his smooth voice, "you didn't tell the inspector everything, did you? And he almost caught you on it."

Amy brushed a hair away from her face and looked at Boye with puzzled eyes.

"What are you talking about?" she asked.

"You told him you were only with Rainer for a brief moment, and that you had simply asked him to come back into the hall."

"So?"

"So that's not what happened. You were with him for several minutes. I heard you arguing."

"Arguing about what?" said Beggs.

"About certain matters in her and Rainer's relationship," said Boye.

Amy's face became fully flushed. Her eyes opened wider.

"There's no need to be embarrassed," Boye said. "I think that everyone in this room, with the possible exception of our American professor, knows that you and Rainer were having an affair."

Her gaze accelerated around the table. There was a definitive lack of surprise in the eyes of her colleagues, confirming Boye's statement.

"Okay," she said softly. "Rainer and I may have had words in the courtyard. But they're of no consequence to his disappearance."

Frontis, who was rocking steadily, paused. He looked up with a glare and said, "They are if Rainer is dead. They have great consequence."

"What are you implying, Iain?" said Simpson, coming to Amy's defense.

"Nothing. Just that why should she lie to the police about what happened in the courtyard?"

Amy looked across the table to Simpson, thinking of the painful grip Rainer had put on her arm before he was pulled away.

"*Why?*" said Simpson. "To protect her relationship with Rainer, of course."

"What I'd like to know," said Cheverton Beggs, "is how young George here knew that Amy and Rainer were arguing if he never left the hall. Do you have X-ray vision, George, or were you, like Amy, not telling the truth to the inspector?"

Boye disliked Beggs almost as much as he did Gräss. His hand involuntarily popped a couple of the bubbles on his bubble wrap.

"George?" asked Frontis.

"I slipped out to go to the loo as well," said Boye. "But only for a moment. When I came out of the courtyard portal, I heard Amy and Rainer arguing. When I saw them, I quickly retreated. I have enough trouble with Rainer already. I didn't want to be caught spying on him. After all, what does a man do alone out in the dark with his mistress?"

"You bastard," said Amy.

Gaines Simpson rose abruptly from his chair and grabbed Boye's collar.

"Apologize," said Simpson.

"Sit down, Gaines," said Frontis, watching the seminar disintegrate into a near melee.

"Make him apologize," Simpson repeated.

"Sit down, Gaines," Frontis repeated.

Simpson didn't sit down. Instead, he pushed himself away from Boye, picked up his notebook from the table, and, without excusing himself, stormed out of the room.

Silent stares ringed the table.

"Listen," Frontis said, looking at Boye, then at the others, "I think we should adjourn for today. Everyone's edgy. Let's meet again on Monday."

Frontis rose and departed, and one by one the group filed out of the room. Ramsgill was the last one out of the room. He decided to go over to Fiona's office to see if he could catch Hill. He wanted to tell him about George Boye and Ghislaine Gräss. And about Boye's having lied about leaving the hall.

But Hill had already left and Fiona was on the phone. So instead Ramsgill climbed the stairs to the second floor, to the temporary office the department had supplied him. As he was unlocking the door he could hear voices in the room next to him, Cheverton Beggs's office. Ramsgill opened his door and stepped inside, leaving it slightly ajar.

"You lied too, Cheverton," said a female voice, which Ramsgill recognized as that of Maria Lendtmayer.

"I'm quite sure I don't know what you are talking about," Beggs said.

"The inspector asked if anyone else was out of the hall," said Maria. "During the time that Rainer went missing. You accused George of lying, yet you were out of the hall for a good long time, too."

"And how do you know that?"

"I saw you. Just before I saw Iain."

There was a long pause. Ramsgill started to close his door. But then Beggs spoke again.

"Okay, Maria, maybe I *was* out of the hall for a short time. I guess that means we were all out at one point or another. What of it?"

"If Rainer is dead, it might mean a great deal."

"*If* he is dead," said Beggs, "which nobody around here seems to know. You usually have a body on hand to confirm that someone has expired. Or maybe, Maria, the good *Herr* Gräss simply had a transfiguration, right out there in the Cloister Court of Queens', right up to heaven. What do you think?"

"I think that the police are going to find his body."

"So you don't believe he's gone off on holiday or a drunken binge?"

"No."

"But no one saw him leave the college, my dear. Did he jump off the Mathematical Bridge and float downriver? Or was he pushed? That's an interesting theory, given that you live on the water."

"I'm afraid I don't have a motive, Cheverton."

"Nor do I," said Beggs.

"But you had plenty of time out of the hall."

"What on earth are you suggesting, Maria? That I killed Gräss? For what conceivable reason? Of all the people who were in that room, I am the sole person over whom Rainer holds no power. Your life, as well as that of the other students, is practically mortgaged to Rainer. And Iain was being skewered by him."

"My life is controlled by no one," Maria said. "Why did you leave the hall, Cheverton?"

"None of your goddamned business."

"Very well," she said. "But if the inspector interviews me again, I'm going to tell him what I know."

Ramsgill then heard footsteps leaving the office, and he could see Lendtmayer passing by. Then Beggs left the office too, following her. But he went only a few feet before stopping, right in front of Ramsgill's door. He turned, and could see Ramsgill looking out.

"Well," said Beggs. "An American spy."

Ramsgill didn't know how to respond. He pulled the door open.

"I'm sorry," he said, his face flushed. "I didn't mean to eavesdrop."

"Very uncivilized," Beggs said. He reached out his hand and Ramsgill shook it.

"I'm Jamie Ramsgill," he said. "We've met before."

"Have we then?" said Beggs. "Mind if I come in?"

Before Ramsgill could answer, Beggs had taken one of two chairs that faced Ramsgill's desk. Ramsgill walked around the desk and sat.

"So tell me, Jamie. Do you make it a habit of listening in on private conversations?"

"As I said, I'm sorry. This whole business with Rainer has gotten me upset."

"Indeed," said Beggs. "And I doubt you had seminars of the sort we just had when you were in school here."

"Oh, we used to have fights in seminar," said Ramsgill. "About theory, though, not murder."

"Terrible business all this," said Beggs. He crossed his legs, his eyes taking in the unadorned office. "You were close to Gräss, weren't you?"

Ramsgill had always thought of himself as being close to Gräss, but the picture of the man emerging was different from the one he held in his memory. It was true that as the years had gone by the two of them had drifted apart, and in fact, on his last two visits to Cambridge, Rainer had hardly made any time available for his American friend. Ramsgill had chalked it up to the pressures of Rainer's position, and his lack of free time. But perhaps it was a conscious break on Rainer's part. It hurt to think that their friendship was not as honest as he had believed.

"We were," he said. "But mostly a long time ago."

"Yes," said Beggs. "Rainer was a different person back then. Civil, so I've been told."

"How about you?" Ramsgill asked. "How did you get on with him?"

Beggs shrugged.

"Fairly well," he said. "We respected each other academically. And aided each other. I helped him a couple of years ago with a book project, and now he's doing the same for me."

"There's talk that you wanted to head up the Ph.D. and M.Phil. programs," said Ramsgill, "after Rainer retired."

Beggs laughed. "Who told you that? Iain? Fiona? No thank you. I'm happy doing my survey courses and publishing a book every two or three years. Surely you must agree. Fiona tells me you're researching a book while you're here. What's it about?"

"It's an analysis of Laugier's *Essai sur l'Architecture*. I'll be examining the Boisset papers in the library."

"Interesting period," said Beggs. "In fact, my new book dwells on the eighteenth century. It's entitled *Ruin and Fragment in the Enlightenment*. About the cult of ruins, mostly in English gardens . . . sham ruins, appropriated abbeys . . . that sort of thing. I've finished the manuscript. Rainer was proofreading it for me."

"Congratulations," said Ramsgill. He envied Beggs for having finished a manuscript, whereas he was just beginning his.

"I say, I should have you down to Purdington End," said Beggs. "To talk about it more, and to show you our own ruins, those of Purdington Abbey."

"I cycled through Grantchester today," said Ramsgill. "I believe I passed the estate."

"You can't miss it," said Beggs. "Though why my great-grandfather thought he could keep up such a place I'll never know. He bought it a hundred years ago for a song. Little did he realize that you need a staff the size of an army to keep it up. And help is not so easy to come by as it was in the nineteenth century, not to mention the sixteenth, when the place was built."

"I'd love to see it," said Ramsgill. "Especially the abbey ruins."

"Then by all means let's set a date," said Beggs. He rose and smiled at Ramsgill. "Come over to my office and let me look at my calendar."

Ramsgill followed him next door.

Beggs's office was immaculate and it smelled of cleanliness. Beggs sat at his desk, and Ramsgill took a seat in what he assumed was a reproduction of Josef Hoffmann's *Fledermaus* chair. But as he sat, he saw the worn corners of the radial arms and a fine patina on the black paint, and realized it was an original. The walls of room were lined in glass bookcases, Hepplewhite in design, and the books within the cases were arranged neatly according to size. Several etchings of eighteenth-century Paris hung above the desk. The desktop itself was inlaid with burgundy leather. A computer sat squarely within the rectangle of leather, the single modern accoutrement in the room. Several boxes of software stood neatly on the desk: a word-processing program, database software, even graphics and photography imaging programs. To the right of the computer was a small marble bust of Jean Jacques Rousseau, and a standing picture frame with a photograph of a younger Beggs in a rowing shell.

"How's Thursday afternoon?" Beggs said, thumbing through a leather daybook. "About three?"

"Sounds fine," said Ramsgill.

"Good then. You'll meet Mother, who will welcome the company."

"Fine. Thanks very much."

Ramsgill rose to leave.

"And Jamie, let's respect each other's privacy up here. Shall we?"

Ramsgill looked down at him. "Sure," he said. "But if you don't mind my asking, Cheverton, why *did* you go out of the hall?"

Beggs closed his daybook and slid it across the desk.

"To go to the loo," he said.

"That's something I still don't understand," said Ramsgill. "Why was everyone going across the courtyard? There's no loo in the hall?"

"There's not," said Beggs. "But that's Queens', you know. Frightfully out of date. At Pembroke, all of our food-service areas have loos. And we're the oldest college at Cambridge."

Ramsgill nodded.

"Can I ask you something else? How long were you gone from the hall?"

"I don't know. Ten minutes, maybe."

"And why didn't you tell the inspector?"

"What's the difference? I suppose he'll learn it anyway."

Ramsgill turned to leave. He will, Ramsgill thought, he will indeed, just as soon as I tell him.

Six

"Jamie?"

Ramsgill looked up from his notebook computer to see Iain Frontis standing in the doorway to the office, his silhouette appearing small and rumpled against the hall light behind him.

"Iain," Ramsgill said. "Come in."

Ramsgill took Frontis's rather limp hand and shook it. He had come to know Frontis on his prior visits to Cambridge, and they ran into each other from time to time in academic circles. He liked the Scot, who exuded an innocence that Ramsgill found rare in the higher echelons of academia, and had always enjoyed their discussions on design and theory.

"Have a seat," Ramsgill said.

"Thank you."

"Sorry I didn't say hello downstairs."

"Me too. Good to see you. It's been, what . . . two years now?"

"The symposium in Montreal," Ramsgill said. "That was a lot of fun. I enjoyed your talk there very much. And our dinner afterwards. How have you been?"

Frontis sat in a side chair and stared up at Ramsgill with a look that invited conversation.

"Not too good," he said.

"Rainer?" said Ramsgill as he turned another chair around to face Frontis.

"Yes." Frontis began to rock, with the palms of his hands tucked beneath his thighs. His eyes stared off to nowhere in particular.

"Want to talk about it?"

"There's not much to talk about."

"Try me."

He stopped rocking for a moment, and looked over to the American.

"Okay," he said. "It all goes back several months, when rumors began to circulate that I was being made redundant."

"I heard about that," said Ramsgill.

"Well, I'm not one to sulk," said Frontis. "And until recently I was a bit of a hanger-on around here. So as soon as I heard the talk, I began to make plans. At first, I thought that I might give up teaching altogether and open a practice. I have the Singapore project. But the more I thought about it, the more impractical it seemed. Teaching has been my life, and besides, Singapore will take years to get off the ground. Even though I've won the competition, the money has not yet been allocated. So I began inquiring at various universities, mostly abroad, to feel out the market, that sort of thing. I even wrote your university."

"And?" said Ramsgill.

"I got a wee bit of encouragement," Frontis replied. "Perhaps not as many responses as I would have liked, but the economy is still in the doldrums, and schools all over are cutting back. Then, in the midst of my search, Rainer comes to me and tells me, don't worry. He can see how much this is affecting me. He tells me that he has been contemplating retirement anyway, and that he's decided to take it early, to allow me to stay on."

"You must have been happy," Ramsgill said.

"I was thrilled, don't get me wrong. I love Cambridge, and I can't imagine myself anywhere else. Which is why I was so shocked to hear his change of heart at the party. And then he goes missing . . . and though it's a terrible thing, I found myself wondering if he would come back. If he doesn't return, then I'll be asked to stay on. But now . . ."

He paused.

"Now what?"

"Now, they're saying that I . . . I murdered him."

Ramsgill rose and walked over to the door. He closed it quietly. "Who's 'they'?" he said.

"The rumor mill. Undergraduates maybe . . . I don't know. One of my third-year students told me about it."

Frontis paused long enough in his rocking motion to retrieve a cigarette from the pocket of his flannel shirt. He stuffed it into his mouth and nervously frisked his body for a match. When he couldn't find one, he seemed to forget about the cigarette. Ramsgill sat again.

"Someone said I put something into Rainer's port," Frontis continued, jabbing the cigarette in Ramsgill's direction, like pointing a finger. "Since I had retrieved the bottle from the cellar."

It hadn't occurred to Ramsgill that the port might have been tampered with, concentrating instead on how the murderer had gotten Gräss out of college in the first place. Certainly, tampering with the wine was a possibility—as was subduing him physically. Tampering hardly seemed feasible, though. With everyone together in the hall, how could the killer be sure exactly when the drug would take effect? If Gräss passed out at the table in front of the others, then there would have been no way for the killer to get him out. In fact, the more he thought about it, the more the whole idea of killing Gräss at the party seemed like lunacy. If someone had wanted to kill him, why do it at the party, where there would be so many witnesses? Why not kill him somewhere where the odds of getting caught would be lessened?

"*Did* you put anything into the port?" Ramsgill asked cautiously.

"No! I swear it."

"What happened to the bottle once it got to the table?"

"I don't know," Frontis said. "I didn't pay attention. But he was drinking from it. And it remained on the table."

"Could someone else have tampered with it?"

"Of course. It was an informal atmosphere. I doubt Rainer would have noticed."

"Did you see what time he left the hall?"

"It was as Amy said. Shortly after midnight. I kept hoping for him to say something to me after his announcement. I was sure that he was going to tell me that he was joking. I waited, sitting across the table from him, looking for a sign. But he ignored me. He truly ignored me. My blood was boiling, and I felt as though I were going to explode. The embarrassment was unbearable and the fact that he had made his announcement in front of everyone, disgusting. I've always felt like an outsider to begin with. I'm sure that Beggs was savoring every moment of it, in his elitist way."

"I can't explain it, Iain," Ramsgill said. "But let me ask you this, and please don't get offended: When you went out to get wine the second time, was that really at about twelve fifteen?"

"Yes."

"Besides going for the wine, were you hoping to bump into Rainer, and tell him how you felt?"

Frontis had been rocking briskly, and he now slowed, almost to a stop.

"Yes. I suppose so."

"Did you find him?"

"No. I looked in the loo and in Old Court, but I didn't see him. I was about to go through to Cloister Court when I ran into Maria. She told me Rainer had gone back into the hall."

"You asked her where he was?"

"No. Come to think of it, I didn't. I guess she assumed I was looking for him."

Ramsgill recalled Maria's statement to DCI Hill regarding her having left the hall. She had said that she went to use the telephone, but he didn't think she said how long she had been gone. Why would she have told Frontis that Gräss had returned to the hall, without his even having asked? And, since Gräss never returned to the hall, either she was lying or mistaken. Ramsgill sighed and stared up at a Japanese paper-lantern light fixture, which dominated the office the way a full moon dominates the night sky.

"What did you do then?" Ramsgill asked.

"I retrieved the wine. Two bottles of Domaine de Verquière, 'eighty-five."

"And were you really only gone ten or fifteen minutes, like you told Inspector Hill?"

"Yes, Jamie, and I know what you're driving at." He rolled his words in a poetic Scottish lilt.

"I didn't murder Rainer. It was true that I was upset after what he did, but *nothing*, including a cozy faculty position, is worth killing over."

"Do you have any idea who might have killed him?"

"We don't even know that he's dead. If he is, there are reasons enough."

"Such as?"

"Well, let's see. I don't think it's a secret that he and Boye had gone at it. And something was going on between him and Beggs."

"What was that?"

"Oh, more than the usual. The usual involved Rainer's treating Beggs with disdain, which, I might say, is not wholly unwarranted. There are several of us in the school who believe that Beggs is here only because of his father's legacy. He treads water within the department. He doesn't exactly drown, but he doesn't move forward, either. You know as well as I do, Jamie, that you have to move forward in academia to survive. And he's jealous of Rainer's reputation."

"So that's the usual. What's the *more* than usual?"

"I've heard them arguing lately. Seems to me Beggs is constantly defending himself against Rainer. I wouldn't swear to it, but I think it has something to do with Beggs's new book."

"Why do you think that?"

"At least once, when they were arguing, Rainer had the manuscript out, and he was referring to it, to make a point. That was just last week."

"Did you notice if Beggs was out of the hall at the time Rainer disappeared? Maria Lendtmayer said that he was."

"As a matter of fact, yes. When I got back with the wine, he was gone. He had complimented me on it earlier and he was one of the people who had requested more. Upon my return, I was going to pour him some, but he wasn't there."

"Did you notice what time he returned?"

"I think that he was gone fifteen minutes, or thereabouts. But as I say, he was gone when I returned, so it could have been longer."

"What about Boye? Did you notice how long he was out?"

"No."

Ramsgill leaned back, trying to form a mental picture of the party that night. He had a number of versions of events. What he didn't have was a fresh image of Queens'. It had been years since he'd been inside the college walls.

"Iain, could you get me into the college?" he asked.

"I suppose I could," said Frontis warily. "I'm going over for undergraduate supervisions at three."

Ramsgill took a look at his watch. It was 2:15.

"Meet you downstairs in thirty minutes?"

"I'll be there."

As Lyndsay Hill drove back to headquarters, he considered what, if anything, he had learned from his interviews at Scroope Terrace. He couldn't get it out of his mind that at least one, but more than likely several, of the attendees of Rainer Gräss's retirement party had lied to him. He was nearly sure that either Amy Denster or Maria Lendtmayer wasn't telling the truth. He had learned in his profession that lying came with the territory, and that behind the big lies that criminals tell are the little ones that are stumbled across in getting to the truth. Often the key to solving a case was being able to separate the two.

He pulled into the car park, and he and Turtonham made their way into the rear of the building. They went straight to the situation room he had had Chris Detler set up in a conference room on the first floor.

Detler was sitting at a long table, shirtsleeves rolled up, talking on the telephone. Two other officers milled about in the background, and when they saw the chief inspector walk in, they pretended to make themselves busy.

"Right," said Detler. "Thank you very much, then. We'll look into it."

He hung up the receiver to the phone, pretending to shoot himself in the head with a finger.

"Witness?" said Hill.

"Yet another one," said Detler. "A lady over in Cherry Hinton. She claims she saw Dr. Gräss in a car Monday evening with two . . . quote . . . *swarthy creatures . . . Arabs I would expect.* Only problem is that it was at the same time he was at the party."

Hill shook his head, leaning over the table and picking up a copy of *The Cambridge Evening News.* The story about Gräss's disappearance was at the bottom of page one, with the photograph Ghislaine Gräss had supplied. The calls had begun coming in, as he had expected.

"Anyone else come forward?" he said.

"Three or four. But so far, all cranks."

"It's still early, Chris."

Detler pushed his pad away and took a sip from a can of soda.

"How'd it go with the interviews?" he said.

"Nothing much," said Hill. "The usual white lies."

"We pretty much wrapped up our search of the college and the river," said Detler.

"And?"

"Nothing of great promise. We turned Queens' upside down this morning but didn't find a thing."

"Who was in charge of the college search?"

"Jameson, sir. But don't worry. He did a good job. I was there half the day myself. We interviewed the porters, the kitchen staff, the bedders, and a number of students. The professor is not on the grounds."

"How about the night of the party?" said Hill. "Did any of the college staff report unusual commotion?"

"No sir."

"Any strangers sighted in college?"

"No sir."

"Did any of the party goers leave the grounds?"

"Just Ms. Mallow, boss. Left by the Silver Street Gate at ten forty-five."

"Right," said Hill. He stroked his chin, then looked at Detler.

"I want you to follow up on one thing there," he said. "One of the people at the party, Gaines Simpson, is a member of college. He lives in the Fisher Building. He says he left the party for a good twenty minutes, to go to his room and change his shirt. Find out for me if he really did that."

"Sure," said Detler.

"And how about the river?" said Hill. "What did you find there?"

"Not a lot. We had two men on the water most of the day, going north all the way to the locks at Jesus Green, and south down to

Newnhamcroft. And we searched the surrounding land from Vicar's Brook up to Saint John's."

"And you didn't find anything?"

Detler shook his head.

"Did you use the dogs?"

"Yes, but they didn't arrive until after lunch. They did pick up Gräss's scent around the area of Queens' punts."

"Good. What did you do with that?"

"The forensics team from Huntingdon vaccumed the punts and searched the ground around. And we cordoned off the area."

"But what about the scent? Where did it lead?"

"It didn't lead anywhere by the shoreline. Which I suppose means he got into a boat. So we started with the dogs heading north."

"And what did you find?"

"In the end, nothing. They lost the trail at Trinity College."

"So you gave up?"

"For today we did."

"When will the dogs be back?"

"Bright and early tomorrow, sir," said Detler.

"How bright and early?"

"As early as you like."

"I want them out at seven A.M.," said Hill. "The longer we wait, the colder the trail. Do you understand?"

Detler did. He had worked for Hill in the investigations unit prior to Hill's taking the top job, and knew that as an investigator, Hill was ruthless on everybody. Including himself.

"And how about Mrs. Gräss, Chris? Did she come in?"

"Yes. I interviewed her myself. There doesn't seem to be much to report. In any other situation, I might suspect that she had something to do with his disappearance. They're estranged, and she makes no secret about her disdain for him."

"Hmm . . . but because she wasn't at the party, you think she had nothing to do with it?"

"Right."

"Well, we shall see. When did she see her husband last?"

"Last Thursday. He's been sleeping at the school, or at one of the other faculty member's flats."

"Whose?"

"Professor Frontis's."

Hill walked around the table and retrieved the pad on which Detler had been keeping phone notes. As was usual when the police asked for witnesses in a case, several people had come forward. The only problem was that, like the lady from Cherry Hinton, none of their stories held up. Hill had purposefully crafted the newspaper article such that it made no mention of Queens' College. He had done so in order to separate credible witnesses from those out to gain a little notoriety. The story had simply stated that Gräss had gone missing from the city center sometime Monday evening.

"How about the hospital?" said Hill. "Did you check that again?"

Detler nodded.

"And what about PNC?" Hill's reference was to the national police computer network.

"We've put the word out, sir. And we've contacted seven surrounding jurisdictions directly. But I thought you believed the body was nearby."

"I do. We can't overlook any possibility though. Turtonham?"

PC Turtonham had been standing in the corner of the room quietly.

"Yes sir."

"Let's see Dr. Gräss's things."

Turtonham brought over three large clear plastic bags. Hill retrieved a pair of latex gloves from a box on the table and carefully opened the first. It was Gräss's overcoat, heavy wool, charcoal gray. He searched the pockets and found nothing more than a writing pen, a wad of tissues, and a book of matches. He set it aside and opened the second bag, which contained Gräss's briefcase. He opened it and pulled out several items. The first was a present, wrapped in plaid wrapping paper. He opened it. It was a wristwatch, Gräss's reward for having given the department twenty-odd years of service.

The second item was a green vinyl date book. He opened it to the current week. Most of the appointments were academic in nature, with the exception of an appointment for 2:45 P.M. Monday, the afternoon before the party. It was with a Dr. Hargreaves at Granta Surgery.

"This is interesting," he said.

"What's that?" said Detler. He leaned forward and looked at the book. "What do you think that means, sir?"

Hill was rubbing the back of his head.

"I don't know. I had pretty much discounted suicide, because of the fact that Gräss's body hasn't shown up. Nor has a note. But maybe he got some bad medical news from this doctor. I'd like you to follow up on this, Chris."

"Yes sir."

Hill thumbed backward and forward through the date book and, once satisfied that it held nothing else of interest, he set it aside.

He then picked up a thick sheaf of papers wrapped by a large rubber band. He read the cover. *Ruin and Fragment in the Enlightenment.*

"What is it?" said Detler.

"It's Cheverton Beggs's new book manuscript. Jamie Ramsgill told me that Gräss was proofing it for Beggs. Seems they help each other with their work."

"Do you think it's of any importance?"

"I don't have a clue. But I can't look at it now."

He set the manuscript aside. He then went through the rest of items that had been in the briefcase. There were several student papers, some of Gräss's lecture notes, an empty thirty-five-millimeter camera, a folder of thirty-five-millimeter slides, and a letter from the university's Senior Proctor, Dr. T. J. M. Massingale of Downing College. The letter regarded Gräss's charges of plagiarism brought against George Boye. It stated that the Proctors had received Dr. Gräss's correspondence on the matter, and that they would begin their review at their February congregation.

"Okay," said Hill. "Look, let's get this up to Huntingdon for the lab to look at. Make me a photocopy of Beggs's book manuscript and the letter about Boye. And by the way, Beggs's fingerprints, as well as those of Amy Denster, will probably be all over this material."

Detler nodded.

"Also, Chris, I want you to review Turtonham's notes from Scroope Terrace," said Hill. "I've got some work to do in my office. I'll try to check back in an hour from now."

Detler started to tell DCI Hill to take his time, to do what he had to do. But before he could get the words out of his mouth, Hill was out the door and disappearing down the hall.

Iain Frontis and Jamie Ramsgill walked together up Trumpington Street, which at three o'clock in the afternoon was brimming with activity. Throngs of bicycling students pedaled in all directions, cars fought for their own piece of the road, and tourist buses made the circuit of the city center, taking advantage of a warm winter's day. Newsmen strolled up and down the thoroughfare hawking the afternoon paper, and booksellers showed their wares in front of their shops.

The bells of Great Saint Mary's Church chimed the hour as they turned onto Silver Street. Just past Saint Catherine's College they turned again, this time onto Queens' Lane, entering Queens' College by the gate there. Frontis pointed Ramsgill in the direction of Old Hall, then excused himself to the Junior Common Room for his supervisions.

Ramsgill crossed Old Court to a portal on its far side. In a shadowy passage he pulled back the low oaken door to Old Hall. Stepping over a raised stone threshold, he entered the room. The room was voluminous, perhaps as tall as it was long, the ridge of its peaked roof some fifty feet overhead. Its heavy wooden rafters alternated in color between vermilion red and forest green, and they were stenciled with sunbursts and flowers. Great arched tie beams spanned the room crosswise, accented in white and gold. The floor of the room was a giant mosaic of brick and stone, and a high, ebony-colored, raised-panel wainscot ran the circumference of the chamber. At the wall opposite the door, the wainscot rose to a height of twenty feet, and there it was studded with fluted half-round pilasters. Portraits hung between the columns, and swags, urns, and cartouches filled out the composition. Ramsgill pulled out his sketchbook and began to draw. Five minutes with a pen was all he would need.

The hall was furnished with four long dining tables, including the high table at the end of the room. The high table was normally reserved for college Fellows, situated beneath the portraits and within the realm of the Corinthian dais. The walls of the room above the wainscot were stenciled in a myriad of stylized floral ornaments, colors and patterns clashing in the overabundant pseudo-Gothic style of G. F. Bodley, who had restored the hall in the mid-Victorian period. Two large stained-glass windows and an oriel bay dominated the wall to the right. Two more windows flanked an overscaled fireplace on the wall to the left. The fireplace was eccentrically majestic, and above its richly carved oak mantel, a high frontispiece rose almost to the height of the windows, its surface clad with handmade tiles, attributed to William Morris and his Pre-Raphaelite associates.

When he was finished sketching, Ramsgill stepped forward, and the sound of his heels reverberated in the vacant hall. The college's main dining hall was now in Cripps Court, across the river, leaving the Old Hall to special dinners and small private parties like the one held for Rainer Gräss on the night of his disappearance. Ramsgill tried to picture it in his mind, when, he guessed, the group had occupied the high table. If it had been anything like the departmental affairs Ramsgill had attended during his time at Cambridge, it would have been a bacchanalian affair, where drink took precedence over food. The meal would have been potluck, no doubt adequate, but the wine would have flowed like water, and only the most reserved attendee would have escaped without the decimation of a few brain cells.

But if indeed Rainer had been murdered, at least one of the guests had kept his or her head. Ramsgill thought of Boye and of Beggs, both of whom had lied to Hill about not having been out of the hall. He thought of Frontis, of Maria Lendtmayer, and of Amy Denster. One of them was lying also, because their separate accounts of when they had been out of Old Hall, and for how long, were inconsistent. And the key to it all was who had been out of the hall when Rainer was out, and for how long. The matter of timing would correlate to how far away from college Rainer (or his body) could have been transported. For instance, if Gaines Simpson was responsible for Rainer's disappearance, then his being away for twenty minutes meant that Rainer could have been taken ten minutes downriver, giving Simpson ten minutes to return.

Ramsgill looked around the room one last time, then made his way outside. He headed west out of the passageway and found himself in Cloister Court. Like most of the older colleges at Cambridge, Queens' was not so much a collection of buildings as it was a collection of courtyards. Cloister Court was among the most picturesque at the university, an irregular rectangle surrounded on three sides by medieval edifices, and on the fourth by the Georgian Essex Building, which fronted Silver Street to the south. On the north side of the quad was the long gallery of the President's Lodge, a half-timbered structure dating from the sixteenth century. The court itself was formed of a lawn, so thick and green as to appear artificial. A path of gray stone led through its center, and its edges were lined with evergreen shrubs and empty planting beds.

He crossed Cloister Court, making his way west toward the building known as the Range. An arched portal took him into another passageway, and the passageway led to the Mathematical Bridge. The Mathematical Bridge was a Tinkertoy of wooden engineering, built in the early twentieth century as an exact replica of a pedestrian bridge that had stood on the site since 1749. Popular belief had always maintained that the bridge had been designed by Sir Isaac Newton, which was as untrue as the story that the entire span was held together without pegs or screws of any sort. Nevertheless, it was an attractive work, with crisscross bracing and high side rails, impossible, Ramsgill realized, for Rainer Gräss, even drunk, to have fallen off.

Standing on the bridge, Ramsgill looked around him. To his right, at the end of the span, was the portal through the Range, the direction from which he had just come. To his left, on the west side of the river, was a footpath that led to modernist Cripps and Lyon Courts, newer additions to the college. South of Cripps Court was the Fisher Building, where Gaines Simpson had gone to retrieve a clean shirt. To the south, closer still, was Silver Street Bridge and a high iron fence preventing access to the road.

The scene confirmed for Ramsgill that the only way out without being seen was by water. And with the Anchor Pub just to the south of Silver Street Bridge, he was sure that north was the direction in which Rainer would have been taken. Ahead of him, to the north, was the bridge at King's College, and beyond that, though he couldn't see past the river bend, were the bridges at Clare and Trinity, and the public footbridge at Garret Hostel Lane. On the east side of the river in that direction were the older colleges of the university. To the west was the succession of great lawns, gardens, and cow pastures known collectively as the Backs. Ramsgill realized that the Backs particularly offered the perfect environment in which to get rid of a body.

He decided he would take a walk in that direction, perhaps in the morning, as the sun was already dropping out of the winter sky. Right now, he had to head back to college to telephone Elena and then Lyndsay Hill. He had tried to call him from the school earlier, but Hill was unavailable. Ramsgill had still not told him about Ghislaine Gräss and George Boye, nor about Boye and Beggs having lied about being out of the hall.

As he left the bridge and made his way toward the Porters' Lodge at Silver Street, his eyes caught one more thing. Six punts were moored on the west bank of the river, just at the end of the bridge. Strands of yellow police tape surrounded them, and Ramsgill wondered if Hill and his men had already been north on the river, where certainly the mystery of Rainer Gräss's disappearance would come into focus.

Seven

"You ever think of moving south, Chris?"

Detective Chief Inspector Lyndsay Hill was staring out at the dark police-station car park, where a fine drizzle drifted through the illumination of the street lamps and looked not unlike falling snow.

"South, sir? You mean to Brighton, or somewhere like that?"

Hill unwrapped his crossed legs and removed them from the windowsill behind the long table in the situation room. He swiveled in his chair to face Chris Detler, who was seated across the table from him, and who was twirling a Biro between his teeth.

"No, I mean really south," he said. He rolled his chair closer to the table to get a better look at Detective Sergeant Detler. "Portugal, Spain, Florida. That kind of south."

"Can't say as I have, sir. And the wife would miss her mother something awful."

"Mm-hm," Hill mumbled. "Well, I do. I'd like to live in a place where if I looked out my office window at four thirty on a Wednesday afternoon in January, I could see something akin to daylight. And where it rains about once a month, instead of on the hour. Anyway, what are we doing here?"

Detler sent a confused look his way.

"We're discussing the case of the missing prof. . . ."

"Right," said Hill. "What more have we got?"

Detler cleared his throat.

"Like I said, we've got nothing, boss. Three more phone calls from supposed witnesses in the last two hours. But that's it."

"None of them legit?"

"No sir."

"What about the Simpson boy? Did he really go change his shirt?"

"Don't know yet, sir."

"How about Gräss's appointment with the doctor?"

"Still checking, boss."

"Forensics have anything?"

Detler was used to Hill's driving investigations forward, but did the inspector really believe that any lab work would have been completed in an afternoon?

"No, sir. Tomorrow or Thursday."

"Then we might as well go home, Chris."

Just then a knock came at the open door to the conference room.

"Hello, Sarah."

Sarah Fray was standing large in the doorway, with a polite smile on her face.

"Evening, guv . . . Chris. There's a man downstairs what wants to see you, guv."

"His name?"

"I didn't catch it, sir. But he says it's important."

"Aren't they all," Detler said sardonically. "I can handle it, boss." He started to rise.

"No, he wants to see the guv'nor," Sarah said. "It's about that story what was in the newspaper."

Hill's eyes shifted, before he arched his eyebrows.

"What do we have to lose?" he said. "Show him up."

A few moments later the sound of footsteps came slowly up the hall, one pair, Hill noticed, with the arrhythmic beat of someone who walked with a limp. Sarah popped her head back in the door and said, "This is Mr. Fortthompson, Mr. Dennis Fortthompson."

She stepped aside and a stump of a man entered Hill's office. He was well on his way to sixty-five, with a flat bald head that was covered on the sides by silvery hair. He had a thick walrus mustache and a sizable nose, and the full cheeks of a baby.

Sarah left them alone.

Hill rose from the table and introduced himself. Fortthompson settled into the chair next to Detective Detler, and Hill noticed that his limp was in his left leg.

"Officer Fray tells me you have some information related to the missing professor," Hill said.

Fortthompson's eyes shifted back and forth between Detler and Hill, obviously nervous.

"Why don't you just start from the beginning," Hill said calmly.

"All right, then," he said. "I was cycling home on Monday evening and I believe I seen the man what's picture was in the paper."

Chris Detler began jotting notes on his pad. He knew that protocol would require a formal statement from the witness, but Hill had shown no interest in that yet, probably wanting first to hear if Fortthompson's story was credible.

"Where did you see him?" asked Hill.

Again, Fortthompson looked at the two policemen nervously.

"On . . . on the river. I know this might sound like a queer story, but I saw him in a punt, heading downriver."

"In a punt?"

"Yes."

"And you're sure it was him, Dennis? Do you mind if I call you Dennis?"

"Oh, no. And yes, I'm sure it was him. You see, he was faceup on the bottom of the punt. I could see his features plainly. I work as a night porter at Smithson College, and I was on my way home. I was right atop Garret Hostel Lane Bridge when I seen him."

"He was lying in the punt?" said Detler. "Then how was the boat moving?"

Fortthompson stroked his thigh, and grimaced.

"Do you mind if I have a cigarette, sir?"

DCI Hill shook his head. Fortthompson pulled a packet from the pocket of his leather jacket, which was wet from the rain. Chris Detler had a lighter to the cigarette by the time it got to Fortthompson's lips.

"Thank you," he said. He took two long drags on the cigarette before speaking again.

"There was someone else in the boat, see, piloting it like."

"What did this second person look like?" Hill asked. He had retrieved an ashtray from the table. He slid it across.

"I'm not sure. It was dark."

"Tall, short, fat, thin, blond, brunette?"

"Not blond, I don't think. Medium height, I would guess. Darkish hair."

"Male? Female?"

Fortthompson shrugged. "I guess I assumed it was a bloke."

"What did this person look like? Any distinguishing features?"

"I can't really say, sir. See, the punt was moving away from me, and all I saw was the back of his head."

Hill's gaze intensified.

"How do you know it was the professor?" he asked.

"He just looked like that picture," Fortthompson said. "He had the same white hair, though even longer. I thought the moment I seen his picture in the paper that it was him. See, there was something quite odd about the scene. And to find now that he's missing, well, it just has to be the same bloke."

"What else was odd?" Hill asked.

"He was in shirtsleeves. No coat, nor sweater. And he wasn't moving. In fact, I wouldn't swear to it, but he looked to be tied up. At first I thought he was asleep. But then I thought he might be hurt."

"Did you offer assistance?"

"No." Fortthompson's eyes dropped to the floor. "You see, I'd had a bit to drink, and it was such a strange sight and all, that it wasn't until the punt was well away from me that I realized it was real."

He looked up at Hill and took a puff on the cigarette, drawing his cheeks in.

"What time did you see the punt?" Hill asked.

Dennis exhaled and reached over to the ashtray. He rubbed the cigarette out, and a smolder of smoke rose above the desk.

"Dead on twelve thirty-five, I would imagine."

"How can you be so sure?"

"I've taken that route home for the past seventeen years. Always on the same schedule. I get off work at quarter to twelve and go straight to the bar. Last call is at quarter past, which is what time I order my last drink. I finish it off in ten minutes. It's a ten-minute ride from college to that bridge."

Hill smiled at Dennis. He was sure that he had a reliable witness and the fact that Gräss was lying in the boat, bound and not moving, made it almost certain that Gräss was dead. But he still didn't have either a body or a description of the second person in the boat.

"Dennis, I want you to think again about the second person," Hill said calmly. "There must have been something you noticed about him we could use."

Dennis shrugged.

"Let's go over it again. You think it was a man?"

"I think so, but I'm not positive."

"And he wasn't blond?"

"I don't believe so."

"What was he wearing?"

"I don't remember. I would say dark clothes, but again, it was pitch black. So I'm not sure."

Hill looked over to Detler and his eyes seemed to inquire if Detler had any questions.

"The second person, the one piloting the boat," said Detler. "Were they sitting or standing?"

"Standing. Up on the boards."

"Were they paddling? Or punting?"

"Punting," Dennis said.

"How fast was the boat going?" Detler asked. "I mean, did the second person seem to be adept with the pole?"

Dennis let out a long breath and considered the question.

"Fairly good, I would say. I remember that the pole moved up and down nicely. Oh yes, and hands, I now remember the hands. They were quite pale. I remember the clothes being dark, but the hands, I guess because of their movement, caught my eye. Very pale, they were."

Fortthompson let out a sigh, and Hill could tell that he was still nervous.

"Just a couple more questions," Hill said. "You said the boat was going *down*river, and that the second person's back was to you."

Fortthompson nodded.

"So they were heading north, toward Trinity and Saint John's?"

"That's right."

"Did you see where the boat went after passing under the bridge?"

Fortthompson stared down at the table and shook his head. "No," he said. "It was like it vanished. Again it was pitch black and misty."

Hill looked to Detler, then back to Fortthompson.

"All right then, Dennis. I'm going to have Sergeant Detler take you downstairs and get a formal statement from you. And we may want to call you back for an identity parade. Do you think you could manage that?"

Fortthompson nodded. Hill rose and shook his hand, then asked Fortthompson to wait out in the hall for Detler.

"There," Detler said after Fortthompson had left the room. "Now we have something, boss."

"We do indeed. Look, Chris, let's have another search of the river and the Backs tomorrow. This time with more men. And more dogs, if we can get them. Drag the river again. Call Wingate at Huntingdon Lab, and get him over here first thing in the morning."

"Yes, sir."

Hill pushed himself back from the table and gave Detler a smile.

"What do you make of it, Chris?"

"Murder, sir. No doubt about that."

"And the murderer?"

Detler looked down at his pad.

"Doesn't sound as though it was one of the women, sir."

"No."

"Doesn't sound as though it's the black chap either."

"Why's that?"

"Fortthompson said that the hands were pale. From your description of Boye, he's got rather dark skin."

"But don't you think that if there were a murderer, he would have been wearing gloves?"

"I see, sir."

"What kind of person wears light-colored gloves, Chris, possibly white?"

"Of the people at the party? Someone high-brow."

"Like Cheverton Beggs? The rich descendant of a famous historian?"

"Yes. Or a lady perhaps. Or someone trying to look like a rich descendent of a famous historian."

Hill looked again at the front page of the newspaper, which was still

99

on the table from earlier in the afternoon. Twenty minutes ago he was dubious about the challenge. Now, his adrenaline was flowing freely and he looked eagerly to what lay ahead.

"Take his statement, Chris," said Hill. "Then come back up. We've got work to do."

"Is that you?" said Ramsgill.

"*Ciao*, lover."

Two words were all it took. Even with the Atlantic Ocean and 3,500 miles between them, Elena Piruzzi's voice stroked Ramsgill's heart.

"I miss you," he said. "No, let me back up. I've *been* missing you for . . . thirty-nine, maybe forty hours."

"Then why haven't you called?"

"I did. I tried last night, but you were out."

"At what time?"

"I don't know. I suppose around six your time."

"I was here, Jamie. I got home from Philadelphia at five thirty."

"Well, no one answered. If you hadn't made me get rid of the answering machine, Elena, you would have *known* that I called."

"Answering machines, *Che invenzióne!* Why do Americans feel the need to be in touch twenty-four hours a day? It's crazy."

He hadn't called her to argue about answering machines.

"How's work?" he said.

"Not good, not bad. We sold one painting yesterday, but today not a soul has come into the gallery."

"What's the weather like?"

"Snowing. So far eight inches."

"I hate to tell you, Elena, but you aren't going to sell any paintings today. Philadelphia shuts down at the mention of snow. Why doesn't Marilyn let you go home?"

"Because she has gone home, Jamie. She's the owner."

"Right." He wanted to tell her to go anyway. Working for Marilyn Foster's gallery, even though it was one of the best in the city, was not without its share of pain. Foster treated her employees like dirt, and Elena was far too qualified to be baby-sitting paintings. She had a Ph.D., and enough money of her own to buy a dozen galleries.

"How are things there, Jamie?"

"As a matter of fact, not good. You remember my speaking about

Rainer Gräss, my former mentor? Well, he's disappeared. Possibly murdered."

"No."

"I'm afraid so. He went missing during that retirement party I was going to attend."

"How did he *go missing?*"

Ramsgill explained about the closed nature of Queens' College, and the fact that Gräss hadn't been seen for a day and a half. He told her about the people who had attended the party, and how Frontis, Beggs, Boye, and Simpson might have had motives to kill him. He told her how Amy Denster and Maria Lendtmayer had possibly lied to DCI Hill. And he told her about the river and the punts.

"It really boils down to this," he said, speaking with more authority than he actually had confidence in. "Gräss left the Old Hall at shortly after midnight. He was noticed missing forty-five minutes later. Each of the others left the hall too, at various times. Somehow, he was taken away from the college, and the killer, if that's what we're talking about, got back before twelve forty-five. And as far as we know, no one had left the hall for more than twenty or thirty minutes."

"Which means," said Elena. "Just a minute, Jamie. I have a customer." She put down the phone, but returned almost immediately. "I'm sorry, Jamie. It was just the postman."

"I told you you weren't going to sell any paintings today."

"*Basta*, Jamie. Now where was I? Oh yes, which means that if Rainer was taken upriver, he couldn't have been taken far."

"Precisely."

"Do you think that one of these boats . . . what do they call them . . . was used?"

"Punts. And yes. At least it's possible. They're right there at the end of the Mathematical Bridge. And it looks to me like the police think so too. The area was taped off when I went by there today."

"Well, I'm sure you'll figure it out, Jamie. Just like you did at father's villa."

"That was different," Ramsgill said. "For one thing, there were no police around at your father's villa. It was a matter of survival. And the inspector here, Lyndsay Hill, already has a half dozen investigators working on it."

"Ah, the English and their chief inspectors. Dalgliesh, huh?"

"Actually," said Ramsgill, "Hill and I were at Darwin College together. We had a drink together last night. He's a nice guy."

"Good. What are your plans for tonight?"

"I don't know. Fiona asked me to dinner, but I'm tired. I think I'll just get a quick bite in town."

"Fiona?" Elena said.

Christ, Ramsgill thought. He had never gotten up the nerve to tell Elena about Fiona. He had wanted to, but instead, had thought that she might be jealous. After all, he was going to be in Cambridge alone, his former lover was the person in Cambridge whom he knew best, and she, conveniently, happened to work for the architecture school. So Jamie had passed her off as merely an old acquaintance, someone he hardly knew.

"Yes, Fiona Mallow. I told you about her, right?"

"You mentioned her," said Elena. "But I didn't know that you were on a first-name basis."

"Well, sort of. I mean, I knew her when we were at school. I think she was just being nice to invite me over."

"Really?" said Elena. "I see. She must have been very old when she was at school, Jamie."

"What do you mean?"

"I mean, you've talked about her in the past as if she were an old lady. You said that she was practically Rainer's Gräss's mother, the way she organized his department."

"I meant that figuratively."

"Oh, never mind."

"Don't just say never mind."

"Never mind. It doesn't matter. I don't care. Go to dinner at her house. I'll be thinking about you while I drive forty miles in the snow."

"Elena, please . . ."

"It's all right, Jamie, I understand."

She didn't understand. And she only knew the half of it. He was a jerk, and he knew it. But how could he tell her about him and Fiona now? He was trapped by his own lies.

"I love you, Elena. And I miss you terribly."

She didn't respond. She was upset. He would have to endure two weeks of this now, all because he had been afraid to be up-front with her.

"I'll call you tomorrow?" he said.

"Call me tomorrow."

And then she hung up.

Amy Denster dropped an armload of books onto the table, perhaps too loudly, for several students at work in the Smithson College Library turned her way and glared.

"Sorry I'm late," she whispered to Maria Lendtmayer, removing her coat and offering an apologetic grimace to the eyes trained upon her. She draped her coat on a bent *finply* chair of Scandinavian design.

"No problem," said Maria softly, sitting across the table with a full compliment of books, notepads, papers, and index cards spread before her. She reached over and gently touched Amy's hand, just as Amy was about to sit.

"I fancy a cigarette," Maria said. "Could we take a walk? I'll tell you what I've done so far, and then we can divide up the rest of the presentation."

They left the library and made their way out into the hall. Smithson College was modern in design, built in the 1960s to the specifications of a well-known Finnish architect. The hall was actually a series of shallow-pitched ramps, separated by short landings on which bay windows, with upholstered window seats, projected out toward the Fellows' Garden. They made their way downward. Just before the Porters' Lodge, they turned and opened a glass door that led out to the garden.

A penetrating cold greeted them. Maria lit a cigarette, and blew the first puff up and into the cold, early evening air. The drizzle had stopped, but a fine mist remained in the air. They strolled out from the building between tall conical yews, then, at the end of the path, they turned.

"I know you haven't had much time to prepare," Maria said, referring to the joint paper that she and Amy were supposed to deliver Monday morning in Cheverton Beggs's history seminar. "So I've written the Ledoux part myself, and have some of the source material outlined on Boullée. I can write that too, if you just want to edit what I've done on Ledoux."

"Thanks, Maria, but you really needn't do all that."

"Why not?" she said. "Amy, you've had a terrible two days. I'm sure you'd do the same for me if I were in your shoes."

"Maria," Amy said, "I lied to the inspector this morning."

"What do you mean?"

"I was out of the hall longer than I said. Rainer and I met in Cloister Court. Thank you for covering for me about the time."

Maria's face turned and looked down into Amy's brown eyes.

"It was nothing," said Maria.

"Maria, I think that Rainer was attacked . . . in the court."

Maria's face became sober.

"Why?" she said.

"Well, we argued. It was dark, and I didn't see what happened, and in fact everything happened so fast. But I remember that he was about to hit me. And then suddenly I didn't see him anymore. It was like he'd vanished. I was so distraught that I ran back into the hall. I *was* crying, like Gaines said. And confused."

Maria took a long drag of her cigarette. She began to walk on a new path, this one parallel to the rear elevation of the college and at a right angle to the first.

"Did you hear me?" said Amy, scurrying to catch up with her taller friend. Amy looked to Maria, but in her mind all she could see was Rainer's arm thrusting toward her. She could almost feel the sharp pain of his fingertips clamping down on her forearm. She was confused, and she really didn't know what she felt about Rainer's disappearance. Part of her still wanted him, wanted him badly, but the other part of her had been hurt too much ever to care for him again. She caught stride with Maria and the pair continued to stroll in silence. As they reached the end of the path, and the northwest corner of the garden, Maria stopped at the edge of a partially frozen reflecting pool. She looked down and, in the darkness, tried to find the carp that inhabited the water. She came to this spot quite often to check on the fish, to see if they were surviving winter.

"Perhaps I should tell the inspector what happened," Amy said.

"No," Maria snapped. "Never."

"But he knows I'm lying. I was out in the courtyard much longer than I told him."

"It doesn't matter. Listen to me, Amy. . . ."

Maria grabbed her by the wrist, then realized she was squeezing too hard. She eased her grip.

"I'm sorry," she said. "But please, Amy. Leave it alone."

Amy stepped away from her, then spun back on a heel in her direction. Maria's eyes were still on the pool.

"There's something else I have to tell you, Maria. I'm pregnant."

Maria's head snapped in Amy's direction.

"Amy, no."

"Yes, ten weeks. I'm frightfully worried and I don't know what to do. I tried to talk to Rainer about it, to see if we could come to some agreement. He told me before that he might leave his wife."

"So he's the father?" asked Maria.

"Yes."

"But you're not considering keeping the baby, are you?"

"I was. But that was before Rainer disappeared. I tried to discuss it with him, but he just got upset. That's why he was attacked in the courtyard. Someone saw him attacking me over my badgering him to leave Ghislaine."

Maria put a comforting arm around Amy's shoulder and pulled her closer. Maria was torn between her friendship with Amy and the police finding out what happened that night.

"Still, you can't keep the baby, Amy. Even if Rainer does come back. He doesn't want it, and how can you possibly afford it?"

"But, maybe he will . . ."

"Forget him. He's not going to take care of you. And he's not going to leave his wife, either."

"Then I'll raise the child myself."

"On what? You hardly have enough money to live on as it is. Were it not for your college stipends and bursaries, you wouldn't even be here. When you graduate, you'll be working full time, not taking care of a baby. And what hope will you have of ever meeting the right person if you're twenty-seven years old with an illegitimate child?"

Amy began to cry, in slow explosive sobs. A second-story window opened across the garden and a head momentarily popped out. Maria took another drag of her cigarette and dropped it to the path. She wondered how much Amy really knew, and about the consequences of her telling Inspector Hill what had happened in the court.

"Then what will I do?" Amy said, wiping her eyes with a tissue Maria had given her. "What option do I have?"

"There's *only* one option," said Maria. "Abortion. Don't even think about carrying the baby to term . . . and giving it up for adoption."

Abortion, Amy thought. That's what the doctor and Rainer had talked to her about. She had resisted it, thinking that Rainer was going to leave his wife and come with her and the baby. But then he shot that down.

"How would I go about it?" she asked.

Maria thought for a moment. She needed a plan.

"I have a friend at the Women's Resources Council in London," she finally said. "I'll call her. Maybe you could go down there tomorrow. Wouldn't that be better than doing it in Cambridge?"

Amy nodded. She *would* have a difficult time of it in Cambridge. An anonymous facility would be better.

"Why does it have to be tomorrow?"

"The sooner the better."

"Will it be kept secret?" Amy asked. "If my mum ever finds out, she'll kill me."

"Let me take care of it," Maria said. "Just keep your head. The only thing I'm unsure of is how long you'll have to wait if it's done by the National Health Service. Do you have private insurance?"

"Of course not. How could I afford that?"

"Do you have *any* money?"

Amy looked up to the window that had opened earlier. It was closed now. She thought of Rainer's offer to pay for the abortion. But now he was missing.

"I suppose I could scrape together a bit; perhaps my brother could help. Wait . . . what am I saying? Of course I have money. Well, not now, but someone owes me money. A decent amount."

"Who?"

"It's not important who. But I'm sure it's enough. Yes, certainly."

"Good," said Maria. "Now let's go back inside. I'll call my friend later."

"It'll be all right, then?"

"Yes. I'll take care of everything."

The phone rang and Lyndsay Hill snatched it up, and leaned back in his chair with the receiver to his ear. His eyes made contact with Chris Detler, who was back from taking Fortthompson's statement. Detler was sitting across the table from him and eating a sandwich, while Hill's still unwrapped sandwich lay on the table.

"DCI Hill," the inspector said.

"Hello, Lyndsay? This is Jamie Ramsgill."

"Hello, Jamie."

"I tried to call you earlier . . ." said Ramsgill, "but you were unavailable. I wanted to tell you of a few things I learned about Rainer's disappearance."

"I'm listening."

"This morning I cycled out to Rainer's cottage and spoke with Ghislaine."

"Yes. We interviewed her earlier today."

"Did she mention George Boye?"

"The African lad?"

"Yes."

"No. Why should she?"

"Well, it seems that Rainer wasn't the only one having an affair. I saw George Boye come out of her house this morning, apparently having spent the night. She admitted that they are seeing one another."

"Interesting," said Hill.

Chris Detler was scrutinizing the chief inspector, trying to glean what he had learned.

"She also told me that Rainer told her he wasn't going to retire until he took care of his complaint against Boye. I guess he wanted her to know so she'd suffer."

"Cruel enough," said Hill.

"Agreed," said Ramsgill.

"Well, she certainly didn't mention that when we interviewed her," said Hill. "And it's odd she'd tell you. It puts suspicion right on Boye."

"I honestly don't think she realized that," said Ramsgill. "She told me that Boye was incapable of hurting a fly."

"The least likely are often the most guilty, Jamie. Anyway, you said you learned a few things. What else?"

"This doesn't bode so well for Boye, either," said Ramsgill. "He lied to you about not having been out of the hall when Rainer was out. After you left the library today he admitted having been out."

"Doubly interesting."

"But he wasn't the only one."

"No?"

"No. Cheverton Beggs was out of the hall too. I overheard Maria Lendtmayer confronting him about it. And Iain Frontis confirmed it for me. Beggs says he was only out for ten minutes, but Frontis says longer. Maybe fifteen or twenty minutes.

"Boye also said he was only out briefly," Ramsgill continued. "But his reason is interesting. He says that when he left the hall he came upon Amy Denster and Rainer. And they weren't just talking. They were arguing."

"Arguing?"

"Yes. But she didn't tell you that, right? You knew there was an inconsistency to her story."

"Either hers or Lendtmayer's. I didn't know which. So she was with Gräss longer than she let on?"

"Apparently. That means you have Frontis, who was going to lose his job. I talked to him today, and although he seems harmless, that's a pretty strong motive. And you have Boye, who might be sent down because of Rainer, not to mention the *affaire du coeur* with Ghislaine. Then there's Gaines Simpson, who used to date Amy. And Amy herself, who argued with Gräss right before he disappeared."

"How about Beggs and Lendtmayer?"

"I can't think of anything on Maria," said Ramsgill. "But Beggs and Rainer had their problems, too. Iain Frontis told me that Beggs and Rainer had argued about Beggs's book manuscript."

Hill looked across the table to the photocopy of the manuscript that Detler had made for him. He picked it up and tossed it to a chair behind him, over which was already draped his coat. He would try to look at it at home.

"I have a copy of the manuscript," said Hill.

"You do?"

"Yes, it was in Gräss's briefcase."

"What else was in the briefcase?"

"Not too much," said Hill. "There was an appointment book. Perhaps the only interesting thing in it was a doctor's appointment for Monday afternoon. I thought before it might be significant, that perhaps Dr. Gräss had found something out about his health. Perhaps he had cancer, or something, and that maybe he'd committed suicide. Those things do happen."

"What do you mean, you 'thought before'? You've changed your mind?"

"Yes. We have some news too, Jamie. A witness has come forward who saw Dr. Gräss in a punt on the night of the party. He was heading downriver, with another person."

"I knew it," said Ramsgill. "Who's this witness?"

"I'm afraid I can't tell you that."

Hill paused, then Ramsgill spoke.

"Fair enough," he said. "But where'd the witness see the punt?"

"Just under Garret Hostel Lane Bridge. He thinks Gräss was injured."

"How?"

"He didn't know. He only said that Gräss was lying on the floorboards of the punt. Thought he might have been bound with rope."

"Did he identify the second person in the boat?"

"Not exactly. He thought it was a man, but his back was to him. Medium height, dark clothes, pale hands. That's all he remembers."

"Did he say what time he saw them?"

"Twelve thirty-five."

"Rainer was last seen at Queens' at twelve ten," Ramsgill said.

"By Gaines Simpson, in Cloister Court," said Hill.

"Maybe," said Ramsgill. "Maybe not. He says he *thinks* he saw him, remember? And you really don't know what time it was. If Amy lied and Simpson didn't leave the hall until she got back, then he might have seen Rainer at more like twelve twenty or twelve twenty-five. Of course, he could be lying too."

"In any event," said Hill, "someone subdued Rainer, got him into that punt, and up to Garret Hostel Lane Bridge by twelve thirty-five. How far do you think that is?"

"I haven't the slightest," said Ramsgill.

Hill covered the mouthpiece of the receiver with his hand.

"Chris, how far do you think it is from the Mathematical Bridge to Garret Hostel Lane? By water?"

"About half of a kilometer, I'd expect," said Detler.

"Detler thinks it's a half a kilometer," Hill said into the phone. "One way must have taken a good five minutes."

"So the punt couldn't have gotten much beyond Garret Hostel Lane," said Ramsgill. "Because your witness saw it at twelve thirty-five, and the group was back together at twelve forty-five."

"We really need to know when each of them was out of the hall, and for how long," said Hill.

"And what happened to the body," said Ramsgill.

"We searched the area today," said Hill. "But no sign of him."

Just then, the wail of sirens came from outside the conference-room window. Hill turned to see two panda cars bouncing out of the car park. He listened until the sound faded away.

"Listen, Jamie," said Hill. "I'm afraid I have to run. We're going to try to get an identity parade together tomorrow. Hopefully our witness will recognize someone."

"With any luck," said Ramsgill.

"Thanks for calling. Look, we should have dinner or something. But at the moment I'm eating from a paper bag. Perhaps after we get somewhere on the case. Good-bye now."

"Good-bye," said Ramsgill.

Hill hung up the phone, then reached across for his sandwich.

While eating, he explained to Detler what he had learned. As he was wadding up his sandwich wrapper to throw it away, the door to the situation room opened.

"Turtonham," Hill said. "Good evening."

The skinny policeman entered the room.

"Sir, you wanted me? Sorry, but I've been out on call."

"No problem, Clive. Look, I thought you were going to get me Dr. Gräss's wallet from the evidence room. I still haven't seen it."

Turtonham brought his hand up to his head and scratched.

"I put a note in your pigeonhole this afternoon about that, sir. Didn't you see it?"

Hill had not had time to go through his pigeonhole at the end of the day. He shook his head.

"We don't have the wallet, sir."

Hill and Detler exchanged glances.

"What do you mean, we don't have it? Did we lose it?"

"No sir, we never had it."

"Then who rang up the architecture school yesterday morning, saying they were the police?"

"I don't know, sir."

Hill shook his head as if he were trying to jump-start his brain.

"I don't believe this," he said.

He leaned forward, but then he froze. Biting his cheek, he rose silently and walked over to the chair that held his coat. He looked back to Detler, who was still sitting across the table.

"I need a drink," he said.

Detler rose before he spoke.

"Make mine a double," he said.

Eight

The basement studio space at Scroope Terrace would hardly seem inspiring to future architects. It was a rabbit warren of confined, interconnected rooms, hemmed in by thick foundation walls of whitewashed brick and seven-foot ceilings below which hung heating pipes. It was just after six on Wednesday evening, and Gaines Simpson was at work on his independent design project, trying to concentrate against the deficiencies of the space. Pipes banged as steam worked its way from the basement's boiler room to the floors above. The odor of chemical developer and stop bath from the unventilated darkroom across the hall permeated the basement, fusing with the aroma of burned coffee from the drip coffeemaker in the studio next door.

Simpson's drafting table occupied a corner of his particular atelier, which at least offered a high window that looked up toward Trumpington Street. As he sketched with marker on yellow tracing paper, his eyes wandered out to a glimpse of a street lamp beyond the wrought-iron fence at the edge of the school's small front yard. It had been drizzling off and on for most of the afternoon, and the mist made a halo around the light. Another fifteen minutes, he thought to himself, and he would knock off for dinner.

The clang of a metal door came from somewhere in the near distance, and Simpson listened as footsteps echoed down the hall. Just across from his desk was an opening through one of the masonry walls, and into the opening stepped George Boye, whose desk was next to Simpson's. Simpson had not seen Boye since the interview with the police inspector in the library earlier in the day. His presence surprised him, as Boye hardly made it a habit of spending time at Scroope Terrace during the requisite daytime hours, much less in the evening. Boye looked back at Simpson's glare with nonchalance. He walked over to his desk, set down his book bag, then stared at the pile of sketches that Simpson had temporarily parked on his tabletop.

"Do you mind?" Boye said.

Simpson got up from his stool and took his papers. He placed them on the floor behind him, returned to his seat, and set about drawing again.

"The sketches have been there for a week and a half," Simpson said. "Which shows how often you actually do any work."

Boye pulled a few books from his bag.

"Go to hell," he said.

Simpson swiveled to face Boye, not in the least intimidated by him.

"Listen, George. I've never had anything against you, other than the fact that you're a leech. But I won't stand by while you cut Amy to the bone like you did today. She didn't deserve that. I'll break your fucking legs if you do it again. You'll wish you were never born."

The books Boye had removed were library books, all of them three weeks overdue. He had forgotten to bring them to school for the second day running, and as the library had closed at six, he would leave them now on his desk, as a reminder to return them. But he wasn't going to stick around with Simpson here, even if he too should be working on his independent project. He began to rezip his book bag.

"Always the white knight," he said, looking over at Simpson. "Why don't you just give up on Amy, Gaines? Let her go."

"Because she's vulnerable," Simpson said. "And nobody's going to take advantage of her."

"Nobody?" said Boye. "Does that include Rainer?"

"What's that supposed to mean?"

"It means I wonder how far you'd go to protect her. And if you'd lie about it to the police."

"Are you implying something?" Simpson said.

Boye smiled impishly.

113

"The inspector already caught Amy in her lie," he said. "Thank God Maria came to her defense. But of course if Maria hadn't, then you would have made up another version of events to protect her. Just like you made up the bit about having possibly seen Gräss in Cloister Court."

"Get to the point, George."

"You didn't *possibly* see him, you spoke to him. Or should I say confronted him."

Simpson capped his Magic Marker and took a sip of bitter, almost cold, coffee.

"You seem to know just what everyone else was doing that night, George. Too bad no one saw you. Especially given your motives for wanting to see Gräss dead. Which one weighs more heavily? The fact that he's going to have you sent down, or the fact that you're fucking his wife?"

Boye moved toward Simpson, bumping him off his stool. Simpson fell backwards, pulling his coffee mug from the desk. Coffee sloshed from the cup, splattering his sketches on the floor.

"You fuck!" Simpson yelled.

He caught his footing and charged Boye. He came for Boye's head with the mug, but Boye snatched his arm between his massive fingers.

"Break my legs, huh?" Boye said. He held Simpson stationary, then thrust him backwards. Simpson met the brick wall with a thud. He clutched his elbow and cowered. He was breathing heavily, his eyes burning.

Boye seemed unfazed.

He picked up his book bag and looked down at Simpson's ruined sketches.

"Looks like you've got work to do, Simpson."

He then turned and left.

Jamie Ramsgill had dinner alone at a restaurant in Sidney Street, then cycled back through Market Hill. As it was after eight o'clock, the market square was quiet, the long rows of striped canvas stalls creating a miniature village, empty until tomorrow morning. Great Saint Mary's Church stood sentry over the square, the light of the church's interior framed by the severe perpendicular-style stained-glass window of its eastern façade. Past the church he came upon the university's Senate House, its courtly Palladian outline reflected in the wet pavement of Trinity Street. Students sat on the low wall in front of the building in groups of twos and threes, talking quietly.

Ramsgill turned onto the small lane behind the Senate House and alongside Caius College, and after two more sharp turns found himself approaching Garret Hostel Lane Bridge. For the whole of dinner, and in fact since he had phoned Lyndsay Hill, he had thought very little about Rainer Gräss's disappearance. His phone call to Elena had jarred him. He now regretted having not been up-front with her regarding Fiona Mallow. The exchange would only rekindle Elena's assertion that Ramsgill was unable to make a commitment.

He had met Elena eighteen months ago at her father's villa on Lago di Garda. Until that time he had been complacent in his bachelorhood, perhaps still reeling from the shock of Fiona's marriage to Dick Mallow almost eighteen years prior. Elena stirred in him feelings he had thought vanquished, and he knew almost immediately that he wanted to be with her. But the transition to being bound to someone, even Elena, came not without some tribulation. Almost two months after she came over to Princeton, she had begun to make suggestions about deepening their commitment to one another. After all, she told him, she had left her friends and family and country behind to be with him. It was not that she wanted marriage but, perhaps even more alarming to Ramsgill, she wanted to conceive a child. He'd told her honestly that it would take a little time for him to think about that.

As he pedaled to the top of the bridge, he wondered if she really believed he still held something for Fiona. He knew that he should make up his mind, and he resolved to come to some decision before returning from Cambridge.

Garret Hostel Lane Bridge was the least attractive of all of the bridges that traversed the Cam in the area of the Backs. It was a simple concrete structure with metal railings, functional in a plain sort of way. Ramsgill got off his bicycle and leaned it against the rail. He tried to picture Lyndsay Hill's witness on the bridge that evening, and what he or she had seen. The thing that struck Ramsgill most immediately was the darkness and isolation of the spot. Hill's witness had said that the second person in the punt was wearing dark clothes, and he characterized the person's hands as being "pale." What about the killer's clothes? Hill had not asked what everyone was wearing that night. With a start, Ramsgill remembered the photograph that had been taken just before the party had disbanded. He would remind Hill to inquire about it.

Ramsgill now looked around him. To the east, Garret Hostel Lane was no more than eight feet wide, lined by the rears of several colleges. To the west, the lane continued on out to Queen's Road, with Clare College's Fellows' Garden on one side and Trinity's great lawn on the other. South of the bridge, back in the direction of Queens' College, he could see the triple-arched stone bridge at Clare, and Clare's buildings set back from the river. To the north, up toward Saint John's College, he could just make out a similar-styled bridge connecting Trinity College on the right, with its lawn across the river to the left.

But he could also make out something else, something out of place in the otherwise placid scene. He could see the silhouettes of tall Lombardy poplars, which lined the walk at Trinity known as the Avenue, a pedestrian way that connected Trinity's bridge with Queen's Road to the west. The Avenue cut directly through Trinity's great lawn, bisecting it. But on the other side of the Avenue, in a dark area of lawn just beyond the willows near the water, the lawn had been defaced.

He took his bicycle and walked to the western end of the bridge, and then crossed the great lawn, heading north toward the Avenue. The grass was wet and cold, and the whole area black under a moonless sky. As he approached the path, he could sense a swaying of the trees and noticed a light breeze.

Ahead of him, dark and almost formless, was a construction site. A solid fence six feet high ran around its perimeter. Several pieces of large earth-moving equipment rose above the fence, looking not unlike large-scale dinosaur models. Building materials were stacked haphazardly around the grounds, and in at least two areas there were mounds of excavated earth. To the north, in the distance, the black outlines of site huts could be seen.

Ramsgill leaned his bicycle against a tree and walked closer to the fence. Small holes had been cut into it, offering views into the site. Even in near darkness Ramsgill could see the outline of the building being constructed. At this point, it consisted of an excavation perhaps one hundred and fifty feet square, of unknown depth. The eastern edge was about twenty-five yards from the river, and on that side Ramsgill could see that there was no fence.

Ramsgill turned and walked down to the water. Across the narrow river he could see the college's Wren Library. The building was long and two stories high, classical in style, its long upper story containing the library proper. Yellow light shone through the thirteen arched windows, casting a pale glow on the construction site.

The fence ended just at water's edge. He stood still, thinking, for a moment, wondering what was being constructed behind the fence. He had seen no sign announcing the project, though he was sure it was a building for Trinity. It was a shame, he thought, because the vista across Trinity's great lawn from Queen's Road, with the library as a backdrop to the lazy course of the Cam, was one of the university's truly exceptional prospects.

His thoughts returned to the night of Rainer's disappearance, and he realized now that two things weighed more heavily than all the rest. First, Lyndsay Hill had told Ramsgill earlier in the evening that his witness had seen the punt from Garret Hostel Lane ten minutes before the group got back together. Second, no body had been found.

Ramsgill looked south, where in the dim light he could see Garret Hostel Lane Bridge, some three hundred feet in the distance. He told Hill that the punt could not have gone much beyond the bridge, because otherwise the killer wouldn't have been able to get back to Queens' on time. And between the bridge and where Ramsgill was standing, there was no place for a body to be hidden. The great lawn occupied the area west of the river, and Trinity's New Court was on the other bank.

Ramsgill returned his gaze to the fence. He walked down to the water's edge, stood motionless for a moment, then did something that surprised even himself.

He scaled the fence.

He dropped down to the other side and found himself inside the construction site. To his left he could now see an area where materials were stored, and beyond that, one of the earthen mounds. The other stockpile of earth was to his north, beyond the excavation. Two modular site huts, made from customized caravans, anchored the northwest corner of the site, one with lights burning inside.

He began to walk, careful of his footing, and soon came upon the open excavation. He could immediately see that it consisted of more than the trenches for the building's footings. The entire square had been dug out to a depth of perhaps fifteen feet, preparation for a basement to the building. The walls of the basement and the foundations below them would be formed of concrete. Ramsgill couldn't actually see concrete, but he could see plywood formwork around the perimeter, into which liquid cement would be poured.

He knelt and looked beyond a trench at one such form just below him. It was about twenty-four inches wide and had iron reinforcing rods poking out of its top. He looked up and around the basement's perimeter, to see if he could tell how many sections of the foundation wall had already been poured.

He then stood and looked in the direction of the site huts. From somewhere in the distance he could hear tree branches rubbing together, more persistent when the wind gusted. And then to his right, a lapping sound, as small riplets of water were blown against the riverbank.

He had a good idea what had probably happened that night.

He turned and followed the excavation perimeter to the side that fronted the water. The earth between the excavation and the river itself was muddy, but there was no trench on the back side of the foundation wall. Here the earth had been replaced against the outside of the formwork, which Ramsgill knew wouldn't have been done until the wall had been poured.

He walked up to the edge of the basement. Kneeling again, he touched the top of the formwork, coming into contact with damp fabric. He removed several layers of the fabric, and his hand reached down again. This time he felt a hard, cool surface, somewhat abrasive, and almost at a level equal to the top of the plywood forms.

It was freshly poured concrete.

He didn't know whether to laugh or cry.

Just then, he heard something from beyond the fence to the north, the sound of footsteps on gravel. He looked up, then froze as he heard a bolt being thrown, followed by the groan of unoiled hinges. In the faint light some fifty feet beyond the edge of the excavation, he could make out a person, coming through a gate in the construction fence.

The person was carrying a flashlight whose beam swung haphazardly across the ground, then almost immediately stopped. The light then snapped up in Ramsgill's direction, landing squarely on his face. At that point he could see nothing, just the blinding aura of white. He felt completely vulnerable.

The way Rainer Gräss must have felt that night, when whoever had killed him caught up to him in the courtyard, just before the boat ride that would take him to this hideous grave.

Cheverton Beggs sat before a computer in his ground-floor drawing room, a room delineated by walls of bloodred damask. The drawing room was situated in the center block of Elizabethan Purdington End, a tall room capped by a fan-vaulted ceiling of Limousine oak, with three pairs of French doors that opened to a rear terrace. Antiques of exceptional provenance cluttered the chamber, and two of Beggs's grandfather's famous Landseers hung above the limestone fireplace. A fire crackled softly in the hearth.

Ever since he was a child Beggs had wanted to be an artist, surrounded as he was growing up by some of the finest pictures in England outside of the National Gallery and the Tate. His father wouldn't let him pursue it, however, convinced that his son had no artistic talent. He tried instead to convince the young Cheverton to follow in his footsteps, to become an art historian like himself. At first Cheverton rebelled against the suggestion, and instead studied computer sciences at Essex University. He ultimately came around to his education in art history, but only after realizing that his father's connections would bode well for him once he finished school. Years later, he ironically found the art world and the world of computers merging to some extent, the latter finally allowing him to create his own quite adequate pictures, without so much as lifting a pencil.

Beggs was working on such a composition now, thirty minutes after finishing the latest revisions to his book manuscript, revisions that given Rainer Gräss's disappearance, would probably be the last until he submitted the manuscript to his publisher. The process of "playing at pictures," a hobby of Beggs's almost to the point of addiction, involved the manipulation of file images brought into the computer by any number of means: photo CDs, PICT and TIFF files from stock art libraries, scanned photographs. Once into his photographic manipulation program, he could produce any number of special effects, including twisting, distorting, inverting, solarizing, posterizing, and "embossing." It allowed him to take a perfectly normal image such as a PICT file of Paolo Uccello's *The Battle of San Romano* from the National Gallery and superimpose it with fragments of the *Wilton Diptych*, as he was presently doing. Once the two pictures were collaged together and after blending them seamlessly such that elements of the first appeared to be integral with the second, he could further run the file through various "filters." This was the truly intuitive part of the experiment (at least in Beggs's mind), which made the file appear as a watercolor rendering, as a pen-and-ink sketch, as an etching, as charcoal, as color pencil, and so forth and so on.

He was using a "lasso" to isolate one of the *Wilton* angels, which he intended to copy and paste into the Uccello's battle scene, when the phone rang. He grabbed the receiver after the first ring so it wouldn't wake his mother, who was sleeping upstairs in the east wing of the house.

"Hello," he barked.

"Cheverton?" It was the voice of Amy Denster.

Beggs didn't respond.

"Cheverton? I'm sorry to be calling at this hour. But I had to speak with you. Before tomorrow."

Beggs typed *alt-s* on his keyboard to save his file. He then shifted back in his chair and removed his eyeglasses.

"Well?" he said. He lifted a cup of tepid Lapsang souchong tea and took a sip.

"Cheverton, I need the money. I told you before that you could pay me whenever, but something's come up, and I need it right away."

"Hiring a consulting detective, Amy? To find Rainer?"

"No."

"Then what's the rush?"

"I can't tell you. But I need it. In cash. Tomorrow."

"Tomorrow? Are you quite mad? Five hundred pounds in cash by tomorrow. Don't you think that might be difficult even for me?"

Beggs had no problem with giving her cash, in fact he had intended to do so anyway, in order that there be no record of the transaction. It was the short notice that perturbed him.

"No," Amy said frankly. The tone of her voice had shifted from whimper to demand.

"Well, I'm afraid it is. I'd be happy to give you cash, but it will be at least Friday before I can get it."

"Don't lie to me, Cheverton. I know you have it. And even if you don't, it would be no problem for you to get it in the morning."

"Sorry, old girl."

"It's you who might be sorry," Amy said. Her words were emphatic. This wasn't the Amy Denster he knew, the tiresome little plebeian whose social class, thirty years ago, would have blackballed her from a Cambridge education.

"What are you going to do, Amy, have Gaines strong-arm me? Is that what happened to Rainer?"

There was silence on the line. Finally, Amy cleared her throat.

"What if I go to the Proctors?" she said.

Beggs's lower lip tightened, and curled downward.

"And implicate yourself as well, my dear?"

"I don't care. What I do care about is getting the money. As I said. By tomorrow."

Beggs gently lifted his glasses and returned them to his nose. He considered whether she was bluffing.

"Okay," he finally said. "But you'll have to meet me at the school. At around ten. I have a supervision at eight, and I won't be able to get to the bank until after that."

"I can't wait that long," she said.

"Then you'll have to come out here. Before eight. And I won't have cash. I can only give you a check."

Again there was silence on the line. Beggs was beginning to tire, and while he waited for a response he shut down the computer.

Amy finally spoke.

"Very well," she said. "I can't wait until ten. In fact, my . . ."

She started to say that her train left at seven for London.

"Is six thirty too early?" she asked. She would have to taxi to Purdington End in order to get there and back to town by seven.

Beggs paused.

"That'll be fine," he said.

"Bye then."

She waited for a response, but he simply hung up.

*   *   *

The flashlight moved closer and Ramsgill stood up, unwilling to meet whoever was coming toward him from a position of disadvantage. He arched his back and brought his hands out to his sides. He was about to say something when the figure spoke, in a refined voice of Carribean tone.

"Don't be going anywhere."

Ramsgill stood still until the figure reached him.

It was a black security guard, with a full, black beard. He held the flashlight in one hand and a set of keys in the other. He had no intention of removing the bright beam from Ramsgill's eyes.

"It's not what you think," said Ramsgill.

The guard stared at him silently, trying to discern what this fellow with the American accent was doing here and whether he posed a threat.

"I'm sorry," Ramsgill continued, holding his hand to his brow to shield his eyes. "I know this looks bad, but I can explain everything."

Still no word from the guard, but Ramsgill noticed that his posture had softened.

"I'm sure you can," said the guard. "And will."

"I was just—"

"You can either come with me to the caravan, where I am going to ring up the police," broke in the guard, "or you can stay put. But don't try to flee."

The guard looked Ramsgill over once more, top to bottom. He then walked past him cautiously, heading in the direction of the caravans. Ramsgill followed him around the excavation and to a caravan door. The guard entered but made Ramsgill stay outside. The guard found a telephone number and dialed.

"Ask for Lyndsay Hill," said Ramsgill through the open door.

"How's that?"

"Lyndsay Hill," Ramsgill repeated. "He's the detective chief inspector at Parkside. Tell him that it's Jamie Ramsgill you found."

The guard wrote down Ramsgill's and Hill's names.

"Yes," he said into the phone. "My name is Stuart Jones. I'm with Rattner and Davids construction at their Trinity College project site. We have a man whom I caught trespassing on the property. Now, I would normally contact the college and ask them what to do with him,

122

but your office had investigators by here today, searching the river for that missing professor. I was questioned by a Detective Sergeant Detler. He told me if I saw anything suspicious, I should contact him directly."

The guard listened intently for a moment, then spoke again into the receiver.

"He's not there?" he said. "Then how about Chief Inspector Hill? The man I caught says he knows him. No? Okay. Well, then if you can't reach him right away, would you please have a uniformed constable drop by? What? His name is Ramsgill."

Again there was a pause, then the guard said, "My number here? 332986."

And then he hung up.

"He wasn't there?" Ramsgill said.

"No. They will try to reach his pager."

"Thank you," said Ramsgill. "By the way, did you say that Chris Detler was by here today?"

Jones didn't respond, staring back out the door at Ramsgill with questioning eyes.

"Are you American?" he asked.

Ramsgill nodded.

"Can you tell me why you were creeping around this project site?"

"For the same reason Detler interviewed you," Ramsgill said. "The professor who disappeared was a friend of mine. We suspect he was murdered, only the body hasn't shown up."

"So the police told me," said Jones. "And they also told me that the killer might return. To retrieve the body."

"I'm afraid it won't be so easily retrieved," said Ramsgill.

Jones looked at him suspiciously.

"You've hidden it well, then?"

"I've hidden nothing," said Ramsgill. "I was on an airplane over the Atlantic when Rainer Gräss was killed. But I can tell you where his body is."

"Clairvoyant, huh? Well, the detective and his men searched the whole site today and found nothing."

The phone rang and Jones snatched it up.

"Hello. Yes. Right. Very well."

He rang off.

"The inspector was just on his way home," he said to Ramsgill. "He will be here in a few minutes."

"Good," said Ramsgill. "By the way, were you on duty Monday night, Mr. Jones?"

"I've already been over Monday night with the detective sergeant. He knows that I was here."

"The whole night?"

"From midnight on."

Jones looked skeptically at Ramsgill, then rose from his desk and walked over to a warming plate. He poured himself a cup of hot water and doused an already used tea bag into the cup. He let the bag steep for a couple of minutes, never asking Ramsgill in. By the time he was finished, Ramsgill could hear the sound of a car pulling up north of the site, just behind the caravan.

"Must be him," Jones said. He looked through a window and could see a car on the access road, which ran right past the caravan. He got up and stepped through the doorway, using his flashlight to illuminate a path over to the north gate. He returned a moment later with Lyndsay Hill, whose tie was loosened after a long day.

"Hello, Lyndsay," Ramsgill said.

Hill didn't reply.

"Mr. Jones," he said, "do you mind if I have a talk with Mr. Ramsgill? Alone?"

Jones shook his head and pointed to the second caravan.

"Light switch is to the right of the door," he said.

He returned inside and Ramsgill followed Hill next door.

"What in the name of Joseph and Mary are you doing, Jamie?" asked Hill once the two of them were seated in the second caravan.

"I was just looking . . ."

"We don't need you to look, Jamie. This is a murder investigation. Not a parlor game."

"Look, Lyndsay. I was coming home from dinner and remembered that your witness saw Rainer in the punt under Garret Hostel Lane Bridge. I then saw the construction site and came over to take closer look, thinking that the body might have been stashed here. There's no way the punt could have gotten much beyond this point and I had no idea that there'd be a night watchman here. I thought the place would be deserted."

"Let's say a body *was* here, Jamie. What do you think would happen if the murderer came back and just happened to find you traipsing around out there?"

"He won't be coming back," Ramsgill said.

"Oh really?" Hill's expression conveyed sarcasm.

"He has no need to, Lyndsay. Don't you see? This is the perfect place to have gotten rid of the body. The building's foundations are concrete. Some sections have recently been poured. There's easy access from the water."

"Hold on, Jamie. You're telling me that the body was dumped into the foundation formwork and then covered with concrete?"

"It's certainly the way I would have done it. Did the dogs search this area today?"

"I believe so. Apparently they were quite active around the riverbank, but then, according to Detler, they lost the scent."

"Precisely," said Ramsgill. "So we've got to look at the foundations."

Hill folded his hands together while he studied Ramsgill's face. There was a boyish excitement on it, as if the investigation were a treasure hunt.

"*We* is the police, Jamie. Not you. What if Jones had rung up the college's dean? I don't think he'd be too thrilled with your little intrusion."

"But still. Don't you think it's worth looking at?"

"First of all, Jamie, we have no idea if any of these walls were poured on Tuesday or today. We would have to talk to the builder. And even if they were, what do you suggest? That we jackhammer every wall out there until we find what we're looking for? It's a little bit like looking for a needle in a haystack, isn't it?"

Hill had a point.

"Also," Hill continued, "how do you know that the murderer didn't just transport Gräss from the site? He could have had a car waiting here. I came in on the temporary access way. It leads back up to Queen's Road."

Ramsgill thought for a moment, then said, "It wouldn't have worked. The access road leads right past these caravans. Jones would have heard a car. He was here Monday night. Besides, the murderer went back to the party, right? Which means he would have had to have an accomplice drive the car."

Hill leaned back and crossed his arms.

"Still," he said, "we can't go ripping out all of these walls."

"You don't have to rip them *all* out. Just the ones that have been poured since Tuesday."

"*If* any have been poured since Tuesday."

"I'm willing to bet on that. And . . ."

Ramsgill stopped midsentence and his eyes widened.

"I have an idea," he said. "Maybe we don't have to rip anything out. Can we go next door?"

They went back to Jones's caravan and convinced Jones to let Ramsgill make an overseas telephone call. Ramsgill got an international operator, and a few moments later had the home number for Nick Wells, a structural engineer on the faculty at Princeton.

"Hello?" The voice of Wells came on the line.

"Nick? This is Jamie Ramsgill."

"Where are you Jamie? You sound like you're on a another planet."

"I'm in England, Nick. Cambridge. I'm over here for a couple of weeks doing research on a book."

"Nice. So what's the call for? Want me to shovel your driveway? We've got fourteen inches of new snow and it's still snowing."

"I need to know if you know anyone over here who does noninvasive concrete testing."

"You're writing a book on noninvasive testing?"

"It's not for my book. I need to know if radar or sound impulse would find a body encased in concrete."

There was a lengthy pause.

"What kind of concrete?"

"A basement wall."

Another pause.

"Theoretically it would. Pulse echo or impact would for sure. Concrete has a dielectric constant of about sixty. A body has one of only ten. Radar should work, too, though I'm not sure of the radial density of flesh and bones. Lord, Jamie, this is pretty morbid. What are you up to?"

Ramsgill proceeded to fill him in on enough of the details to make sure that Wells would be able to tell him with reasonable assuredness that it would work.

"So do you know anyone over here who does what you do?" Ramsgill asked again.

"Well, let's see. There's Blanco Lage in Madrid. And Doerstling in Germany. Nygaard and his wife in Oslo, and . . . wait, where did you say you were?"

"Cambridge."

"Of course. There's a guy right there. I met him at last year's ACI conference in San Francisco. Cleeve, Greeve, something like that. He's on the faculty of the engineering school."

"Perfect," said Ramsgill, writing on a notepad as quickly as he could.

He thanked Wells and hung up.

"There's a professor at the engineering school," said Ramsgill. "He can find your body, and he'll be able to do it without destroying a thing."

Ramsgill tore off the note and handed it to Hill.

"Are you sure about this? I'm going to look bloody stupid if—"

"Believe me, it'll work."

Hill sighed. "Okay, I'll get him over in the morning," he said.

"And we should talk to the contractor," added Ramsgill. "To find out which walls are fresh."

"They'll be here bright and early tomorrow," said Jones, who had been listening to the conversation. "The site supervisor is a man named Brian Moss; he'll know."

"Will you still be here?" asked Hill.

Jones shook his head. "Oh no," he said. "I go off at midnight. But we can leave a message with my replacement."

"Do that," said Hill. "Tell Moss that we'll be here tomorrow around eight and we're going to want to search the grounds again, as well as talk to him about the concrete."

Jones nodded. Hill and Ramsgill then excused themselves and walked out of the site by way of the gate. Hill's car was parked on the gravel access way.

"Can I give you a lift?" Hill asked Ramsgill.

"No thanks. I have my bike."

Hill nodded.

"By the way," he said. "I appreciate what you're doing, Jamie. But I want you to leave it to us. I mean that."

"He was a friend, Lyndsay."

"He's a dead friend, Jamie. Your efforts aren't going to bring him back. We are going to find his killer but what I really don't want to do is to have to investigate *your* murder."

Ramsgill shrugged. He looked off in the direction of the excavation, wondering what they would find.

"I'd like to be here tomorrow," he said, "when you look for the body."

Hill looked frustrated, realizing that his caution had no effect on Ramsgill.

"Sure," he said.

"You know," said Ramsgill, "I was thinking about what your witness said about the second person. You know, that he was wearing dark clothes and had pale hands. It made me wonder what was everyone at the party wearing."

"I intend to ask them that," said Hill. "Tomorrow."

"Oh, but I was thinking you could just look at the photograph. Photographs don't lie and, as we already know, suspects do."

"What photograph?" asked Hill.

"The one that was taken at the end of the party."

A look of puzzlement came over Hill's face.

"I know nothing about a photograph," he said.

Ramsgill paused.

"No? Well, Fiona told me that they took a group picture, right as the party was breaking up."

"I wondered about the camera in Gräss's briefcase. But there wasn't any film in it."

Ramsgill shrugged. "Better ask Fiona," he said.

"I certainly will."

Hill opened the car door.

"Has anything happened at the station since I spoke to you earlier tonight?" Ramsgill said.

Hill let out a spurt of laughter.

"You just don't give up, do you, Jamie?"

Ramsgill shook his head.

"As a matter of fact," Hill said, "something new did come up. That phone call about Rainer's wallet being found. It was staged."

"What do you mean?"

"We don't have the wallet," said Hill. "We never had it."

"But I don't get it."

"It was a hoax," said Hill. "But not that of a kid having a go at the police. I think we've got a brazen killer on our hands. Someone who wants to engage in a game of wits. Someone with a sense of the dramatic. And I'm sure it was the killer who made the call, because who else would know that Gräss was on the river?"

"But why make the call?" wondered Ramsgill.

"He's taunting us," said Hill. *"Catch me if you can.* Or the whole thing could just as easily be a ruse. To make us spend time downriver when the body is actually here."

Hill slid into the driver's seat. He rolled down the window.

"A little light reading?" Ramsgill asked.

Hill looked to the seat beside him, where Beggs's manuscript lay.

"Beggs's book manuscript," Hill said. "I was going to try to look at it tonight to see if there's anything in it that might have caused the arguments between Gräss and Beggs."

"Happy reading," said Ramsgill.

"What do you mean?" said Hill.

"Beggs's work can be obtuse," he said. "It's not quantum physics, but he goes out of his way to make things as pedantic as he can."

Hill looked over to the manuscript and picked it up.

Turning back to Ramsgill, he shoved it toward him and said, "Okay, Mr. Detective. You want to be on the team? Then you read it for me. Give me a book report."

Ramsgill smiled and took the manuscript.

"I'll see you in the morning," he said.

Hill put the car into Reverse.

"And stay out of places you don't belong, Jamie. Got that?"

Maria Lendtmayer clicked down the telephone receiver, her arrangements with Amy Denster complete. She then walked to the front hall and removed her book bag from the wicker basket of her bicycle before making her way down the hall to the study beyond the kitchen. At the rear bay window, she placed the book bag on the desk Janice had bought her for her last birthday, a Queen Anne revival bureau-desk of dark rosewood with a multitude of drawers.

She returned to the kitchen and took the narrow stairs down to the cellar. In the far corner of the dimly lit space were the two wine racks where Janice and she kept their small but adequate collection of wine. From the right-hand rack she pulled out a bottle of Rioja. The bottle was cold, as was the unheated cellar, and the label was covered with mildew. Janice had had plans to improve the cellar, even to fit it out as a guest bedroom. But as recently as three weeks ago another builder had looked at it and confirmed the opinions of all those who had come before. Because of the house's proximity to the river and the high water table, they were told to expect dampness. The only way to correct it would be to excavate completely around the outside of the house and put a waterproof membrane on the exterior.

Maria returned upstairs. She opened the wine in the kitchen and poured herself a glass before returning to the study.

She booted up her Macintosh computer, and the green-blue light of her screen flickered to life. She took a sip and thought of Janice's exceptional talent at choosing wine. Janice had called down to her earlier to come to bed, but that was fifteen minutes ago, and Maria guessed that she was now fast asleep. Maria herself was tired, but she wouldn't be able to sleep, not with so much on her mind.

She slowly removed the contents of her bag, her notes for the Boullée and Ledoux papers, along with a few books on the two eighteenth-century architects. She found the LEDOUX/BOULLÉE ALIAS file on her computer and double-clicked it open with her mouse. While she waited for the file to come up on the screen, she stared out the window into the night. The bay window at the rear of the small but elegant terraced house was her sanctum sanctorum. From the desk, even in the dark of night, she could see the River Cam, just beyond their small summer garden, now no more than a mass of dead foliage. When Janice bought the house two years ago, the first thing she did was remove an old cinder-block wall which, though it offered privacy for the rear garden, blocked the view to the river. Janice replaced it with a low fence of woven ash strips, and a small gate leading to a pair of granite steps at the water's edge. There they kept their punt which, as the house was situated just below Magdalene Street Bridge, put them within a few minutes' reach of the Backs.

Maria returned her attention to the computer. She began to scan her notes, working on the first full draft of the paper on the French-man Étienne-Louis Boullée, the Enlightenment architect whose fantastic and megalomaniacal designs were as revolutionary as the political turmoil of his day. The writing was slow and tedious as Maria's academic area of interest centered squarely on the twentieth century, particularly on the work of the Russian Constructivists. She found eighteenth-century architecture, however radical for its own day, to be rather quaint. She was just going through the motions, preparing a required paper for Cheverton Beggs who, in her mind, belonged in the sentimental premodern world.

Maria's thoughts drifted in and out of her writing, constantly gravitating back to the incident in the Queens' courtyard and whether her decision about what to do about it had been the right one.

Amy told her she would have her money by morning, and Maria had convinced her to come by and pick up the information regarding the clinic before heading to the train station. Amy had protested, saying that it would be too early, and tried to get Maria to give her the information by phone. But Maria wanted to get a sense of Amy's state of mind before Amy headed off to London. She wanted reassurance that Amy had no intentions of going to the police with her version of Monday night's events.

Maria could still see the two of them, Rainer and Amy, standing beneath the dark brick loggia at the north end of Cloister Court, outside the brown-and-white half-timbered President's Lodge. It was dark in the courtyard, with the only light being cast rather eerily from a large copper-and-glass lamp that hung above the rear door to the Old Hall. Fog shrouded the scene, with the mist forming an aura around the lamp. The loggia was lit only dimly, a raking light from the east, and Rainer's back was to the courtyard.

Maria had come upon them on her return from making her phone call to Janice. She had heard that Amy was seeing Rainer, but she hadn't believed it. It was incomprehensible to her that Amy, young and pretty, could be attracted to such an old bastard. At first she watched in silence from across the courtyard as the two of them talked, not loudly, but in rising and falling intonations, which seemed to indicate a quiet argument. Suddenly, Amy let out a short shrill cry, and Maria could hear her sobbing, pleading with Rainer about something. She then saw Rainer's hand locked onto Amy's wrist. Slowly,

Maria started across the courtyard toward the loggia. For a moment she thought she saw someone in the east portal of the courtyard, but as soon as she turned—if anyone had been there—they were gone.

In her mind, Maria could now see herself coming up behind Rainer. She could clearly make out Rainer's hand around Amy's wrist, and Amy's moans. Suddenly Maria saw herself as a young woman on the shores of the Bodensee, Gunthar Krupps forcing himself on her. Amy's view of Maria was blocked partially by Rainer and partially by one of the brick piers. Amy could do nothing to stop him. Rainer was in shirtsleeves, yelling at Amy, calling her filthy names, misogynist names. She pleaded with him to stop, and as Maria got closer she could see Amy's face, though Amy was in such a state that she didn't notice Maria. Amy's tears were raining down, but Rainer kept after her. Then he raised his hand across his shoulder, upwards in a broad, diagonal sweep.

He was just about to bring it down when Maria grabbed his hand, and not with the undeveloped force of that little girl of fourteen. She grabbed it with the full force of someone who lifts weights three times a week and runs ten kilometers every other day. Rainer's hand never reached Amy's face. He wasn't a big man, and Maria jerked him back like a yo-yo, dragging him across the lawn. Amy, either out of fear or shock, didn't follow them. Maria's intention was to just pull him away, but Rainer fought back, once or twice digging his fingers into Maria's neck. So she had to subdue him. She had no choice. When she was finished with him she left him on the ground and smiled, like Krupps had smiled at her. Maria's only question now was, Had Amy seen her, and, if so, what did she intend to do?

After leaving the Trinity construction site, Ramsgill returned to Darwin, put away his bicycle, and checked for any messages at the Porters' Lodge. He then walked across the dark croquet lawn to the hall door of the Old Granary. When he reached his room, there was a note on the door, which said to call Fiona Mallow.

Ramsgill looked at his watch. It was almost ten thirty. He went to the hall phone and dialed Fiona's number. She answered on the second ring.

"Thank you for ringing," she said. "I'm sorry to bother you this late."

"It's okay. What's up?"

"We need to talk, Jamie."

"Okay. How about breakfast? I can tell you what's happened with the investigation."

There was a brief silence.

"It's not about the investigation, Jamie. And I would really like to see you tonight. I wanted to tell you yesterday, but I couldn't. And I don't think I can wait until tomorrow."

"Tell me what?"

"Meet me at the Thistle Pub. Please? It's right off Lensfield Road."

There was an urgency to her voice, and a hint of despair.

"Fine," he said. "I'll be there in ten minutes."

Ramsgill walked into the Thistle, and through a haze of smoke he could see Fiona Mallow in the back room. He got himself a drink and made his way to her booth, removing his blue-jean jacket and hanging it on a hook.

"Hi," he said.

Fiona looked beautiful. She was wearing a pale gold sweater, which brought out the color in her face. Her eyes were radiant, contradicted only by a bittersweet smile.

"Thank you for coming," she said as she watched him slide into his seat.

"What's going on? You sounded so urgent on the phone."

"I want to apologize for last night."

"What about?"

"About my having implied that you walked out on me. It was my fault we separated. You must know that."

"There's nothing you have to say, Fiona. Really. I understand why you left school and I'm sure most people would have done the same thing. Our timing was just bad, that's all."

"But that's only part of the story."

She was cradling a glass of wine between her hands. Her fingers were trembling and seemed almost as fragile as the glass itself.

"When I left," she continued, "I had the full intention of coming back. And though my father was distraught at my mother's death, I could have returned. In fact, he tried to make me. But something happened after I had been home a few weeks, something that kept me away."

Ramsgill took a sip of his drink, his eyes unblinking.

"I found out that I was pregnant, Jamie."

A flood of memories swept over Ramsgill, as if his life were on microfilm and he was rewinding it at full speed.

"You *what?*"

"I was pregnant."

"But I . . ."

"Let me continue," she said. "It wasn't that my father needed me so badly. It was that I didn't want you to know. That I couldn't let you know."

"Why? You mean it wasn't ours? Were you seeing someone else?"

"No," she said. "It was ours. But I didn't know how you would react. I also knew you had to return to the States. I wasn't prepared to go with you and I figured if you knew about the baby, you would have felt you had to stay. Whether I was right or not, I decided that it was better not to tell you."

Ramsgill thought back to all of the times he had tried to go to Kent to see Fiona, and how she had put him off. It wouldn't be good for her father, she would say, or "Perhaps in a few weeks I'll come back to Cambridge." But she never did. And then two months passed, and Ramsgill had to return to the United States. They had corresponded, but slowly, over time, Fiona's letters became devoid of emotion. They reached the point where they read like letters from a pen pal.

"I'm sorry, Jamie. I'm sorry that I never told you, and I'm sorry that I didn't allow you to have a hand in making the decision of what to do with the pregnancy. I'm just sorry, and there's no way I can make it up to you."

Ramsgill looked at her face, and watched as tears slowly fell from her eyes. He reached over and touched her hand, and, unlike the night before, she reached out for him, pulling his hand tightly beneath her own.

"Fi," he said, watching as her eyes looked up to him. "What did you do? About the pregnancy, I mean."

"I kept the baby, Jamie."

"And what happened to it?"

She tried to laugh, but the crying continued too.

"It's not an *it*, Jamie. It's a *she*. Margaret."

"Margaret? But she's only sixteen, Fiona. How can it . . . ?"

"She's eighteen, Jamie. I just never told you that."

"And what about Dick?" Ramsgill said. "I don't understand. I thought she was your and his baby."

Fiona wiped a tear from her cheek, then shook her head.

"Dick turned out to be not such a good person, Jamie. But in the beginning, he was. He married me right after Margaret was born, and he accepted her as if she was his own."

"I see."

"I never meant to hurt you, Jamie. Please forgive me."

Ramsgill was not looking at her now, but toward a stair at the rear of the pub. He let out a near silent laugh.

"What?" Fiona said.

"Elena," said Ramsgill. "She wants to have a baby, and I told I wasn't sure I was ready. And now to learn that I've been a father for eighteen years. It's bizarre."

Fiona smiled.

"If you want," she said, "I'll tell Margaret. And if you want to come back into her life, I won't stop you."

Ramsgill took a sip of his drink, thinking still of the irony of it all.

"No," he said. "That would be too difficult. Difficult for me, but more difficult for you and her. As far as she knows she has a father who loves her, even if you two are no longer married. I'm just a stranger with a funny accent."

Fiona squeezed his hand.

"Jamie, Margaret really is like you. She's smart, sensitive . . ."

"Stubborn?" said Ramsgill.

"A little bit of that."

"A little bit goes a long way."

"Do you think you'll try to have that baby, Jamie? You would be a terrific father."

"I don't know about that," he said.

"I'd like to meet Elena," Fiona said. "To tell her how lucky she is."

Ramsgill smiled, but he knew that it was not Elena who was lucky. It was he, and he realized, just then, that he ought to do something about it.

Nine

*F*iona Mallow hurried to her desk, latte in hand, her croissant still in its bag. She popped the lid to the coffee and sat down, unfolding the morning paper before her.

WITNESS COMES FORWARD IN CASE OF MISSING ACADEMIC was emblazoned in one-inch type across the top of the front page.

She scanned the article, which she had already read once, unable, it seemed, to let the information sink in. The article stated that, according to a "reliable source," a witness had seen Dr. Gräss with another person at the time of his disappearance. The police now suspected that foul play was involved. While the source did not identify the witness, it was said to be an employee of a graduate college. *"The Morning News* has learned," the column went on, that the witness was a man in his sixties who was a porter at Smithson College.

The office door opened and Cheverton Beggs strolled in. He was dressed in a navy wool blazer with a vermilion turtleneck, and he had a cashmere scarf slung once around his neck so that he looked a bit like a flying ace from World War I.

"Morning, Fiona," he said, not looking at her, but rather walking leisurely to his pigeonhole.

"Morning, Chev."

Beggs reached into the box and retrieved his mail. He sorted through it, then suddenly blurted out, "What in heaven's name?"

Fiona looked up.

"The police want me to be in an identity parade this afternoon at the Parkside Station," he said. "How utterly absurd."

"Yes," Fiona said. "They rang up earlier. They've asked everyone who was at the party. So far, the only person I haven't gotten the message to is Amy. You haven't seen her this morning, have you?"

Beggs considered telling Fiona the truth, but only for a fraction of a second. He would be a fool to mention that Amy had come to his estate that morning.

"No," he said. "And why on earth are they having a suspect parade? They're so sure that one of us took Rainer away? I should think he's off on a drunken jaunt."

"You haven't seen this morning's paper, I take it."

She tapped the paper with a finger, and Beggs strutted over to her desk. He read in silence.

"So they must want this fellow from Smithson to have a look at each of you," said Fiona.

The phone rang, and Fiona, in the middle of a sip of coffee, slowly picked up the receiver.

"Ms. Mallow? It's Detective Sergeant Detler again."

"Oh hello, Sergeant."

"Sorry to bother you, but something's come up."

"About the identity parade?" she asked. "I've gotten in touch with everyone but Amy Denster. No one seems to know where she is."

"It's not that," said Detler. "DCI Hill just learned last night that a photograph was taken at Dr. Gräss's party.

"That's right," said Fiona. "A group picture."

"Well, we have Dr. Gräss's camera," said Detler. "But there's no film in it."

"No? Hold on for a minute, Sergeant."

She put the phone to her chest.

"This is the police sergeant," she said to Briggs. "He's asking about the film in Rainer's camera."

Beggs took the phone.

"Sergeant? This is Cheverton Beggs. I'm afraid I sent the film to Barrington Photo first thing Tuesday morning. Did I do something wrong?"

"I suppose not," said Detler. "But can I ask why *you* sent it?"

"I took Rainer's things after the party," said Beggs. "And I also gave Amy a lift home. She said it would be nice to have prints made. You know, for each of us. So my man Cox ran the film over Tuesday morning. We had no idea at that point Rainer was missing."

"Did you get the prints back yet?"

"No. I don't believe I did. In fact, I believe they are to be delivered today."

"All right," said Detler. "I'll call the lab. But if you get the prints, will you let me know?"

"Certainly."

"Bye, then."

"Good day, Sergeant."

Jamie Ramsgill woke with a start, sure that he was late for class. He had been dreaming that he was in Rainer Gräss's theory seminar, and that he was due to give a paper this morning on the influence of American farm machinery on Dadist architecture. The only problem was that in the dream he knew nothing about Dadist architecture, and even less about farm implements.

He sat up in a damp sweat. He looked around him, realized where he was, and that he wasn't due to give the paper after all. But he did sense he was late for something. He found his watch on the nightstand. It was 8:30 A.M. Lyndsay Hill and his men were due back at the Trinity College site by eight.

He jumped out of bed and threw on his clothes, not bothering to check the temperature. He hurried downstairs and got a cup of instant coffee from a machine near the college laundry, then found his bike in the bike shed.

He cycled up Queen's Road. A heavy mass of gray clouds hung over the city, and a cold drizzle filtered down. He was without a raincoat. But he was anxious to get to Trinity, and in five minutes he was at the gate that led into the construction site. A lanky, squint-eyed man in a hard hat escorted him to one of the caravans. He knocked, and the door opened.

Lyndsay Hill was sitting in a swivel-type office chair across from two men, while a third was on the telephone behind him. The room was cramped and chock full of file cabinets, blueprints, and product samples.

"Jamie," he said. "Come in. Gentlemen, this is Jamie Ramsgill. An old college mate of mine from America, and a friend of our missing professor."

Ramsgill shook hands. The two men were introduced as Brian Moss, the site supervisor with Rattner+Davids Construction of Norwich, and Sir Edgar Barnes, Master of Trinity College. Moss was a short, bald man with a ruddy face and Barnes a tall, older gentleman in a dark brown suit. The man on the phone nodded in his direction.

"Has the forensic engineer shown up yet?" said Ramsgill.

Hill shook his head.

"This was your idea, then?" said Barnes, the college master. He had the long, stern face of a Dickensian schoolmaster.

"I suppose," said Ramsgill. "If you mean my idea to look in the foundations."

"I'll tell you something," Barnes said, turning to Hill. "I've got benefactors who expect this building to be completed on time. We're spending several million pounds here, and if your department holds up completion, there's going to be hell to pay. We're already behind schedule because of this abnormally cold winter. And what are you going to find anyway? We pay Rattner and Davids quite a sum of money to have a security guard here each night. No one's been caught on the property, with one exception. . . ."

The college Master leered back at Ramsgill.

"Jamie assures me that this won't take long," said Hill. "And we've discussed his nocturnal wanderings. He's promised to reform his ways."

Ramsgill looked to Moss, the site supervisor for the contractor.

"Did DCI Hill ask you if you've made any concrete pours this week?" he said.

"Yes."

The third man hung up the phone.

"Did you pour Tuesday morning?" asked Ramsgill.

"I believe so," said Moss.

"One of the sections of foundation wall near the water?"

"Actually that whole side."

"I take it you are joking, Brian," said the third man. "It was too cold on Tuesday to pour. I told you on Monday that we should wait until the weather broke."

"Jamie," said Hill. "Allow me to introduce Maltby Sykes. Mr. Sykes is the project architect, from Llewelyn/Prouvé, Limited, of London."

Sykes was a bearded man about Ramsgill's age. After shaking hands, Sykes looked again over to Moss.

"Brian," he said. "About that pour. It was near freezing Monday night."

"I've told you several times," said Moss. "We can provide temporary heat. And our concrete mix is air-entrained to resist freezing. As of the first of January, we were already three weeks behind schedule because of weather. If the college is willing to pay the additional amount for air-entraining and the heaters, I'm not going to sit around and wait for the weather to break."

Moss looked to Barnes, the college Master, who nodded to confirm the additional cost. Sykes sighed deeply. He picked up a metal clipboard and thumbed through a pad.

"My phone notes from Monday are right here," he said emphatically. "It was left between us, Brian, that even if the college approved the extra, we were still to talk to the engineer to make sure that it was okay with him. I specifically told you not to do anything until I got back to you."

Moss rose without saying a word and went over to a long table. He opened a set of blueprints.

"Look," he said. The group of men gathered around the documents.

"Between columns six and twelve, on column line G. That pour was approved via the fax I got Tuesday morning. It's written in red right here on the print."

"A fax from who?" said Sykes. "Not from me."

Moss leaned over, pulling a pair of eyeglasses out of his pocket and putting them on.

"Guy Spencer," Moss said. "Of Culworth Engineering."

"Guy Spencer?" said Sykes. "I know of no Guy Spencer who works for Culworth. Let me see that."

The architect looked over the print, then said, "Do you have a copy of the fax?"

Brian Moss dug through some papers on the table. He pulled one out, which was a fax cover sheet. It had Culworth Engineering's name and logo on top, a steel I-beam turned sideways and underlining their name.

"May I see that?" said Hill. He took the paper and looked at the very top. The time, date, and the fax's telephone number of origin ran across the header in small type, the imprint known as the transmission report. But the origin number was not the same as the fax number listed on Culworth's masthead, and it wasn't a London exchange. The fax came from another number, a local one.

"Anyone recognize this phone number?"

The group of men looked at the number of the origin machine.

"That's probably the architecture department," said Ramsgill. "At least, it's one digit different than their phone number."

"The fax must have come from there," said Hill. "At nine fifty Tuesday morning. So it seems it was forged."

Hill's eyes turned to Ramsgill.

Just then, a knock came to the caravan door, and Moss opened it to see the lanky man in the hard hat standing in front of two men and a young woman.

"Matthew Cleeve to see the inspector," the lanky man said. He moved aside.

Cleeve stepped forward. He was a large, roundish man, with thinning gray hair and the luminous face of a country doctor. He wore a tan Burberry and brown Wellingtons, and the boots were caked with mud the color of creamed coffee. Behind him were a young man and woman, probably graduate students, Ramsgill thought. Both wore hooded anoraks and carried aluminum suitcases.

"Good morning," Cleeve said. "If you don't mind, I'd like to get started. I have a lecture at eleven, and I'd just as soon not have to miss it."

Hill, Ramsgill, and the other men piled out of the caravan and stepped out into the rain. Brian Moss led them around the building excavation to the side adjacent to the river. In daylight, Ramsgill could make better sense of the building. It was as though they were looking at an archaeological dig, without the decay that comes from age. The plan of the building was clear. Though it was essentially a square, its form was actually a modified cruciform. The perimeter walls were delineated by numerous projections, what he guessed were supports for bay windows above. The column spacing of the interior was regular throughout, the one exception being an oblique grid of columns, which Ramsgill guessed was the support for a monumental stair.

"What's being built, anyway?" asked Cleeve once the group had reached the side of the excavation adjoining the river.

"It's a commons building," said Moss. "Three stories, dining, lecture hall, and lounges."

"And what are we going to look at?"

"This area here, which has most recently been poured. From this corner north to that bucket was poured on Tuesday. And we can get down into the excavation right over there."

"Not so fast," said Cleeve, in a tone of voice that seemed accustomed to giving orders. "We won't be going down yet."

"No?" said Hill.

"We'll need to look at the top of the wall first," he said. "Up at grade. Unless you want to spend days here, and I don't, we'll first shoot straight down."

Cleeve had a wart just below his lower lip, and Ramsgill noticed that he fingered it each time he spoke.

"Whatever you say," said Hill.

"And I'm going to need power," Cleeve said.

Moss already had a couple of heavy-duty extension cords waiting for them. Their orange leads ran back to a temporary power panel on a pole next to one of the site huts, some two hundred feet away. Cleeve and his assistants uncased their equipment and set it out on the ground.

"Is this going to work in the rain?" asked Ramsgill.

"Oh, it'll work," said Cleeve. "We do this in any weather. In fact we do it under water, on marine construction."

He was connecting a small black metal box via a long cable to a larger metal box in one of the suitcases. He plugged the larger box into the extension cord.

"What's that?" asked Hill.

Cleeve picked up the smaller box.

"This is a piezoelectronic transducer. It will pick up sound waves from the face of the concrete and feed them into this device, which is an oscilloscope that I've modified into a pulse echo scanner."

Hill nodded as if he knew what the engineer was talking about.

Cleeve then flipped a switch on the front of the oscilloscope and a luminous green screen came to life. The screen was gridded in lighter green lines, with numerical values along the bottom and left side. As Cleeve adjusted the dials on the oscilloscope's front, one of his assistants pulled another device from a second suitcase. It looked like a small artillery shell, with a coil of long, loose wire attached. The assistant plugged it into the extension cord, then slid a toggle switch on the side of the device, whereupon a piston was driven out one end. The device made a popping sound, followed by the piston being recoiled.

"Swedish hammer?" asked Ramsgill.

"Actually, a Schmidt hammer," said Cleeve, fingering the wart on his chin. His eyes moved back and forth, from his oscilloscope to the hammer. "But they're very similar."

"I thought you used pachometers for this type of work," said Ramsgill. The assistant with the Schmidt hammer was now moving to the north end of the foundation. Cleeve had given the transducer to the second graduate student, and she was following her colleague.

"No, no. Pachometers are only good for finding metals," said Cleeve. "They can locate reinforcing steel, but they're dreadful for most of what we do, which is looking for stress fractures, nonbonds, voids. And if our professor is in that wall somewhere, then the only way we'll find him with a pachometer is if he has teeth fillings, or some other heavy metal on his body. And we're just as likely to find something else metal down there, something that might throw us off."

"Such as?" said Moss.

"You're the construction man," said Cleeve. "I don't have to tell you what ends up being poured into walls by accident. We've found lunch pails, tools, keys, cans. . . . Once we even found a toaster."

"But never a dead body?" asked Hill.

"Thankfully no," said Cleeve.

By now, Cleeve's assistants had positioned themselves. The one with the Schmidt hammer held it with the piston facing down, atop the wall in the middle of its width. The young woman held the small transducer in contact with the wall, several inches away.

Cleeve called "Fire!" and the Schmidt hammer let out a loud pop. A second later an image was generated on the screen of the oscilloscope, a brilliant green gash, roughly in the form of an H.

"How does this work?" asked Hill.

"Quite simple, really," said Cleeve. "The hammer projects sound waves down through the wall, not unlike throwing a stone into a pond and creating ripples. Since sound moves constantly through homogeneous material, we can predict its rate of transmission. The sound echoes off the bottom of the wall as if a ripple had hit the shore of the pond, and it returns at a similar rate. If it encounters anything other than concrete, the wave is distorted. The transducer picks up the anomalies and turns them into electrical impulses. It sends them to the oscilloscope, where a screen image is generated. A distortion or blip on the screen means something other than concrete."

"But how do you know one blip from another?" asked Ramsgill. "I mean, how would you know the difference between a toaster and a person?"

"Ah," said Cleeve. "That's where the art of it comes in. Something I keep trying to drum into the heads of these students of mine. I've developed software that generates a three-dimensional image based on a number of factors: size of the object, mass, its dielectric constant, and so forth. Once we go down into the pit, I'll show it to you. The software is loaded onto the notebook computer in that third suitcase."

"Fire!" he called again. Once again the green H emanated from the screen of the oscilloscope. He made a few more adjustments, then said to his assistants, "All right. Let's start it up. We'll do two firings at each location. I think we can move a meter for each new firing. All I want to do up here is to determine where there might be objects in the wall. We'll look at them better once we're down in the pit."

For the next fifteen minutes, Cleeve and his assistants worked with near-silent efficiency. The rain continued to fall, but it didn't seem to bother them. They shot the hammer twice at each location along the top of the wall, and after each firing they moved south the distance of one yard to the next location. Cleeve didn't say much, having the graduate students halt on occasion so that he could play with the dials of the oscilloscope, and once or twice pausing to jot down some numbers on a rain-soaked legal pad. As the two assistants finally reached the southern portion of the wall, Cleeve said, "Okay, we've got two irregularities. One at eighteen feet from north, and one at roughly sixty. Let's go into the hole."

The group moved down into the excavation. By now, whether because of boredom or because they sensed a rising expectation that something was about to happen, several of the police and construction personnel on the site had joined the group.

"We'll start here," said Cleeve, motioning the crowd back from the wall.

Cleeve's assistants arranged the equipment as before, and this time Cleeve opened the third suitcase, connecting a small gray notebook computer to a port in the rear of the oscilloscope.

"We'll try it through the plywood," said Cleeve, looking at Moss but speaking such that his assistants could hear. "If we get too much distortion, though, then I'm afraid I'll have to ask you to remove the wooden formwork."

Moss frowned, as did Barnes, the college Master.

Again, the trio went to work, this time along the face of the wall, in an area about six feet wide, at the first of the two locations where Cleeve had found anomalous readings on his oscilloscope. The wall was at least ten feet high, and the two graduate students started atop ladders provided by Moss. This time they moved the Schmidt hammer and transducer in very small increments, a grid of perhaps one-foot centers. It took them a good twenty minutes to work their way to the bottom of the wall, then Cleeve said, "We've got something, definitely."

Ramsgill and the others moved toward Cleeve. Cleeve booted up the notebook computer and navigated his way into a program that opened with a view of a cube in axonometric form, a wire-frame model defined by lines of indigo blue on a white screen. A menu of graphic interface tools ran down the left side of the screen, and a color palette along its bottom. To Ramsgill's eyes it looked not unlike a computer-aided design, or CAD, program. The x, y, and z dimensions of the cube had values of one foot each, representing the height, width, and depth of the cube. Clicking on the numbers one by one by means of the computer's track ball, Cleeve changed their values. He made the height of the cube eleven feet, the depth two feet, and the width six. Graphically, the 3-D object on the screen now approximated the section of wall that had just been tested.

He then exited the program and went into the computer's control-panel folder, where he accessed a file-sharing panel that allowed him to communicate with the oscilloscope. After a few moments he brought over a file named "TRIN.NUM.VALS.0–10.," the file that Ramsgill presumed held the values recorded by the transducer. Placing the file on the computer's desktop, he again opened the CAD program with the view of the wall. Once opened, he pulled down the "Import" command from the menu at the top of the screen, and imported "TRIN.NUM.VALS.0–10." into the CAD program.

Almost instantly, a small amoebalike blob of chartreuse green formed within the lower left-hand corner of the wall.

"What is it?" Ramsgill asked.

Using a number of deft keystrokes, Cleeve rotated the wire-frame model of the wall, turning to different views as if the model were truly three-dimensional and he were holding it in his hand. The amoeba was formed of "wire mesh" lines to give it three-dimensional definition, and Ramsgill guessed that it was about two feet high and two feet wide at its widest point. It was almost at the bottom of the wall, and one side of it appeared to be somewhat compressed. But no matter how the model was rotated, it didn't look human, at least not to Ramsgill.

"It's nothing more than a void," said Cleeve. "It's about six or eight cubic feet in size, but it has virtually no mass. It's not something I would want in my foundation wall if I were Trinity, but it's not a human body."

Hill was about to ask how Cleeve could be so sure when Cleeve walked over to his male assistant and gave him some instructions. He seemed to be losing patience now, and he moved with an expedient air. In ten minutes the high-tech bivouac had set up again, before the new section of wall, twenty-some-odd yards from the north end of the pour. Again, Cleeve's assistants climbed the ladders, and again they moved methodically down the wall with hammer and transducer. By the time they reached the bottom, the rain seemed to be dying out. It was quarter past ten. Ramsgill thought that if they didn't find something in this next section of wall, then Cleeve would leave the site for his eleven o'clock class, not returning until afternoon. For two days now, Ramsgill had hoped that Rainer Gräss's disappearance was an aberration, and that he would again appear as if nothing had ever happened. But now, soaking wet and standing in thick mud, with time diminishing, he simply wished that the ordeal would come to a resolution.

Cleeve followed the procedures that he had followed on the earlier

wall. When he accessed the oscilloscope, he brought over a different file, "TRIN.NUM.VALS.11–20." He then opened the CAD file again, and imported it. Nothing happened for a moment, then a window of text popped up onto the screen. It read, *Unable to import, due to error type-28.*

"Bloody hell," said Cleeve.

Cleeve clicked *OK* on the message screen, and exited the file. Ramsgill wondered what the fix for the error message was, but as he watched Cleeve pull down "Get Info" on the CAD program from the main menu, he realized that it was a simple lack of RAM memory allocated to the program. Sure enough, Cleeve increased the memory for the CAD program, from 1,024k to 8 megabytes. He then went back into the program.

When he again tried to import the numerical values from the oscilloscope, the image that appeared within the wall caused a palpable, and almost comical, gasp from the group watching Cleeve's screen. There, in the absolute middle of the wall, as if it were levitating within air, was a long, tapered, wire-frame amoeba. It was without discernible appendages, but it did show what could only be construed as an egg-shaped head, which connected to the amoeba by a more narrow connection, which was surely a neck. Cleeve rotated the model until he had a three-quarter side view, and what could now be seen as feet projected in a perpendicular manner. The body, because there was no doubt in anyone's mind that it was a body, slumped forward in the side view, and the head was tilted unnaturally, against what Ramsgill guessed was the reinforcing cage at the front of the wall.

Ramsgill stared at the abstract image, trying to imagine it as something tangible. As Rainer Gräss. It was so uncomplicated as a wire-frame CAD model, an entity with no organs, features, psyche, or life. It wasn't a man, with a wife, who was a teacher, and who had once been a father. It didn't have an intellect. It was a symbol for Rainer, really, in the same way that a dot on a map represents a city. It was one with the wall, outlined in colorful, geometric vector lines.

Ten

On the third ring, a man who looked surprisingly like Vladmir Lenin, but in reality was a college porter picked up the phone.

"Smithson College Porters' Lodge," he said, in a smooth and assured voice.

"Yes, quite, hello. Hello, my name is Jenkins, Thomas Jenkins from *Crime Enders*, on Channel Four."

"Yes?"

"You probably know our program. Thursday evenings at eight."

"No."

"Ah, right. Yes. Well, it's a true-crime program. Each week we do three stories on unsolved crimes, in documentary fashion, you know. The circumstances of the case, profiles of the victim and the investigating team, that sort of thing. At the program's end, we ask for the public to come forward with any information that might help solve the crime. If you haven't seen our program, you've probably seen one of the ones that the other channels do like it."

The porter breathed deeply, and let out a long, slow sigh.

"I don't have a television," he said.

"I see. Well, I'm ringing up about the Rainer Gräss case. The missing professor, there at the university."

"Yes?"

"You know about the case?"

"Yes."

"Well, we've heard that a witness has come forward. A porter from your college."

Hamish Thornebury, the porter, twisted the point of his Van Dyke with his thumb and index finger. It was all over college that one of his co-workers, Dennis Fortthompson, had supposedly seen the missing professor on his way home Monday night. Thornebury was not convinced, as he considered Fortthompson to be a rather unreliable chap when sober, much less after a few pints, which undoubtedly he had had on the night in question.

"So?" said Thornebury.

"So it wouldn't be you . . . the witness, that is?"

"No."

"No, quite. Well, we're patching together a story for next week's program on the disappearance. And, of course, we would be mad keen to talk to the witness. Do you know him?"

Thornebury considered whether there was any reason he shouldn't tell this fellow that it was Fortthompson. He didn't like the sound of the chap's voice—high pitched, affected and almost like that of a woman—something he could tell that the fellow worked at. On the other hand, it might be rather entertaining to watch Fortthompson deal with the maggots from the press, an ordeal that Thornebury was sure he wasn't up to.

"What's in it for me?" Thornebury asked.

There was a pause on the line, followed by a surprise offer.

"We could pay you a hundred quid," the fellow Jenkins said.

Thornebury was a mathematician by training but, like many mathematicians, he had never found a job commensurate with his education. He quickly calculated that a hundred quid for a one-second answer translated into six thousand pounds per minute. Three hundred and sixty thousand pounds per hour. Not a bad return for a painless piece of work.

"And how do I get paid?"

"By check. If you'll confide in me now, and only now, I'll have the check in tonight's post."

"But how can I trust you? If I give you the name, how do I know that I'll get the money?"

"You don't. But if you don't give me his name, somebody else at your college will. And they'll be the hundred pounds richer."

Thornebury realized that the man had him figured. It sounded as though he was used to dealing with people this way.

"Okay," he finally said. "His name's Dennis Fortthompson. He supposedly saw the missing professor being taken downriver by punt the night he disappeared." Thornebury started to say that he didn't put much stock in the story, but he figured if he wanted his hundred, he'd better keep his mouth shut.

"Is Fortthompson there now, by any chance?" said the caller.

"No. He should be in tonight, but let me just check the schedule. He alternates between Thursday or Friday off."

Thornebury reached across his desk and found the porters' work schedule. There he could see that Fortthompson's night off for this week was Friday.

"He'll be in tonight," he told the man called Jenkins.

"What time?"

Thornebury pulled a silver pocket watch from his trousers. It was almost noon.

"He'll be here from four until midnight. Ring back later."

"Okay. Thanks very much. And as I said, I'll drop your check in tonight's post. Cheerio, then."

Thornebury started to hang up, but caught himself.

"One minute," he said, "you didn't even ask my name."

"Ah. No, I didn't then. How stupid of me. What is it?"

"Thornebury, Hamish Thornebury."

"Well, thanks very much, Mr. Thornebury. You've been jolly helpful. Bye now."

"Good-bye."

After he hung up, Thornebury went back to sorting various announcements from the Dean's office that he was to stuff into the college members' pigeonholes. As he finished sorting, he thought of something the fellow named Jenkins had said, something incongruous for a voice that was at once erudite and assured.

How stupid of me, Jenkins had said.

He paused for a moment, and looked back toward the phone. Was he really that stupid or was I, for giving him Fortthompson's name?

Amy Denster had been aware of the cold for what must have been the better part of an hour now, sliding in and out of a fitful slumber. But when she opened her eyes, it was the darkness that surprised her. She couldn't sense the position of her body in space. She lifted a head capsized in sleep, and realized, without the benefit of being able to observe herself, that she had been lying. She was resting atop something dark and hard, and she thought she was dressed in her heavy coat and scarf. It reminded her of how she had slept as a child, in the tiny three-room flat her family had let from the vicar at Yarm. She and her brother had shared the same hard floor mattress in the dull, cramped addition to the vicar's grit stone house that overlooked the River Tees. Back then, sleeping in her coat and scarf had given her a modicum of comfort against the harsh North Yorkshire winter, when inevitably her family couldn't afford to feed the heat box with fifty-pence pieces those last few nights of each month.

Now, as she tried to regain a sense of her existence in the present, she wondered why she was dressed as she was. Her head ached. It was a dull, numbing pain that felt as though her temples had been slowly squeezed between a vise. Had they done it? she wondered. She felt no pain down there. She couldn't remember. In fact, she couldn't even remember going to the clinic.

Maria had assured her that there was nothing to worry about, that the doctors and staff of the clinic would treat her kindly. It was a clinic run by and for women. It would all be over in a matter of hours. It would be performed as an outpatient procedure, and she would spend the night with her brother in Crawley. On Friday she would be able to return to a normal life. But then why was it dark now, and where was she?

Her mind seemed incapable of holding on to a thought, other than the desire to get warm. Suddenly she was aware that she was hungry, too. She pulled back the sleeve of her blouse, but she couldn't see her watch. They had taken it from her. What kind of place was this? It even smelled, she now realized. Not the pungency of antiseptic, nor the false naturalness of cedar-scented cleaning solution, but it smelled moldy. Had Maria betrayed her? she wondered. Had Amy collected the five hundred pounds to ensure proper treatment for herself, only to be sent to some mews butcher who performed abortions with a coat hanger and a little tea and sympathy? Why was Maria so intent that she go to this clinic in the first place? And what did she really know about what had happened in Cloister Court the night that Rainer disappeared?

Her mind shifted to Rainer. It was weird, but she wanted to hold him. He wouldn't hold her back—he never did—but at least he could make her warm. He had made her warm before, in his own bed, at the cottage in Coton, when his wife had gone to visit her mother in Nîmes. For three nights they had lived like lovers, Amy having full access of the cottage, able to roam Rainer's study, to hold his venerable books in the lap of her bare body while he slept off the effects of too much drink. It wasn't love, but it was attention, something she had rarely been given in her life. And he was cultured and had money, two things that she had always hoped for. Where had they gone wrong? If she just closed her eyes, she thought, maybe he would appear. But he wouldn't. And it was too dark in this cold prison to see him even if he did.

By midafternoon the Trinity construction site had been transformed. The east wall of the foundation had a gaping swath cut from it, a four-foot-wide by eleven-foot-high void. The enormous piece of concrete that was removed had been lifted by crane to an area near the site huts, and laid horizontally on the muddy ground. Portable arc lights had been situated over the concrete slab, the whole looking not unlike an operating theater for a giant.

Three stonemasons were busy at work trying to extricate the body from the section of wall. One of the masons worked with a cumbersome hand-held diamond-tipped power saw. He was cutting away concrete in a rough outline of the body to match that provided to them by Cleeve, now traced on the face of the concrete in marker. Cleeve had added a good six inches of additional area around where he thought the body was to compensate for the possibility of an inaccurate reading. DCI Hill didn't care if it took two days to get the body out, just as long as it was done with care, not destroying any part of the corpse.

The other two masons worked in a manner that befitted Hill's mandate, carefully chipping away flecks of concrete, but at the rate they were working, it indeed might take two days. Finally, one of them offered the suggestion that they make two single saw cuts lengthwise along the top and bottom of the slab, centered along the axis of the body within. They could then drive splitting wedges into one of the saw-cut cracks, and if they were lucky, the slab might split along the cut, not unlike the method of removing slabs of stone from a quarry.

Hill agreed to the suggestion, and within twenty minutes the first saw cut was made. Then a strap was attached to one end of the slab, and the crane was used to lift and tip it to its other side. This time it was wrestled onto two heavy timbers, parallel to one another, which kept it suspended above the ground. Then, once again, a cut was made lengthwise. The masons began driving in the wedges, slowly at first, until nearly a dozen wedges were driven in at equal distance from one another along the length of the crack. The masons then situated themselves at third points along the crack, and using sledgehammers instead of the smaller mason's mallets, they began to pound the wedges. It took only four hits with the sledges before a definitive crack was heard. Immediately the right side of the slab split apart from the left, and slid off its timber with an enormous thump. Inside was the dusty gray body of Rainer Gräss.

The body, without anything to support its left side, emerged from the cement. At least most of it did. Gräss's feet were bound together by rope and still embedded in the concrete but all it took was a series of hammer blows by two of the masons to free them. Quickly, members of the police investigative team picked up the corpse and carefully carried it to a makeshift table set up a few feet away. The group of people surrounding the slab followed the body to the table, and DCI Hill gave Jamie Ramsgill a brief, appreciative nod.

"Move back, gents," said Hill, pushing his way to the edge of the table. The arc lights were now being resituated overhead.

Ramsgill stepped in next to Hill, and across the table noticed Matthew Cleeve, who had missed his class after all. Next to him was the college Master Barnes, an impassive stare planted on his long face.

"Is that him?" Cleeve asked.

Ramsgill nodded. He then looked down at Gräss's corpse. At first, the uneasiness Ramsgill feared he would feel was minimal. He was simply relieved that the ordeal was over and, if not completely resolved, at least what had happened to Rainer was now known. The body, with the exception of a rather grotesque open mouth that was filled with concrete, was the picture of placidity. His eyelids were closed, and his eyelashes rested snugly against his high cheekbones. The body was stiff from rigor mortis, but not shockingly so, the rigor undoubtedly having been retarded by the body's encasement for three days, without the accelerating effects of exposure to climate. The arms were bound around the torso, which would have made it easier for the murderer to get the body between the reinforcing rods. Another length of rope ran free, attached to the back of the torso, and was probably used to lower him into the forms. There was a fine gray-white dusting of cement covering the body, which hid the discoloration caused by death, making it look more like a limestone sculpture than a human being. The only exception was the reddish brown coloring of the back of his skull.

"What kind of wound is that?" said Hill, addressing his question to John Wingate, a youthful, academic type who was head of Forensics at Huntingdon Laboratory.

"Looks like a laceration, or even an incision to the posterior parietal," said Wingate. "Right side."

"Do you think he was dead when he got here?" asked Hill.

"Definitely not," said Wingate. "The fact that he took concrete into his mouth meant that he was alive."

Ramsgill tried to think of how horrible it must have been for Rainer. He wondered if Rainer's killer had relished the suffering he had caused, or whether it was simply expediency that prescribed the method of entombment.

"He might have been alive," said Ramsgill, "but he must have been unconscious. How else would he have remained within the formwork of the wall for what . . . ten hours . . . before the concrete was poured?"

Wingate nodded.

Ramsgill considered what they had learned, other than that the death must have been horrible. He had already pondered the legerdemain required to get Rainer out of the college in the middle of the party. In answer to some of his earlier questions, it now appeared that Rainer was knocked unconscious prior to being placed in the punt. How was the blow exacted, and where had he been overtaken? Since the blow was to the back of the head, it more than likely came as a surprise.

John Wingate pressed a gloved finger against Gräss's right temple, turning his head to the left. His white hair was matted down and completely brown in the area of the cut, but the wound, which was fleshy and more red than the other hair, stood out clearly. The laceration was about two inches long, and slightly curved. Torn tissue could be seen, and the wound was wider in the middle than at the ends.

"What kind of an instrument leaves a mark like that?" said Ramsgill.

"We once had a woman beaten to death over in Newmarket," said Wingate. "By her husband who was a blacksmith. He used a very heavy horseshoe, but only a portion of it left an imprint. Same curve, and with a sharp, square edge to it, like this wound. See, there's some bridging of the tissue here, like you would expect in a laceration, but the margins of the wound are sharp, and there appears to be little bruising. Which means that it wasn't a blunt instrument, a tire iron, for instance. No doubt it was something with a sharp, or at least square, edge to it."

Just then the north gate in the fence opened. A short man with heavy black eyeglasses stepped through. In his arm he carried a large leather case.

"Gentlemen," he said as he arrived at the table.

"Good afternoon, Dr. MacCaig," said Hill. He shook the Home Office pathologist's hand.

"I'll need a little free space, Lyndsay," said the doctor.

"Right," said Hill. "Okay, everybody. I'd like us to get out of Drs. Wingate and MacCaig's way. Let let them do their work. In fact, I would like everyone with the exception of the police to please clear out. You can go to the caravans or outside the gate. But we need to clear the area."

Most of the construction personnel returned to the caravans. Cleeve and his assistants had already packed up their gear and, after appreciative thanks from Lyndsay Hill, left the site. Ramsgill resolved to return to Darwin, where he needed to call Elena and get into some dry clothes. Hill walked with him toward the gate. As they were about to say good-bye, Chris Detler appeared before them, having spent most of the day tracking down leads.

"Afternoon, Inspector. Mr. Ramsgill."

"Hello, Chris."

"Do you have a minute, boss?"

Hill walked over to his car, which was parked at the end of the access way. He turned and leaned against the bonnet, facing Detler, and Ramsgill, who was still standing nearby.

Detler flashed his eyes in Ramsgill's direction, not sure if Hill wanted Ramsgill to hear what he had to say.

"It's all right, Chris," Hill said. "I've given up on trying to keep Jamie out of this."

"Very well," said Detler. "Here's what I've got, sir. First off, the phone call about the wallet. We tried to trace it back through British Telcom, but no luck. We know it was a local call, but that's about the extent of it."

"I figured that would be the case," said Hill.

"Lyndsay?"

It was Ramsgill speaking.

"I was thinking about that on my way back to college last night. Fiona told me that the phone call about the wallet was made to her at about ten o'clock Tuesday morning, the morning after the party."

"Yes?"

"Well, I know that she was in her office at the time, and I believe that Frontis and Beggs were there with her."

"Meaning that neither of them could have made the call?"

"Right. And if it was the killer who made the call, because he was the only one who knew that Gräss had even been on the river, then it would seem to give Beggs and Frontis an alibi. At least an alibi for not having made the call."

"Interesting," said Hill, scratching his nose. "A point well taken. What else do you have, Chris?"

"Gaines Simpson did go to his room that night, to change shirts like he said. Two students saw him."

"And?"

"They say it was at about twelve forty, maybe later."

"It couldn't have been much later," said Hill. "Remember, the group was back together at twelve forty-five."

"So say somewhere between twelve forty and twelve forty-five," said Detler.

"That means," Ramsgill broke in, "that he was out of the hall for twenty to twenty-five minutes."

"How are you figuring that?" said Hill.

"Well, he said that he left the hall after Amy returned. And if she's really lying, and was out in the court until twelve twenty, then he couldn't have left the hall before then."

"Still enough time to have come here," said Hill. "And we only have his word to go on that he didn't leave the hall before Amy returned. He could be lying."

"There's something else of interest about Simpson," Detler said.

"What's that?" said Hill.

"One of the students I talked to told me that Simpson's shirt wasn't just stained. The pocket was ripped, also."

"Now that is interesting."

"I found him at school today," said Detler, "and asked him about it."

"And?"

"He said that he'd had too much to drink, and that he must have caught it on something. I think he's lying."

"Most likely. Then again, aren't they all? What else did you come up with, Chris?"

"I must have spent half the day on the phone with Barrington Photo."

"Who's that?"

"That's where Cheverton Beggs sent the film from the party."

"Beggs? What was he doing with the film?"

"He had taken Dr. Gräss's things home from the party. Ms. Denster suggested that it would be nice if they could have some prints made. So he took it upon himself to have his valet send off the film to the lab."

"Even with the guest of honor dead?"

"It went to the photo lab first thing Tuesday. Before anybody knew Gräss was missing. Anyway, when I rang up Barrington today, they told me that they had already delivered the prints to Beggs. Yesterday. But Beggs said no, that they're supposed to be delivered this afternoon. As it turned out, Beggs had another job at the lab. That's what was delivered yesterday."

"So did you get them?"

"No. By the time I straightened everything out, they were already on their way to Beggs. To his estate in Grantchester. I can run out there now, if you'd like."

"Bugger it," said Hill. "What's one more day at this point? Just ring Beggs up and tell him we want the prints first thing in the morning."

"Right, sir."

"Now, what else is happening?" said Hill.

"It seems that Amy Denster's missing."

"Tell me you're joking."

Detler shook his head.

"I wish I was. This morning I had alerted the others to the fact that we wanted to have an identity parade, and I also knew that you wanted to question her again. But she's nowhere to be found."

"Have you been to her college? Checked with her friends, family?"

"We're doing that now, sir."

"I don't like the sound of this. At all."

"There is one possible explanation," said Detler.

"What?"

"I rang up that doctor today. The one in Gräss's daybook. The appointment with the surgery Monday wasn't for Gräss. It was for Amy."

"Then why'd Gräss have it in his book?"

"He went along with her, sir. She's pregnant and Gräss was the father."

"Hmh." Hill pursed his lips and let that thought hang for a while.

"The doctor, Hargreaves, said that Ms. Denster was unsure of what to do about the pregnancy," continued Detler. "He got the feeling that she wanted to keep the baby, but that Professor Gräss wanted her to abort it. Gräss asked him during their consultation how long she would have to wait if the procedure was done via the National Health Service. Hargreaves told him perhaps a month. That was unacceptable to Gräss; he wanted it done straightaway. Hargreaves told him it could probably be done immediately if it was paid for directly, or through private insurance."

"And?"

"Gräss apparently tried to convince her to go through with it. Said that he'd pay for it. Hargreaves says that at one point she seemed willing to, but then reneged. So Gräss left the office in a huff."

"I see."

"Hargreaves also says he didn't want to sway her one way or the other. So he suggested she confide in a friend, to get an opinion from someone without a stake in the matter."

"I know one thing," Ramsgill said. "When Amy met up with Rainer in the courtyard, I doubt it was the brief exchange she claims. She probably hadn't seen him since the doctor's appointment and I'm sure she vented some frustration."

"You may be right, Jamie."

"But I still can't see Ms. Denster having anything to do with his disappearance," said Detler. "You'd have to be in good shape to get Gräss across the bridge and into the punt, then up to here, dump him, and return, all within roughly twenty minutes."

"Agreed," said Hill. "But at this point I'm not discounting anybody."

"There's something else," said Detler, his voice low.

"What?"

Detler handed Hill a copy of the morning paper.

"Did you see this?"

Hill didn't respond. He carefully read the front-page story about a witness having come forward. When he was finished he looked up at Detler and Ramsgill.

"Bloody fucking hell," he said. "They might as well have given the poor fellow's name, for Christ's sake."

"Can I see it?" said Ramsgill.

Hill handed him the paper, and Ramsgill hurried through the article. He realized Hill's ire when he got to the part about the paper having learned that the witness was a porter at Smithson. Hill had wanted to keep it confidential.

"How did the paper find out about this?" said Hill.

Detler's face was red.

"I don't know, boss. Somebody at headquarters."

"I'm going to have to ring up Fortthompson," said Hill. "I don't want him skipping out on us. If he gets scared, we're nowhere."

Hill pushed himself off the car and walked around to the driver's door. He opened the door and slid into the seat. A moment later, he still hadn't made the call to Fortthompson.

"What is this?" he said.

Detler and Ramsgill looked through the front passenger-side window, but they couldn't see well enough, so Detler opened the door. Hill had an envelope in his right hand, and an unfolded sheet of white writing paper in his left. He handed the paper over to Detler.

Detler read it.

"Where was this?" Detler said.

"On the steering wheel," said Hill.

Detler handed the paper to Ramsgill. Neatly typed in the middle of an otherwise blank page was:

DID YOU FIND HIM? THEN TRY THIS:
PARIS, WHY, OH WHY, DO I LOVE PARIS?

"What the hell?" said Ramsgill.

"What is it?" said Detler. "A joke?"

Hill thought back to the phone call the murderer had made to Fiona about the wallet being found in the river.

"It *is* a joke, Chris, the kind I'm getting tired of. It's from the murderer."

"So what does it mean? Our killer's a Francophile?"

"I don't know," said Hill.

Ramsgill handed the note and envelope back to Hill. Hill placed them on the seat beside him.

"I'll have Wingate check them for prints," said Hill. "And the graphologist should look at it."

"It's a shame," Ramsgill said, his eyes cast downward.

"What's that, Jamie?" said Hill.

"Well, your man must have been here within the hour. He got into your car when we were preoccupied, I suppose when we were down in the hole. This gravel might make for a good access road, but it's too bad, with all this rain, that you can't get footprints."

"No," said Hill.

"He *is* theatrical," said Ramsgill. "It took balls to put that in your car with us not a hundred feet away."

"He?" said Hill. "Or she? Let's don't leave sight of all the possibilities."

Possibilities, thought Ramsgill. At this stage, they were all they had.

Eleven

George Boye's room at Darwin College was simple, with two lateral walls of solid wire-struck brick and a broad plate-glass window that overlooked Silver Street. He walked to a desk beneath the window, turned on a CD player, and the smooth voice of Majek Fashek wailed to an Afro-reggae beat.

It was twilight, and through the twisted web of branches that brushed against the second-floor window, Boye could see the neo-Gothic Fisher Building of Queens' College across the street. He had unbuckled his belt and was about to remove his trousers when he heard a light knock at the door.

"Just one minute," he said.

He had just returned to college and his blue jeans were damp from the rain. He removed them and draped them on the desk chair before retrieving a new pair from a closet. He pulled the new jeans up over his thick legs and drew them together at the wide girth of his waist.

He opened the door to find Ghislaine Gräss standing before him, looking surprisingly good. She looked a decade younger than her forty-seven years, her face made up in a pale, natural-looking yellow with subtle eye shadow that mitigated the normal shadowy circles beneath her gray eyes. She wore a smart white silk blouse beneath a long black jacket, a knit miniskirt, matching hose, and black pumps with silver buckles. On her ears she wore loop earrings, and the lapel of

161

her jacket held an antique pin made from silver and champlevé. But the most important change in her appearance was her hair. She had cut it. All of it. Just yesterday, it had been thick and wavy, of medium length. It was now shorn to a uniform one inch, as short as a man's, with a jagged fringe that lay straight down on her forehead. The length made her appear to be almost adolescent, while drawing attention to the subtle proportions of her head.

"May I come in?"

As she passed, Boye caught the faint scent of jasmine, and he thought of doing her here, now, in his dorm room, with his mates all around him.

He closed and locked the door as she turned around to face him. She threw her purse and raincoat onto the bed and said, "How are you?"

He loved the way she spoke. After twenty years in England, she still had her French accent, and pronounced each word with precision.

Boye stepped beyond her and lowered the volume on the CD player, then, instinctively, turned back to her and reached around her waist. This was the first time she had ever come to college, and he wondered who had seen her. He wondered if Tidiane's door had been open just three rooms down and if he had seen her pass on the way to Boye's room. He fantasized about the whole of college knowing that he was hitting on Ghislaine Gräss, in his room, at five o'clock in the afternoon, when most of them were studying.

He raised his broad hands to the lapels of her jacket, and slipped it off. The inner lining of the jacket's sleeves slid effortlessly over the arms of her silk blouse. The jacket dropped to the carpeted floor. He pulled her to him. He could feel the points of her breasts, swelling within her bra, pressing against his torso. With one hand, he reached down and pulled up her skirt and with the other he touched the back of her head. The newly cropped hair there felt unusual, and yet sensual all the same. He pulled her toward him, and their lips met. They fell to the bed. Boye thrust his thigh between her legs, with his still-exploring hand beneath him. She was wearing stockings and a garter belt, and silk underpants that his fingers slipped beneath with ease. As he felt the first contact with the flesh of her groin, she reached down and grasped his hand.

"George," she said.

"What?"

"The police came out to the cottage again today."

"So what?"

He dug deeper with his fingers, but she wrapped her own fingers around the tips of his, making it impossible for him to explore farther.

"They're asking all sorts of questions."

"So?"

"I want you to tell me what you know, George."

She squeezed, and her nails dug into the backs of his fingers.

"Don't," he said. "That hurts. You know you want it."

He changed strategies and brought his other hand through the overlap of her blouse, penetrating her bra. His breathing became louder, and he was beginning to get hard. Again, she blocked his advance.

"If you want me, George, you're going to have to tell me what happened at the party. I'm being harassed by the police, and I can't tell them with a clear conscious that I don't know anything. Either you did something, or you *know* something."

"I don't know anything, baby."

His groin rubbed more tightly against her body.

She pushed her hand between them and unzipped his fly. She grabbed him, and just as he thought he was on his way, her hand stopped, holding him solidly, but not stroking. She pulled her face away from his so that she could see his eyes.

"George, if you want to make love, tell me what you know."

Boye sat up on the bed and Ghislaine pulled her hand away. His eyes roamed around the room, defeated, while he debated what he had to lose if he told her. He was sure he hated her husband more than she did. You don't stay married to someone for twenty years without some affection for them, even if there was nothing left of the marriage. Boye, on the other hand, had never felt anything for Rainer Gräss.

"Okay," he finally said. "I did see something."

"What?"

She waited for him to speak again.

"Just after midnight, at the party, I saw Rainer out in Cloister Court with Amy Denster."

"And?"

"They were arguing. Quietly, but seriously. At one point Rainer raised his arm to hit her. Maria Lendtmayer, the big German girl, sort of came out of nowhere. I hadn't seen her before, but she rushed across the courtyard opposite from where I was standing and prevented him from doing it—hitting Amy, that is. She grabbed him like she was yanking a fish out of water. He didn't have a clue as to what was happening. It was dark, and he was drunk. She was crazy. She dragged him across the court and was just hitting him. She didn't stop."

Ghislaine's eyes hardened.

"And what happened then?" she said.

"He was hurt, gasping for breath, and cursing. Amy fled back to the hall and Maria went after her. I was in the shadows beneath the south loggia and they didn't see me. Rainer sat on the grass in the corner of the courtyard, moaning to himself, just rocking back and forth."

"But he didn't go back into the hall?" asked Ghislaine.

"A moment later Gaines Simpson came across the courtyard."

"He's the American boy?"

"Yes. He has a room in college and he told the police that he was going there to change shirts. But what he didn't tell them was that he stopped, and that he too had words with Rainer."

"What happened?"

"I don't know. Rainer tried to get Simpson to help him, he kept grabbing up at him. I could hear them arguing too, but I then thought I heard footsteps walking toward me, under the loggia. So I retreated into Pump Court, which is farther to the south. I climbed the stairs near the Old Kitchen, figuring that I didn't want to get messed up with what was happening."

"Who was it you thought you heard under the loggia?"

"I'm not sure. It was someone who walked with a long stride. I saw their silhouette, but it was from a distance. It could have been Beggs, or Frontis, or even Maria returning. She was livid."

"How long were you on the kitchen steps?"

"Um . . . about five minutes."

"Did you see or hear anything else?"

caught the coxswain, the cause of the near collision, slouched down within the shell's paper-thin mahogany hull, now silent, gripped no doubt by fear that Simpson would lodge a complaint with the university boat club about the Pembroke boat. He could see that the coxswain was a young woman, dark of complexion, Indian or Pakistani. She looked him out of the corner of her eye, and as she glided past she could see that his eyes were staring her down. She offered yet another apology.

"Sorry . . . frightfully, sorry."

He waited until the Pembroke shell was clear and free in the water and the eyes of the coxswain had returned upriver.

"Fucking Punjabi bitch," he muttered.

He watched for a reaction. Her tiny head turned back toward him for a brief second—perhaps it turned fifteen degrees—before freezing. But it never made the complete turn.

"Pick it up!" yelled the coxswain, eager no doubt to get her boat well away from the American with the acerbic tongue, and now thinking of lodging her own complaint. Simpson watched as the boat pulled away and disappeared beyond the bend.

He then slowly rolled forward on his slide and squared his blades in the water. He extended his arms and brought his knees up into his chest. His strong hands wrapped the oar handles tightly. His blue eyes stared off to the riverbank, to the flat, grassy fen dotted with cows, lazily grazing in disregard of the cold and the constant rurr of traffic just beyond the pasture.

He began his catch. His powerful legs drove the slide backwards, and his forearms brought the oar handles to his chest. Soon he was back into his rhythm and glad to be rowing on his own.

Five minutes later, Simpson's shell passed under Elizabeth Way Bridge, his workout over. He guided it slowly through the area of university boathouses, taking intermittent strokes and steering through a flotilla of shells. He approached the Queens' boathouse and feathered the shell up alongside the concrete apron, and as he glided in he began to remove his stocking feet from the sneakers attached to the stretcher boards.

"Gaines."

Simpson looked up to see Amy Denster standing at the boathouse

Boye rubbed his hands across his thighs as if he were wiping away imaginary crumbs.

"George?"

He looked back at her with the most serious look she had ever seen on his jovial, boyish, face.

"I heard . . ."

He paused, and clumsily bit his lip.

"I heard a thud, and then another, like him . . . well . . . maybe like him falling to the ground. And then I heard a wail . . . a short, high-pitched wail, Rainer's voice crying for help, followed by silence."

Ghislaine reached out and touched Boye's hand.

"And then?"

"And then nothing. I was scared, because I knew something dreadful had happened. I didn't move. My only thought was that we'd killed him."

"*We?*"

"Did I say that? I meant them."

"Who's them?"

Boye was rubbing his hand across his face, his eyes closed.

"I don't know. Simpson. Or the person who came down the loggia. Beggs, or Maria. Frontis. Or maybe a couple of them together. I was confused. I know that I should have gone to help, but I was afraid. If someone had really killed him, then they might kill me, too. It happened quickly, but people do live around those courtyards. I kept thinking someone would appear."

Ghislaine pushed her hand through an opening in his shirt.

"George," she said softly, "you have to tell the police."

He stared at her blankly.

She stood up.

"Where are you going?"

"I don't know."

"But what about . . . ?"

"I can't make love now, George. You must understand that. If you'd like to come out to the house later, please do. If not, I'll ring you up in a day or so. I just need a little time to be alone. And you have to talk to the police."

He rose, and walked her to the door. As she stood in the hall, she leaned in and kissed him on the cheek.

"One more question," she said.

His head tilted slightly, a gesture that he was ready to answer.

"You are telling the truth," she said, "about what happened?"

He nodded and she walked away.

Ramsgill returned to Darwin, changed into dry clothes and then checked for messages in his pigeonhole. Elena had not called, but there was a message from Cheverton Beggs from earlier, stating that Beggs would be unable to show Ramsgill his ruins because Beggs had to take his mother to the doctor in Peterborough. Ramsgill had completely forgotten about their appointment and, as he had been at the Trinity construction site, he wouldn't have been able to make it anyway. He then telephoned Fiona Mallow at home and told her about their finding Rainer's body. Fiona took it calmly, as he suspected, and she offered to go out to Coton to tell Ghislaine. Ramsgill was appreciative, as he didn't feel up to the task. He could still picture Rainer's rigid corpse sliding out of its concrete mold, and he was sure it was an image that he wouldn't soon forget.

He had dinner in the college dining hall, and then phoned Elena at work. Marilyn Foster told him that she was away from the gallery, and took his message to return the call. As usual, Elena's boss was arrogant and terse, assuring Ramsgill that Elena would get the message but that she wouldn't be returning the call from the gallery. Expect it after five o'clock our time, Foster had said, when Elena will be off the clock.

Ramsgill hung up, wondering how Elena could subject herself to Foster's torture but satisfied, at least, that she would get the message.

By seven-thirty he was back in his room. He thought about going down to the Darwin Library to work on his book, but he couldn't get Rainer's death out of his mind, nor the odd note they had found in Hill's car. He propped himself up in the desk chair next to the window and rifled through *The International Herald Tribune* for anything of interest. After confirming that the Philadelphia 76ers six-game losing streak was still intact, his eyes caught Cheverton Beggs's manuscript on the desk. He folded the newspaper and tossed it to the floor. He had told Lyndsay Hill that he would have a look at the manuscript, as there was still the issue of Beggs and Rainer having argued about it.

He removed the clip that held it together and separated the pages. He flipped to the table of contents and saw that the book was divided into five chapters: "Melancholic Pleasures," "Reading the Ruins," "The Hand of Man," "Future Ruins," and "The Cusp of Modernism." Knowing the kind of books that Beggs had written in the past, *Ruin and Fragment in the Enlightenment* would ultimately be filled with many pictures (and quite nice ones at that), and it would be a large-format book, perfect for the coffee table. It would sell for a good £40, the pictures would be printed in four-color offset on heavy stock, and at least until it found its way to the clearance table at Dillon's, it would be a respectable seller. It would get full complimentary treatment from *The Times Literary Supplement*, but no serious student of the Enlightenment would expect to be truly edified by what was contained within its pages. Most of it would be rehashed from other sources, stitched together by Beggs into a neat little patchwork quilt, with too-easy theoretical leaps and one-off deductions, but under the guise of pseudo-intellectualism. Serious historians would write letters to the historical journals about Beggs's dilettante approach to the subject matter, but no one, other than a handful of academics, would read them. In another two years Beggs's publisher would welcome his next work.

Ramsgill turned to the first page of the first chapter, "Melancholic Pleasures," and read:

> In the eighteenth century, that century of great discovery and unparalleled social tumult, fascination with ruins held a certain exalted status in the pantheon of European artistic culture, unmatched by any other phenomenon. Ruins were sketched by artists on their Grand Tours, eulogized by poets, debated by politicians, studied by archeologists, denounced in some instances by clerics, built by country gentlemen, and admired by architects. The power of their stimulation is one of the most unique phenomena of the century, crossing the boundaries between aesthetics, science, religion, politics and literature.

That century of *great* discovery . . . *unparalleled* tumult, thought Ramsgill. *Exalted* status . . . *pantheon* of European artistic culture? *Most* unique? Histrionics, right from the get-go. Well, somebody had to popularize history, to dramatize it, and better Beggs than him. At least the general public would read Beggs's books, which is more than Ramsgill could say about his own work. It still bothered him, though. It was so forceful, so bang-you-over-the-head black or white. Boil something as complex and mysterious as an entire century down to its constituent parts, then serve it up on a platter of rhetoric and hyperbole. Did Beggs really believe it was this simple?

He read on. The first chapter, "Melancholic Pleasures," told him how the whole phenomenon of ruins had begun in the first place, growing out of a fascination in the eighteenth century with picturesque theory and the sublime, as well as the grand tours western Europeans took to Italy and Greece. The next chapter, "Reading the Ruins," dealt mostly with contemporary accounts of how ruins "spoke" (Beggs's term) to eighteenth-century man, primarily accounts of perambulating Britishers like William Gilpin and the writer Thomas Whately. The third chapter, "The Hand of Man," discussed the incorporation of ruins into the building designs of noted architects like Sir William Chambers and Robert Adam, along with the relationship of those two Englishmen to the Roman architect and *vedutist*, Giambattista Piranesi. "Future Ruins" dealt with the Temple of Philosophy at Ermenonville, France, built by the Frenchman René Girardin, an ironic shift in the ruin phenomenon. Girardin had it built for himself on his estate, but rather than building a sham ruin, i.e. a picturesque garden folly that evoked the feelings of decay espoused by Edmund Burke, the Temple of Philosophy was a building purposefully not completed. Ramsgill had always been fascinated by the temple, but Beggs's account of its design and construction was nothing he hadn't read elsewhere before. Finally, Ramsgill arrived at the last chapter, "The Cusp of Modernism."

The final chapter was thirty-five pages long, and Ramsgill read it straight through, captivated by its content. In essence, it involved the comparison of two eighteenth-century texts about ruins, the Englishman Robert Wood's *The Ruins of Palmyra*, and the Frenchman Constantin François Volney's *The Ruins: or Survey of the Revolution of Empires*. Beggs had used the two texts as metaphors for an inherent struggle that was at the heart of modern aesthetic culture— namely the use of fragmentation in either a positive or negative way. Wood's book revered the ruins, and he tried to use them in a way that emphasized the positive threads between the architecture of his own day and classical Greco-Roman architecture. Volney's book, on the other hand, took an almost existential attitude, seeing the negative notion of fragmentation as no more than an aesthetic device that could be appropriated for the architect's or artist's own use, a kind of "art for art's sake." It was a rare and sobering view, and quite modern considering that it was written in the eighteenth century. And Beggs, much to Ramsgill's surprise, had understood the importance of the appropriation. His treatment of it was a well-thought-out piece of writing.

Ramsgill put down the manuscript, thinking that finally Beggs had expounded an interesting, lucid, and extremely perceptive argument. The analysis of Wood's and Volney's books in "The Cusp of Modernity" was better than all of the other chapters in the book combined. In fact, in Ramsgill's mind it was better than Beggs's earlier three books and numerous articles combined. Ramsgill wondered why Beggs hadn't devoted more of the manuscript to the subject matter, as Ramsgill himself could see a whole book being written around the premises developed in the last chapter.

Gräss must have liked the last chapter too, as it was completely devoid of his editorial corrections. Whereas the other chapters were filled with Gräss's marks—including syntax and spelling corrections, notes about Beggs's assumptions, citations in the margins of other sources Beggs should look at—the final chapter had absolutely none. The corrections to the earlier chapters were made in cursive script, in what looked to be pen. Since his was a photocopy of the original, though, Ramsgill wasn't quite sure if the writing were indeed pen, nor what color ink had been used, but he was sure that it was Rainer's handwriting.

Stimulated by his reading of "The Cusp of Modernity" and glad that he had persevered through the other, more mundane chapters to get to it, Ramsgill returned to the fundamental question that had gotten him to read the manuscript in the first place. What was in the manuscript that Beggs and Gräss could have argued about? And, though not necessarily related to that question, why had Rainer not edited that last chapter? He thumbed through the text again. This time he wondered whether Rainer simply hadn't gotten to the chapter. Perhaps he ended proofreading at "The Temple of Philosophy."

Perhaps he was still working on it when he disappeared.

Ramsgill flipped back to the cover page. In the upper right-hand corner, written in the same cursive script as the editorial comments, was the short note: *Reviewed and Complete, 16 Jan. RGG.*

Rainer *had* finished the manuscript. Ramsgill turned to the table of contents and scanned the chapters. Each chapter was checked off, with a date that Ramsgill assumed was the date Rainer had proofread it. Next to the final chapter, "The Cusp of Modernity," were Gräss's initials, along with a date of January 14.

Just then a knock came at Ramsgill's door. He rose from the bed and looked at his watch. It was almost 11:20 P.M. He realized he had been reading for nearly four hours.

He opened the door and a lanky graduate student, who didn't introduce himself, said, "Are you Ramsgill?"

He nodded.

"Then there's a phone call for you downstairs. At the pay box, other end of the hall."

Ramsgill thanked the fellow and followed him down the hall, which twisted twice before leading to a stair. At the bottom of the stair he found the receiver to the pay phone dangling from its steel cord.

"Hello."

"Jamie, is that you?" It was Elena.

Ramsgill tried to gauge whether she was still upset with him. She sounded congenial, which gave him a modicum of hope.

"It's me," he said. "And I want to apologize about yesterday."

"Why?" she said. "I was going to apologize to you."

"Not when you hear what I have to say. About Fiona and me."

She went silent. He closed his eyes, wanting to tell her everything, realizing that he had to tell her everything.

"Elena, I *did* lie to you. Or at least I didn't tell the truth."

He could hear her soft breathing, and he could picture her, sitting with her legs curled up beneath her, on the stool next to the phone in their small kitchen.

"Fiona and I lived together for a time. When we were in graduate school. She left Cambridge two months before I finished my thesis, because her mother had died. She didn't come back, and we never saw each other after that. I returned to the States and she got married. She has three children. And is divorced now."

He exhaled, realizing that he had gotten out most of what he had to tell her—at least the easy admissions.

"I see," said Elena.

"And I'm very sorry I didn't tell you. When I decided to come over here to do my research, her being here had nothing to do with it. If anything, it made me *not* want to come. Because I knew that I was too afraid to tell you the truth, but worse than that, afraid that you'd think I still had an interest in her."

"Do you?"

"No. I have an interest in only one person, and I'm speaking to her. Before I met you, I used to wonder what would have happened had Fiona and I stayed together and when she got divorced, I even thought of contacting her. But I swear, I swear to God, I think of nothing but you every night. And when I get back, I'm going to change."

He could still hear her breathing, but now he also thought he heard sniffles. He wondered if she were crying.

"Elena?"

"What?"

"There's something else. Something I just found out. And even if you could see a way to believe everything I've told you so far, I'm afraid to tell you this. Very afraid. Because of what you might think or do. But I can't keep it from you either. It's not fair, and it would kill me."

She didn't say anything.

"Fiona's oldest daughter, Margaret, is my child."

The line went silent, now not even the hint of Elena's breathing.

"Not that it matters, but I didn't know that until yesterday," he continued. "And it changes absolutely nothing of what I've said so far. I told Fiona that I don't want Margaret to know the truth, nor do I want to be a part of her life. She's a nice girl, but she has a father, even if he doesn't live with her. And I want my own children, with the person I love."

"What are you saying, Jamie?"

"Just that I've thought things over. And I want to have the baby. Pretty soon we'll be too old to enjoy it. I don't want to be a dottering old man when the kid goes off to college. Seeing Margaret as an eighteen-year-old makes me realize just how fast the time goes. I want to have time to enjoy children, and grandchildren. And I also want to rethink my priorities, number one of which is you."

"Jamie, I don't know what to say, except to wonder if you've gone mad."

"Probably," he said. "But, Elena, I'm not offering the baby as a way to placate you for not telling you about Fiona. I really do want it. I mean that. And you deserve to be mad about Fiona, and especially Margaret."

Ramgill stared down the empty hall. At the end, a small window looked out to the black night.

"Jamie, you should have told me about Fiona. I might have been upset, but I would have understood. If we can't trust each other when we're apart, then what's the point of having a relationship anyway?"

"But what about Margaret?" he said. "She's not just a little indiscretion. She's the legacy of Fiona's and my relationship."

"How can I be angry about that?" said Elena. "There are things I've done in my life that you don't know about. Our relationship has nothing to do with what happened twenty years ago. It's about now, and about sharing a life together. Besides, Margaret is a living person. Could either of us, or Fiona, actually believe that it would be better if she had never been born?"

Ramsgill's own eyes began to swell with tears. He wiped them away.

"So do you believe me?"

"Jamie, why on earth would you make up a story like this? Of course I believe you."

"I love you," he said.

"And I you," she said.

"When can we start?" he said.

"Start what?"

"Making a baby."

"We can start as soon as you get your *natiche* home. It's rather difficult to do by telephone."

Ramsgill smiled, thinking of how fortunate he was.

"Now, what is happening over there?" she said. "What about your friend?"

"That's not good news, I'm afraid. We found his body today."

"Oh, Jamie, I am sorry. But you say 'we.' What did you have to do with it?"

Ramsgill recounted the story of finding the body, leaving out the more lurid details.

"Are the police getting anywhere?"

"Somewhat. They're tracking down leads and they have a witness now. A porter from one the colleges has come forward. He saw Rainer in the punt with the murderer. They're going to get a police lineup together."

"What is a porter, Jamie? I don't know that term."

"A doorkeeper . . . concierge. In Italian you'd call it a *portinàio*."

"Oh, yes. Who is going to be in this lineup?"

"The people who were at the party. Though I don't know exactly how they'll do it. Usually, you put one suspect in with a bunch of people who are completely unrelated to the case. Here, you've got six suspects."

"Do you believe that one of them is capable of murder? Could it not have been a random killing?"

"No, because of the fact that the college was secured, and that most of the people there had a motive to kill him. And as for whether one of them is capable, listen to this. The murderer telephoned the Architecture Department the morning after the murder, acting as if he were the police. He said that Rainer's wallet had been found in the river, which was simply a way of challenging the police to look downriver. He could have concealed the whole thing, but instead he taunted them. I guess he thought that the police would never find the body."

"You say he, Jamie. Why not she?"

Ramsgill thought for a moment. Both he and Hill had assumed that the phone call to Fiona was from a man. But come to think of it, Fiona had never said whether it was a male or a female voice.

"I don't know," he admitted. "Maybe you're right. But let me tell you something else that happened. When we were at the construction site, down in the excavation, the murderer left another message. Try this on for a clue: 'Paris, why, oh why, do I love Paris?' "

Across the faint intercontinental phone connection Ramsgill thought he heard humming, which slowly got louder. He seemed to recognize the tune.

"You are correct, sir."

"Okay," he said. "But what's the song?"

" 'I Love Paris,' " she said. "From the musical, *Can-Can.*"

"How the hell do you know that?"

"I know more things than you realize, Professor Ramsgill. You had better hold on to me, before you lose a good thing."

"Yes, honey."

"Don't call me honey, Jamie. It might be a term of endearment in English, but it reminds me of bees. You know I don't like bees."

"Okay," he said. "But what the hell does that have to do with Rainer's murder?"

"Why does it have to have something to do with Rainer's murder?"

"Because the murderer left the note on Hill's steering wheel, when we weren't fifty yards away. He started the note by asking, 'Did you find him?' meaning did we find Rainer."

"What was it you called the *portinàio?*"

"A porter."

"And what did you say about a porter?"

"I said that a Smithson College porter saw Rainer in the punt the night of his murder."

"And they have not had the lineup yet?"

"No."

There was a long pause on the line.

"Do you know who wrote 'I love Paris,' Jamie?"

"Rodgers and Hammerstein? Lerner and Loewe? Music's not my forte, Elena."

"No. Cole Porter."

"So?"

"*Capire?* Get it, Jamie? *Cold* Porter."

"My God, Elena, I've got to go."

Twelve

*D*ennis Fortthompson turned the corner and, with a large ring of keys in his right hand, descended the steps to the basement, the last corridor of the college to be checked before he knocked off for the night. In another five minutes he would be in the college bar for his usual quota of three Gold Stars. For most of his life he had assumed that alcohol somehow impaired him, but now it seemed that the barley wine had the effect of righting him, like the weighted keel of a sailboat. At least until tomorrow, when he would have to start anew, the wine would set his mind to the correct frequency, and it would become the filter between him and his wife's tirades.

Of course Lillian would be waiting up for him again when he got home. She had been up for the past two nights, ever since he had gone to the police with his information about the missing professor. She would sit alone at the kitchen table, sipping tea and eating biscuits. She refused to sit at the front bay window, the one with the view down to Mill Road, the direction from which he would come home. She couldn't bear the wait. Despite his flaws, Dennis was a good man, and she knew that he kept the exact same routine every night. If he didn't show by 12:50 A.M., then he wouldn't be coming.

"We got no cause being mixed up in university affairs," she had said just that afternoon. "You think if one of them professors saw you in trouble, that they'd help you out? No, I dare say not. Their sort don't lift a finger. It doesn't pay to poke your head into other people's business."

Dennis wouldn't hear of it. He was doing his duty, as any good citizen of the Crown ought to do. But he had to admit that he didn't feel any safer as such. He was glad that Detective Chief Inspector Hill had called the college that very evening to say that the ID parade was still on, now rescheduled for ten o'clock the next morning. Once he participated in the parade, either the killer would be locked up (if Dennis could identify him) or, if Dennis wasn't able to identify anyone, then he would be off the hook. Either way, by midday tomorrow, it would be over.

Dennis opened the fire door that led out of the stair. It closed by itself with a loud clang, resounding down the dark basement corridor. He reached to his right and found the light switch on the wall, which brought the two overhead fluorescents slowly to life. Some nights he stood at the stair door for a full thirty seconds before finding the switch. Tonight he was lucky, and again he thought of the simple pleasure of going to the Smithson bar. The bar would be busy tonight—it was a Thursday—and most of the students wouldn't even know that Dennis was there. He would stand at the far end of the room with his friend Andrew, the college's clerk of the works. While he downed his Gold Stars and Andrew nursed his gin, they would talk about the government, football, the decline in quality of Smithson's food, how their kids were getting on. Just before last bell Dennis would order his final Gold Star, his £1.20p already stacked neatly beside his glass, and then, without the pressure to beat final call, he would savor the last one before going to the bike shed to begin his trip home. It was a simple ritual, but then life's like that, thought Dennis, no more than a collection of simple rituals, strung together to make a day.

Dennis checked the first two doors on the left, the dry-goods storage and the wine room, and both doors were locked. Farther down the corridor, he checked the door to the electrical room, which was open, as it always was, and the insistent hum of the transformer greeted him at the door. Next it was the boiler room, around the corner and down a second corridor, a short dead-end hallway that led only to that one room.

As he turned the corner and made his way to the doorway, he could see that it too, like the door to the electrical room, was open, as it always was. But something was different. It wasn't the faint smell of oil that invariably met him as he entered the room, nor the low hissing of the boilers themselves. It was the sound of music, almost imperceptible, coming from the rear of the room. He stood in the doorway and listened. It was a recording, he was sure of that, and he could only hear the bass portion of the song. But it was vaguely familiar to him, and in the darkness he looked around him, trying to sense its source. He reached for the light switch and flipped it on, waiting for the lamps to fire up.

But nothing happened.

He could hear the music better now, not that it was actually louder, but his ears had locked onto the sound, in the same way that his eyes were adapting to the darkness. He was aware of the sound of his own breathing, and the jingle of the keys in his hand. He was also aware of the sound of his bum leg sliding across the concrete floor. Just then, his ears picked up the first of the song's lyrics. Something about blue or gray skies. He stepped forward. There were four boilers in the room, two each flanking an aisle, that much he remembered. The air was warm, and dead still. The boilers were set up on high curbs, and he was careful as he walked because he didn't want to trip up on one of them.

He could tell by the sound that he was now beyond the boilers, at the wall where the aisle turned left and led to the back left corner of the room, where the air-handling equipment was. The hiss of the boilers gave way to the low rumble of the air-handlers, and the smell of oil gave way to a dry, dusty scent.

"More and more I re-al-ize," continued the song, and Dennis too continued, now seeing a small red light on what must be the floor at the end of the room, perhaps twenty feet away. The voice on the recording had a hollow ring to it and, as he groped along in the darkness, his arms before him lest he run into one of the pieces of equipment, he remembered the period of the song, if not its title. He was sure that it was from 1953 or '54, a show tune, one of the American musicals. Nineteen fifty-four was the year he and Lillian had first courted, and they used to drive from Cambridge to Clacton-on-Sea at the weekend in his father's old Morris Minor to dance at the seafront pavilion.

"I love Par-is in the spring-time," came the refrain, and he now remembered the song well.

He kept limping forward, the tiny red light in the distance growing like an approaching traffic signal on a dark, empty road.

"I love Par-is in the fall. . . ."

He arrived at the light, and knelt. It hurt to kneel, but again, the sooner he got out of the boiler room, the sooner he would be in the bar. His hand reached out and felt what must have been a portable cassette player. Which of the students had put it here, he wondered, to make old Fortthompson grovel around in the dark? Were they in the room with him now?

He was about to turn the power off when his head snapped back as if he were standing behind a jet turbine when the engine ignited, the force of the blast jerking his neck into contortion, making him bite his tongue.

"I love Par-is ev'ry moment. . . ."

The ring of keys shot across the floor. Suddenly a smoldering suffocation came over him, and his face was enveloped by a tight material, plastic perhaps, grinding his eyeglasses into his nose.

"I love Paris, why, oh why, do I love Paris?"

Tighter now, he couldn't breath, not even a single breath. The material wrapped his face and neck, someone behind him pulling, pulling with the tightening force of a boa constrictor; he thought his face was going to crush . . . Lillian, what? . . . I know—

"Because my love is near."

No air, just a deep canyon. Floating down into it . . . I'm not . . . no, Lillian, I can't. . . . I can't turn around and stop it, because my neck will snap off . . . blood now coming from the bridge of the nose, stop pulling, you bastard! Was it him? . . . Stop! Stop! Dancing . . . it was Cole Porter, I told you, Lillian.

"Because my love . . ."

Lillian?

"Because my love . . ."

Lillian? It was Cole Porter.
"Because my love . . ."
Lillian?
". . . is near."

Thirteen

The hollow echo of dripping came from some distance away, but because of the darkness, Amy Denster couldn't sense its source. Was it in her mind? She didn't know how long she had been here, but the water, if it was water, only tormented her. She was hungry, and still frightfully cold. But mostly she was thirsty, her tongue swollen, her lips caked with dried saliva.

She thought again of Maria, whose idea it had been to go to London. She now realized why Maria was bent on her having the abortion. It was because of Maria's dislike of Rainer, or perhaps her jealousy of him. She wouldn't want Amy to have Rainer's baby, because Maria, despite what she had told Amy after their one and only encounter, still cared for her in a sexual way.

Amy recalled the night. Soon after her breakup with Gaines Simpson, Maria had invited her for dinner. Her friend Janice was away, and they had gone through several bottles of wine, ending the evening together in front of the fire, putting down Gaines, who in Maria's opinion was no different from any other man. All Gaines ever wanted to do was to get off between your legs, Maria had told Amy, with no compass to direct him with regard to your feelings, sexual or otherwise. Maria had told Amy that she had been with many men growing up, but that she had never had a true orgasm until she made love to a woman. Amy had found herself intrigued by what Maria had told her, partially because it confirmed some of what she had felt about Gaines,

but also because she and Maria had grown close during the year. As she lay there, her inhibitions loosened by drink, she began to wonder how much of what Maria had said about making love to another woman was true.

And then Maria pulled her into a platonic embrace, and they lay there as the fire died, finally falling asleep. A stimulation between her legs awakened Amy, and she felt Maria's hand on her groin, and her own hands feeling up Maria's breasts. One gentle touch led to another, and before she knew it they were making love, and it was, as Maria had said, different from anything she had ever felt.

But the next morning, with a clear head, it didn't feel right. She left Maria's more confused than ever, unsure of what would happen to their friendship but knowing that being with Maria in that way was not what she wanted. And then three weeks later, Rainer Gräss came on to her, in his office, like a bolt out of the blue. She had always thought of him as attractive, and she admired him as a scholar. But this was a shock, and she wondered later if requiting his interest in her wasn't simply a convenient way to avoid Maria.

She also wondered now whether Maria had been the one to find them in the courtyard that night, when Rainer and she had been arguing. The one who jerked him away. The one who had taken his hand from her wrists as it clamped down hard on her bones.

Amy began to cry. She didn't know what she had done to deserve to be here. And worse, she didn't think she was going to get out.

Lyndsay Hill had just turned the Austin into his driveway in Chesterton when he got the call.

He was returning from Rainer Gräss's postmortem at Addenbrookes Hospital, hoping to get a decent night's sleep, at least what was left of the night, as it was quarter to one in the morning. The fifteen-minute drive from the hospital had given him a few moments of solace, sufficient time to mull over what he had learned about Gräss's murder.

The forensics team at the construction site had found hairs on the body, eight or ten longish brunette ones, which he had assumed were Amy Denster's. They also found three long, blond hairs of unknown origin and medium length, which along with the brunette hairs had been collected into separate evidence bags. Hill remembered thinking as the blond hairs were being bagged that Gräss's wife had such hair, as did Maria Lendtmayer, and for that matter, Gaines Simpson. Gräss's own hair had been combed by the crime-scene investigators, and his body had been vacuumed. But nothing that had been removed from the evidence-vacuum filters stood out as special. If anything was to come from the vacuuming, it wouldn't show up until they got the laboratory results, when the matter would be scrutinized under a microscope.

As far as fingerprints went, it was doubtful, he was told by John Wingate, the senior biologist, that any latents would be found, even if the perpetrator had been ungloved. The fine dusting left by the concrete had undoubtedly absorbed any sebaceous or eccrine secretions, and even if it hadn't, trying to lift prints via plates would have been futile with the body having been coated with the dust. It was also probable that the chemical reaction of the concrete, as well as the cold, had absorbed any sweat-gland secretions.

The only other item of interest was that Gräss's fingernails had been scraped by the crime team and, at least from the biologist's visual inspection, there was a good possibility that tissue and blood had been found. As to whose tissue and whose blood, no one could say. When pressed, Wingate was evasive, as, after all, he would want the full benefit of lab analysis before reaching any conclusions.

By the time Hill turned onto Grange Road, he could see the orange strobes of the pandas and the red of the mortuary van, electrifying what would normally be a quiet night in Smithson College's neighborhood. He pulled the car up to the college entrance and hopped out, signaling to one of the uniform constables at the curb that he was leaving his keys in the car, should the constable have to move it. He quickly made his way through a glass vestibule and into the college lobby. At least a dozen students stood around the periphery of the lobby, most of them in night dress and all of them bleary-eyed, hoping, Hill assumed, for one brief glimpse of the corpse as it was wheeled out of college.

Chris Detler was talking with one of the students, notepad in hand. He looked up and saw Hill and pointed in the direction of the stair. Hill entered the stair and descended to the basement and walked briskly to the end of a dead-end corridor, where several white-shirted detectives, along with a few medical personnel, also in white, stood at a doorway. He squeezed himself into the mechanical room, where in the far left-hand corner John Wingate stood, and where behind him, sitting on raised concrete, was Jamie Ramsgill.

Sprawled out before them on the floor was the body of Dennis Fort-thompson. The smell of body fluids was strong, and Hill's first thought was that a boiler room was a particularly confining place in which to die.

He knelt beside the body. Lividity had set in, but it was not very advanced. Fortthompson was lying on his back, his left leg straight, his right leg bent at the knee. His hands, fingers spread, were gathered at his face. The face itself was marred by blood, which seemed to have originated at the bridge of his nose. The frames of his wire-rim eyeglasses were bent, and one of the lenses broken, the glass no doubt having caused the bleeding. The mouth was wide open and the tongue was pulled back into the throat, and it seemed to have bled too. The eyebrows were raised in horror. Around his neck he wore a gold chain, and a purple and yellow shadow of the chain was impressed into the neck.

Hill turned and looked up at Wingate.

"Has he been disturbed?"

"Not that I know of. Professor Ramsgill found him. He hasn't been moved since we got here, but I don't know what happened before that."

"Jamie?"

Ramsgill shook his head to signal that he hadn't touched the body.

"What do you make of it?" Hill asked Wingate. "Asphyxiation?"

"No. More like strangulation. Or a combination of both."

"Ligature?"

"Sort of. There are no pronounced marks of ligature, a cord, a belt, finger marks, whatever. But look and you'll see a bit of plastic lodged into the chain and there . . . at the hinge of the eyeglasses."

Wingate leaned over and pointed to the thin pieces of torn clear plastic, presumably left behind by whatever had asphyxiated Fort-thompson.

"Plastic sheeting?"

"I would say so. Perhaps bunched up. You can see that whatever it was left the impression of the chain on the neck. And there's a bit of bruising on the inside of his lips, as if something flat pressed very hard against them. There's also a spot of friction burn on the forehead."

"How did it happen?" asked Hill.

"From behind," said Wingate. "Imagine your face and neck being covered, the murderer behind you, pulling like bloody hell. You bring your hands up, as they are here, to try to remove whatever it is that is across your face. But the bunched-up part must have been down at the neck, causing strangulation. Asphyxiation alone would have taken too long. There would be more of a sign of struggle."

"Okay," said Hill. "Let's say it was plastic. Any idea what kind?"

"We'll do a lab test on the sample," said Wingate. "We should have no problem finding out exactly what it was."

"I was thinking of bubble wrap," said Ramsgill.

"Bubble wrap?" said Hill. "Why?"

"Because it's strong, but made up of thin layers. And, of course, George Boye has that habit of popping it."

Hill looked perplexed.

"You never noticed that?" said Ramsgill. "He does it all the time."

"So you think it was Boye?"

"That, or someone trying to frame Boye. That's assuming you actually find out it's bubble wrap."

"Jamie, how did you come to find the body? What were you doing here?"

"I was on the phone with Elena. She knew the reference of 'Why, oh why, do I love Paris.' It's a line from a Cole Porter tune. Get it, *Cold Porter?* Another tease from the murderer. The minute she said that I rushed over here."

"And?"

"And of course Fortthompson wasn't at the lodge. The college's clerk of the works was in the bar, and he told me that Fortthompson should just be finishing his nightly lockup."

"What time was that?"

"Eleven forty, or so."

"What did you do then?"

"I told him I thought Fortthompson might be in trouble, but he convinced me that if I'd just wait five more minutes, he would walk through the door. He comes in every night, he said. We waited, but of course he didn't come. I now wish I had just followed my instincts. Maybe I would have found him before this happened."

"And maybe you would have found the murderer, too," said Hill. "Or he you." He paused. "Then what?"

"The clerk, Hutchinson, I think his name is, said that he'd check the top two floors of the college if I'd check the ground floor and the basement."

"And you found him?"

Ramsgill nodded.

"What time was that?"

"I suppose it was just before midnight."

"Jamie, this is important. Did you see anyone or hear anything when you came down here? Did you notice anything unusual in the room?"

"When I first got here," Ramsgill said, "there were no lights on and the switch didn't work. Even with the corridor lights on, I could hardly see. I just sort of stumbled onto him. I went and got Hutchinson and we called the police. He brought a flashlight down, and we found several of the fluorescent bulbs over in the corner, behind one of the boilers. He wanted to put them back into the light fixtures, but I wouldn't let him because I figured that there might be fingerprints on them. We got some new bulbs from the storeroom. By the time we got them in, the first of the police cars had arrived."

"That was good. Have you dusted the bulbs for prints?" Hill looked to Wingate.

"We're doing that now."

"Is the doctor on the way?"

"Yes," said Wingate. "And he wasn't too thrilled to be called out again."

Hill pressed two fingers against his brow. "Like I was?"

Just then Chris Detler entered the boiler room.

"Gentlemen . . . boss," he said.

"What have you got, Chris?" asked Hill.

"Fortthompson was last seen in the Porters' Lodge at eleven-thirty. That's when he always leaves to make his final walk around."

"So he was killed between eleven-thirty and midnight?"

"No, sir. Sorry, I'm not being clear. He was last seen in the *lodge* at eleven-thirty. A student on the second floor saw him at eleven-thirty-five. And he was seen near the laundry, at the far north end of the first floor, at eleven-forty. He was working his way down."

Ramsgill considered the fact that Fortthompson had been alive at the same time he was in the bar.

"There's another fire stair at the north end," continued Detler. "He probably came down that, as no one saw him come down the lobby stair. The basement corridor goes in two directions."

"So then it was between eleven-forty and midnight?" said Hill.

"Seems so, sir."

"And Jamie, you started searching about the same time. How did you work it?"

"I went as far north as the laundry," said Ramsgill. "Past the library and the computer lab. I didn't know about the north stair, though, so I returned to the lobby before coming down here."

"By way of the lobby stair?"

"Yes."

"And you heard nothing?"

Ramsgill shook his head.

"So the killer must have escaped by the north stair. Where does it lead?"

"It exits into the hall near the laundry, adjacent to an outside door," said Detler. The door opens to a small walled yard on the ground floor with a bicycle shed. A gate opens to the street, locked from the outside, but operable from the inside."

Hill looked to Detler. "I want the yard secured. And the north stair. And I want a first-rate job done on those areas, John."

Wingate nodded.

"Chris, I want the suspects questioned immediately. Get them out of bed if you have to. See who has alibis."

"We're already doing it, sir."

"Good."

"Anything else you want me to do?" asked Detler. "If not, I'll continue questioning upstairs."

A balding man wearing a necktie, whom Ramsgill recognized from the Trinity site as a detective, entered the room.

"Guv . . . Dr. Wingate," he said.

"What's up, Hugh?"

"We've located the second student, the one who saw Fortthompson in the laundry at eleven forty."

"Good," said Hill. "I want to interview him straightaway."

"It's a her, sir. And Newsham has gone to fetch her. She doesn't live in college. It's the German girl. Lendtmayer."

Hill and Ramsgill exchanged glances.

"I don't get it," said Hill. "Didn't you talk to her, Chris?"

"No."

"Then how did you know she saw Fortthompson in the laundry?"

"Hutchinson, the clerk, told me. He didn't tell me who it was, though. He just said that when he and Jamie were searching for Fortthompson that a student told him she had seen Fortthompson in the laundry. She must have left the college after that."

"Interesting," said Hill. "Well, let's get out of here and let Wingate and Company do their job. The sooner we can get the body out, the sooner we can rid ourselves of the circus upstairs. If we're lucky, maybe we'll get an hour or two of sleep. Hugh, I'll be upstairs. Let me know when the pathologist arrives. And Chris, as soon as Lendtmayer gets here, I want to see her."

Ramsgill followed Hill out and they made their way to the ground floor. As they exited the stair to the lobby, they could see that the crowd had grown, both inside and out. There were more students standing around in front of the Porters' Lodge, and at least three reporters whom Hill recognized standing outside the glass vestibule. They were motioning silently from behind the glass for him to come over to them, the way a visitor goads an animal at the zoo.

"Sod them," Hill said. "Let's take a look at the courtyard."

The two men strode over to the rear window wall, then turned left and walked up a ramp that led to the library. They passed the library and continued down past a couple of meeting rooms on the right, and the computer lab and laundry on the left. At the end of the corridor they exited into the small courtyard. Two detectives were searching the courtyard with flashlights.

Hill walked out on a white gravel path that surrounded a small piece of lawn. His eyes swept around the dark courtyard, landing at the gate to the street.

"Do you think the murderer escaped this way?" said Ramsgill.

"Must have," said Hill. "Though if it was Lendtmayer, she could have walked right out through the front door."

Ramsgill followed Hill over to the bike shed. It was open on the courtyard side, with two short flanking walls of masonry connected into the back wall, which was part of the wall that separated the courtyard from the street. It had a simple wooden roof.

"So what are you thinking?" asked Ramsgill.

"I'm wondering what happened to the plastic," said Hill. "And thinking that I'm going to pay for what happened here."

"What do you mean?"

"I mean that Gräss's death couldn't have been anticipated, but this . . . this was just plain bloody stupid. I was a fool not to put a man on Fortthompson. To guard him."

"It wasn't your fault."

"Then whose was it?"

"Nobody's. How could you have known that we'd find Rainer's body today, or that Amy Denster wouldn't be available for the lineup? If neither of those two things had happened, we wouldn't be here right now."

"And how do you know that?"

"I just do. Plus, it wasn't your fault that someone let the paper get wind of Fortthompson's coming forward."

Ramsgill noticed that Hill's eyes were markedly red.

"You don't understand, do you, Jamie?"

"What?"

"I'm the end of the line as far as investigations go. I have almost ten detectives on this case now. If any one of them screws up, I'll ultimately be held responsible. A single technicality can get a killer off. Basically, in this, you win or you lose. Catch the killer, and you've won. People remember the details of the case, but they haven't a clue as to what went into catching him. Let him get away, though, and the entire country knows that you've made a mess of it. I simply can't believe we let that porter die. This is a bloody awful business."

"It'll work out," Ramsgill said.

Hill sighed. He began walking again. Ramsgill watched him make a half-circuit of the courtyard, until the two men stood opposite one another, across the small green. They stood in silence.

Just then the door to the courtyard opened and Chris Detler and another detective appeared, with Maria Lendtmayer between them. She was wearing jeans and a leather jacket and her long blond hair was pulled up in a bun.

"Ah, Ms. Lendtmayer," said Hill.

Hill crossed the courtyard. Ramsgill followed.

"I was told that you were here earlier," he said.

She nodded, her face as white and impassive as a blank sheet of paper.

"Could you tell me what you were doing?"

"I was washing clothes," she said.

"And what time did you leave?"

"About quarter till midnight," she said.

"Did you see Mr. Fortthompson, the porter, in the laundry?"

"Yes, just before I left. He asked if I would turn out the lights when I left. I was just folding the last of my clothes."

"Jamie?" Hill said. "You didn't see Maria in the laundry? You must have checked it about the time she left."

Ramsgill shook his head.

"Nor in the lobby?"

"No," said Ramsgill.

"I didn't leave by way of the lobby," said Maria. "My bicycle was in the yard. I went out by the gate."

"Newsham," said Hill, speaking to the detective who had brought Lendtmayer back to the college, "did you see fresh laundry at her house when you picked her up?"

"Yes sir," said Newsham, a ruddy-faced man with curly brown hair. "Ms. Lendtmayer was in the living room when I arrived."

"Was your housemate at home?" said Hill, now speaking to Maria.

"No," she said. "Janice is on a business trip to Dublin. But you can see, I was doing wash."

"You could have done it earlier," said Hill. "You say you were folding your clothes when Fortthompson came in, but unfortunately he can't corroborate that. Who else saw you?"

Maria shrugged. "Nobody," she said. "The laundry was empty."

"And did you cycle straight home from college?"

"Yes. I arrived about midnight."

"No one can corroborate that either."

"I guess not," she said.

Just then one of the officers searching the courtyard called out to the other one, and the two of them walked over to Hill's group. In his hand the officer held a sheet of bubble wrap the size of a small towel.

"Found this behind the woodpile, sir."

Hill turned to Maria.

"Did you put it there?"

"No. I don't know what you are talking about. What is it?"

"It's bubble wrap," said Hill. "Fortthompson was strangled with it. I was thinking downstairs that if someone wanted to frame George Boye, they would have left it with the body. But that would have been too simple. We would have realized that Boye wouldn't have left it behind. Much better to make Boye look like he had hidden it."

"I still don't know what you're talking about," she said.

Hill brought a hand up to his face and tried to wipe away his fatigue.

"Maria," he said. "Have you seen Amy Denster today?"

Ramsgill caught the slightest expression of surprise on Lendtmayer's face, as he was sure Hill did too.

"I . . . uh, no."

"Are you sure about that?"

"Quite sure. I already told Fiona Mallow that."

"Maria, did you know that Ms. Denster was pregnant? And that Gräss was the father?"

Maria half shrugged as she shook her head no.

"Ms. Denster and Dr. Gräss went to see a doctor on Monday," said Hill. "They talked about her having an abortion. Gräss wanted her to have it, but she wasn't sure. The doctor suggested she confide in someone. Was that someone you?"

Maria's face became expressionless. Her body went rigid.

"Maria, Amy is missing. Her parents don't know where she is. Her college doesn't know where she is. If you have any idea, I want to know. Right now. Or we can spend the rest of the night at headquarters."

Maria sighed, looking down to her feet, where the toe of her boot swirled gravel.

"Amy has a right to privacy," she said.

"All night, Maria," said Hill. "I've got all night."

He stared at her until she spoke.

"Okay," she said. "Amy went to London this morning."

"Why London?"

"To have the abortion. She wanted to do it away from Cambridge. And she wanted to do it at a private clinic."

"What's the name of the clinic?"

She hesitated.

"Women's Planning Services of East London," she finally said. "In Islington."

Ramsgill considered what he knew about Amy Denster. That she was a scholarship student, with little money.

"How did she get the money for a private abortion?" he asked.

"She told me someone owed it to her."

"When did she tell you that?"

"Last night."

"And she went down to London this morning?"

"Yes," Maria said reluctantly. "First thing. She was supposed to come by my place but didn't."

"She should be back by now," said Hill.

Maria nodded.

"She mentioned her brother," said Maria. "She said she might spend the night with him. I believe he lives in Crawley."

"Chris," said Hill. "Ring up the clinic and find out if she showed. And locate her brother. Hopefully, she's down there. If she is, and she's all right, I want her back up here first thing in the morning. I want to meet with all of the people who were at the party at ten tomorrow morning at the school library. That includes you, Ms. Lendtmayer. And don't think about trying to leave town. There will be a uniformed officer outside your house for the rest of the night."

Maria nodded.

"You can go now. Hugh, have one of the PC's take her home."

Maria followed the detective back inside, and the two other detectives followed.

"Will that be all for me?" said Detler.

Hill nodded. "Yes. And Chris, I want Fiona Mallow there in the morning too. As well as you, Jamie. You are now a witness, so I can't very well keep you away."

Ramsgill nodded. The three men then turned and began to walk back to the door.

When they were inside, and walking down the ramped hall that led to the lobby, Ramsgill said, "What do you think, Lyndsay, that it was Maria?"

Hill paused, and several steps ahead of him, Ramsgill and Detler stopped too. They turned to him.

"I don't know. But if it is her, then we've got eight hours to figure out the motive."

Fourteen

*T*he attendees of Rainer Gräss's re-
tirement party sat around the walnut table in the rare books room of
the Art and Architecture Library, just as they had two days before.
Only Amy Denster was absent from the group. Iain Frontis, George
Boye, Maria Lendtmayer, Gaines Simpson, and Cheverton Beggs
were again joined by Fiona Mallow and Jamie Ramsgill, who sat in
adjacent armchairs in one corner of the room. Lyndsay Hill and Chris
Detler stood at the end of the table closest to the windows, and everyone's gazes, including the bloodshot eyes of the policemen, were
trained on an object before them.

In the center of the table was a wrought-iron candlestick, decidedly
medieval in style, yet with a simplicity particular to a more modern
era. At its base were three splayed legs formed of sharp square-rod
stock, each an inch thick and curved outward, hand-beaten by a metal-
smith. The rods wound together to become the candlestick's shaft,
which was approximately eight inches tall, then they separated again
at the top, flaring outwards before curving together to hold a small
iron cup.

Jamie Ramsgill's sketchbook rested in his lap, open to the sketch
of Queens' Old Hall he had made two days ago on Wednesday afternoon. He thought that he had recognized the candlestick when Lyndsay Hill had placed it on the table, and the sketch, though loose and
vibrant, confirmed it. It was one of four identical candlesticks that

had stood atop the William Morris mantel, and which, now that he could see it up close, he recognized as a Morris design.

"Let's begin," said Hill, his face contorted by fatigue, his gaze brooding.

The eyes around the table rose to look at him, faces void of expression. The week's events had taken it out of everyone, thought Ramsgill. No longer did Boye look smug, Simpson concerned, or Frontis nonplussed. Each had now drawn into himself, waiting patiently for Hill to begin, wanting to know how the events surrounding Rainer Gräss's death might be extrapolated. The candlestick stood for something, surely, as Hill had carefully removed it from a plastic bag, setting it on the table without comment. They were now ready to hear what he had to say.

"I'm going to be blunt," said Hill, his eyes canvassing the group, his lips tight. "Amy Denster was supposed to have gone to London yesterday morning. She never arrived at her destination, nor at her brother's flat outside the city. We have put out a search for her in all surrounding counties, but haven't found her. I suspect that we're not going to find her. She has disappeared because of something she saw or knows about Dr. Gräss's death. Or should I say murder. Because Rainer Gräss was murdered in a most horrific fashion, as was an innocent witness, Dennis Fortthompson. There is nothing we can do about either of those events now. But I might possibly be able to do something about Amy."

He let his words hang in the silence, then said, "We're not going to leave this room until I'm satisfied I know who's responsible."

Still the faces around the table were without emotion. It was as if Hill were a teacher accusing one of them of stealing a pencil and, while the others knew who the guilty party was, they wouldn't tell.

"So let us begin by discussing alibis," said Hill. "As far as I am concerned, none of you has one for the time of Dr. Gräss's murder. We now know that he was subdued and taken across the Mathematical Bridge, then ferried downriver by punt to Trinity College, where he was lowered, still alive, mind you, into the concrete formwork of the new building there. In all, we estimate that at least twenty minutes were needed to complete this rather gruesome task. We also know that each of you was out of Old Hall with sufficient time to have done it.

But in addition to Dr. Gräss's murder itself, the murderer has tipped his hand four times. First, on Tuesday, the morning after the party. A fax was sent from Scroope Terrace to Rattner and Davids' construction site, authorizing the concrete pour which would seal Dr. Gräss's fate. Also on Tuesday, the murderer telephoned Fiona Mallow at the school, acting as a representative of the police. The caller stated that Dr. Gräss's wallet had been found in the river, a good kilometer north of Trinity College. In my opinion the initial purpose of the phone call was to divert attention away from Trinity, but in actuality it served another function. It was the murderer's way of locking horns with us, his way of telling us his secret—what he had assumed had been a flawless murder. This is not an uncommon practice with psychopaths."

Hill again let the words hang.

"But I said that the killer tipped his hand four times, didn't I? The third occasion was yesterday afternoon when the murderer left me a calling card. And finally, there was Fortthompson's murder itself, last night, between eleven forty and midnight, which I will get to in a moment."

Hill paused, moistening his lips.

"So why don't we discuss the fax. It was sent at nine fifty on Tuesday morning from the school. As I understand it, Ms. Mallow, you were out of the office at the time."

"I was," said Fiona, nodding. "I generally take a break in the mornings. I rarely have time for breakfast at home, so I pop over to Greenway's for a coffee and pastry."

"And when you do this," said Hill, "how long are you out of the office?"

"It depends on the queue at Greenway's. But usually five or ten minutes."

"So would you say that on Tuesday it was five or ten minutes?"

"Yes."

"Do you lock the office door when you go out?"

"Heavens no. People are in there all day. There are faculty and student pigeonholes, people wanting to make photocopies, et cetera. But I will say that on Tuesday no one was there when I left, nor when I got back."

"Right," said Hill. "So you were out from, say, nine forty-five until nine fifty-five." Hill gave Lendtmayer a dark look. "Why don't we begin with you, Maria. Where were you at that time?"

"I was running. I do ten K every Tuesday and Thursday morning."

"Is there anyone who can vouch for you?"

"Well, scores of people must have seen me. I usually run up Castle Hill and out of town by way of Huntingdon Road. The road is jammed with traffic. Though whether a commuter would recognize me, I don't know."

"How about your housemate? Where was she?"

"Janice commutes by train to London. She leaves at six, usually long before I'm awake."

"So other than someone you might have seen on Huntingdon Road, no one saw you. You didn't stop for a pastry. A newspaper?"

"No."

Hill's focus released Maria and he turned to George Boye, who was hunched forward in his chair.

"How about you, George? Where were you on Tuesday, at just before ten?"

Ramsgill noticed that Boye was not fingering his usual bubble wrap.

"I was asleep. I didn't get to bed until two. I was exhausted."

"Do you share a room, George?"

"No. It's a single."

"And you never stepped outside the room?"

Boye shook his head. He then said, "I know it would be better if I could say that I was in the dining hall, or at school, but the truth is, I was in bed."

Hill's bronze eyes turned to Simpson. Simpson leaned forward, his jaw moving slowly up and down, as if it were sore.

"And how about you, Gaines?"

"I didn't get to bed until two, either," he said, looking at Boye with disdain. "But I was on the river as usual. Sculling. I work out every day."

"Is there anyone who can attest to that?"

"Amy," he said. "She came down to the river to talk."

"Unfortunately, Amy isn't around to corroborate your story," said Hill. "Anyone else see you?"

"Like Maria's jogging, probably a lot of people saw me. But only for a moment, and generally from a distance."

"What did Amy come to the river to talk about?" said Hill.

"About her and Rainer. She told me she was pregnant, and that he was the father. She told me they had had a row."

For the first time, the faces around the table displayed emotion. Ramsgill watched carefully, noticing surprise on the faces of Boye and Frontis, but not on that of Beggs. Lendtmayer, of course, already knew about Amy's pregnancy.

"Yes," said Hill. "Amy was . . . is pregnant. And if anything happens to her, a court will surely take that into consideration."

He cleared his throat, then leaned over to Detler, who was taking notes. He looked down at Detler's pad.

"But let us continue. Where were you Tuesday morning, Professor Frontis?"

Ian Frontis rocked slowly, staring blankly at a bookcase. When he heard Hill's words, his head snapped back.

"I was on my way to school," he said, "for a ten o'clock lecture. I cycled up Fen Causeway."

"And did anyone see you?"

"Cars on the road, and my cat, of course. I kiss her good-bye in the morning. But other than that, no."

He attempted a smile, but Hill immediately turned his attention across the table.

"Which leaves you, Professor Beggs. Do you have an alibi?"

"Alibi?" said Beggs. "Such a romantic term, one you don't hear too often these days. Read Sayers and Marsh, do you, Inspector?"

Hill frowned, which seemed to lengthen his face.

"Just answer the question please, Professor."

"I was on my way to school, too," Beggs said. "In fact, Fiona, didn't I see you outside, when you returned from Greenway's?"

Fiona nodded. "Yes. You were locking up your bike."

"So there you have it," said Beggs. "And as I know that your next question deals with the phone call about Rainer's wallet, Inspector, you already know that I was in Fiona's office with her when the call came."

"Quite," said Hill. "That puts you in a rather propitious light, Dr. Beggs."

Hill turned back to Frontis. "I believe you were in the room with Ms. Mallow at the time of the phone call, too," he said.

Frontis looked befuddled, then seemed to nod.

"No," said Beggs. Frontis's head froze. "Iain wasn't there. He'd just left."

Hill looked to Fiona Mallow.

"I believe Cheverton's right," she said.

"When did that call come?" asked Frontis, now looking confused.

"Five minutes after ten," said Hill.

"Just after you left the office," said Beggs.

"Well, not long after," said Frontis.

"Where did you go after you left?" said Hill.

"Like I said, I had a lecture."

"In Scroope Terrace?"

"No. At the annex across the street."

"And did you stop on the way?"

"No."

"There is a call box right outside of Greenway's," said Beggs. "He could have phoned from there."

"If you don't mind, Professor Beggs, I'll conduct the interview."

"Sorry."

"Dr. Frontis?"

"I didn't make that call," said Frontis. "I swear it."

Hill folded his arms across his chest, thought for a moment, then squinted in the direction of George Boye.

"I was asleep, like I told you," said Boye, without even hearing the question.

"Do you have a phone in your room, George?"

"No."

"Phone on your hall?"

"Well . . . yes."

"So you could have made the call."

"I suppose."

"And how about you, Gaines?" said Hill. "Rowing still?"

"Sculling. Yes. And now that I think about it, Inspector, I do know of someone who could corroborate my story. There was a novice boat from Pembroke on the water that morning. An eight, with a small In-

198

dian or Asian girl as cox. They almost ran me down, and I let her have it. I doubt she'd forget me."

"Okay," said Hill. "We might check on that. How about you, Ms. Lendtmayer?"

"I was still jogging," she said. "Or perhaps home already, drawing a bath."

"I take it you have a phone."

"Yes."

Hill paused.

"It just occurred to me," he said, "regarding my earlier question, about the fax. Even if you were jogging, Maria, you could have just as easily jogged south from your house as north. To Scroope Terrace, no? To send that fax?"

Maria sat back and made a comb of her long fingers, brushing her hair back.

"It's possible," she said. "But I didn't."

Hill paused again, gathering his thoughts. Ramsgill was impressed with his technique, probing yet not harsh.

"Which brings us to yesterday afternoon," Hill finally said. "And to my note from the murderer. Let's start with you, George."

"You mean, where was I?"

"Yes."

"At what time?"

"Never mind what time," said Hill. "Let's just say I'm interested in the whole afternoon."

Ramsgill remembered that the note had been left in Hill's car sometime around 3:30 P.M. It was a smart move on Hill's part not to tell the suspects the hour.

"I was in class until three," said Boye in a low tone of voice. "Then I went to see a friend."

"Ghislaine Gräss?"

Boye bit his lip.

"No," he said.

"Does your friend have a name?"

Boye nodded.

"Yes," he said. "But look, Inspector, I have something I want to say. Something about Monday night."

Ramsgill noticed Gaines Simpson looking Boye's way, contempt furrowing his brow.

"We'll get to that in a moment," Hill said. "But first this. Does your friend have a name?"

"Valery Jacobs. She lives in Eltisley Avenue."

Detler wrote down the name.

"Dr. Frontis," Hill continued. "Where were you yesterday afternoon?"

Frontis grimaced. He was toying with an unlit cigarette.

"I don't remember. I know that I had a supervision just after lunch, but later in the day . . . can I think about it for a moment . . . ?"

Hill nodded.

"Then how about you, Dr. Beggs?"

"No problem," Beggs said, looking at Frontis with a smirk. "I had to take mother to the doctor's in Newmarket. We left Grantchester around noon, and didn't return until five."

"May I have the name of the doctor?"

"Sure. Whitmore. In the High Street. But we were there only briefly, for a one o'clock appointment. We spent most of the afternoon walking around the Heath, watching the horses exercise. Mother loves horses."

"So your mother would attest to this?"

"Hardly, Inspector. She's senile. She may remember having been there, or maybe not. And even if she did, she wouldn't be able to tell you what day it had been."

Hill nodded.

"Inspector?" said Iain Frontis. "I just remembered where I was. I was in the Fitzwilliam Museum. Looking at Dürer etchings."

"Who saw you?" said Hill.

"The prints curator got them out for me, but mostly I worked alone, in an upstairs study room."

"Did you leave the museum at any time?"

"I don't think so."

"But you could have, and not have been seen?"

"I suppose."

"Maria," said Hill, "where were you yesterday afternoon?"

"At the university library."

"The whole afternoon?"

"Yes. I went there after a one o'clock lecture. I was there until five. And yes, I could have left, but didn't."

"Interesting," said Hill.

Ramsgill considered what Hill had meant by the comment. Undoubtedly it was that the Trinity construction site was just across Queen's Road from the university library. Which gave Lendtmayer ample opportunity to have placed the note in Hill's car.

"And finally you, Mr. Simpson."

"I was in my room at college," he said. "Trying to study for a Latin exam, but mostly dozing off. Conjugations don't exactly move me."

Hill pondered Simpson's answer. He then looked down at his watch.

"Right," he said. "Well, I see that Dr. Frontis could use a cigarette and I could go for some coffee myself. Ms. Mallow, could I impose on you to run across the street? Perhaps everyone would like some. I would ask Sergeant Detler, but I would like him to place a few phone calls. I want to see if we can find that Pembroke cox, Chris, the one Mr. Simpson says saw him. And Mr. Boye's friend in Eltisley Avenue."

Detler nodded. Fiona Mallow rose and took orders, then she, Detler, and Iain Frontis left the room.

Hill took the chair at the head of the table. He sat silently for a few minutes, until Frontis returned. He then reached down for a briefcase below the table and opened it. He pulled out several blank sheets of paper and a handful of pencils. He gave one to each of the five.

"What's this?" said Iain Frontis, sitting just to the left of Hill.

"And what's the candlestick for?" said Beggs. "It's from the Old Hall, right?"

Hill didn't answer.

"I would like it if each of you could write your name at the top of the paper," he said. "In cursive."

He watched, while the group did as they were told.

"Now just below your name, again in cursive, write the name Guy Spencer."

Several heads looked up at Hill, perplexed by the request.

"Just write it, please," said Hill. "G-U-Y S-P-E-N-C-E-R."

Ramsgill suddenly remembered that Spencer was the name of the imaginary engineer from Culworth Engineering, on the forged fax.

The instruction on the fax had been typed, but Spencer's name had been signed. By the murderer.

"Now, if you'll pass them this way."

The group passed the papers to Hill, and he thumbed through them slowly before setting them aside. He made no comment, but jotted a few notes to himself on a small steno pad.

"Now, before we get on to Fortthompson's murder," he said, "I want to explore one more item. That of motive. Since we last spoke as a group, several things have come to light. Of course, it was obvious from the outset that Professor Frontis had a reason to kill Gräss, as he was to lose his position in the department. George, you had a motive also, as Dr. Gräss was bringing the plagiarism complaint against you. And that motive was strengthened by our subsequent discovery that you were in a relationship with Mrs. Gräss. Gaines, you too had a motive—your concern for Ms. Denster and your former relationship with her. Which leaves us with Professor Beggs and Ms. Lendtmayer."

"With Dr. Beggs," Hill continued, "there seemed to be two possibilities. One, that he wanted to take over the Ph.D. and M.Phil. programs, and two, that he had argued with Dr. Gräss about his new book."

"I do not want to take over the program," Beggs broke in. "I don't know who told you that. That's the second time I've heard it and it's rubbish."

"Don't worry," said Hill. "I've already discounted it anyway. It's a cipher because once Gräss announced that he wasn't stepping down, then Iain was sure to be let go. And Iain was your only competition for the job. There would have been no reason for you to kill Dr. Gräss."

Beggs folded his arms, sat back, and smiled.

"But that still leaves us with your book manuscript," said Hill.

"Lyndsay?" said Ramsgill. "I've read the manuscript. I didn't get a chance to tell you that last night."

"*You* read it?" said Beggs, his expression suddenly chafed. "For what reason?"

"To see if he could find what would have caused the argument between you two," said Hill.

"And?" said Beggs. "What did you find, dear Jamie?"

"It was more what I *didn't* find," said Ramsgill.

"What?" said Hill.

The door to the room opened and Fiona Mallow returned. She set a bag on the table and began to distribute hot drinks.

"The manuscript was divided into five chapters," Ramsgill said. "The first four, I'd have to admit, were rather straightforward. More or less a history of the cult of ruins and picturesque theory in the eighteenth century. Nothing I haven't read before. But the last chapter was unusually good. And it broke new ground. It was an examination of Constantin Volney's book *The Ruins: or Survey of the Revolution of Empires* and Robert Wood's *The Ruins of Palmyra*. He used the contrast between the two as sort of a paradigm of modernity, the struggle between the link to tradition and a certain positivistic determinism."

Fiona handed Jamie his coffee, concentrating on his words.

"If you say so," Hill remarked. "But what's your point, Jamie?"

"My point is that the last chapter had absolutely no editorial marks on it. But Rainer had marked up the other chapters considerably."

"Well," said Beggs. "As you say, Jamie, the last chapter was *unusually good*. I'm sure he saw no need for marks."

"Oh, there was need for marks," said Ramsgill. "I noticed some misspellings myself and, as good as it was, there were several minor theoretical points which needed work."

"Maybe Dr. Gräss didn't finish his review," said Hill.

"No, he did. He dated each chapter review in the table of contents."

Beggs appeared momentarily shaken, but then said, "I can assure you I don't know what you're talking about, Jamie. And besides, Rainer's not here to confirm or deny what you're saying. But whether Rainer liked my last chapter or not pales in comparison to any of the others' motives. You don't murder a colleague simply because they don't like your work. If you did, half of academia would be in prison."

"Maybe there was more to it than the fact that he just didn't like it," said Ramsgill.

"Like what?" said Hill.

"I don't know."

Hill took his coffee from Fiona, flipped the lid, and tested it. It was steaming, so he set it aside. He looked at Beggs for a moment longer, then turned to Lendtmayer.

"Let's hold that as a possibility, Jamie," he said. "But I would like to move on to Maria."

Lendtmayer sat still, her hands cradled around a white foam cup of tea. She appeared cold, even dressed as she was in a turtleneck sweater.

"I'll have to admit," began Hill slowly, "that until last night, Ms. Lendtmayer, I hadn't thought of you as a suspect. Dennis Fort-thompson said that he thought the second person in the punt was a dark-haired man, and you didn't seem to have a motive. But there is the problem of your having been at Smithson when Fortthompson was killed and your having lied about Ms. Denster's and Dr. Gräss's rendezvous in the Old Court at the party. Also, the fact that when you saw him in the courtyard that night, you told Iain that Dr. Gräss had returned to the hall. Even without his having asked, and even though, as we now know, Dr. Gräss never went back into the hall. I've been thinking quite a bit about that.

"And yet the one thing we didn't have on you was a motive. Of course, you are friends with Amy, as is Gaines, and therefore you might take it upon yourself to defend her honor. But somehow that didn't seem enough. Frankly, I thought we would come here this morning and that would be all I could pin on you.

"But last night, after I left Smithson, and against my best intentions to get some sleep, I went to Newnham College and examined Amy's room. I went there in the hope that I would find a clue as to her whereabouts."

Lendtmayer remained motionless, not bothering to touch her tea.

"But do you know what I found instead?"

Hill pulled something else from the briefcase and tossed it onto the table. It slid several inches before coming to a stop. Ramsgill, whose position in the armchair was lower than that of the others, could hardly see what it was. He raised himself higher, and looked down. It was a hardbound book, with no title on either the front or the spine.

"What is it?" asked Maria, her voice quavering. She wished she'd gone out for a cigarette.

"It's a diary," said Hill. "Amy's diary. And given our discussion of motives, it makes for interesting reading."

Fifteen

*A*my Denster no longer opened her mouth. She could, if she forced her tongue through her dried lips, but the sensation of air on her tongue only made her need for water stronger. She breathed through her nose now, her nostrils inflamed by the fetid air, her lungs hollow and tender, her throat tight and dry. She hardly moved. Her buttocks were numb from the cold, hard surface beneath her, her fingertips tingly. Her head felt like an inanimate weight, while the past and present melded in a drunkenness of unconnected thoughts.

There was a time, maybe yesterday, when she had gotten the cold sweats. She had tried to harvest the sweat from her forearms, but by the time her damp fingertips reached her lips, they were dry once again.

And now she was hungry again. At first the pangs came and went, as did the headaches that accompanied them. But presently the emptiness was like a chant, enveloping her, rhythmic, unrelenting. She thought she heard someone coming for her once, but the noise evaporated. Even the dripping she had heard earlier was now gone. Now there was just pain, desire for sustenance, and confusion. That was all she had, the sum total of her miserable existence.

Chris Detler opened the door and slipped back into the rare books room. He walked over to DCI Hill, now seated at the head of the table, and whispered something into his ear. When he had finished, he straightened up and returned to his place near the windows.

Detler could see Amy Denster's diary on the table. He wondered if Hill had refrained from going into detail about its contents, as he had said he would. Hill had figured that just showing it to Maria Lendtmayer would convince her that he knew about her brief affair with Amy. There was no reason to air that information in front of the others.

"I was just showing Amy's diary to Maria," said Hill, his words directed back at Detler. "Can you guess what she talks about in there, Maria?"

Lendtmayer shifted in her seat, drawing one foot up beneath her other thigh.

"Perhaps," said Maria. "But I don't see what it has to do with Dr. Gräss."

"Amy believed that you might be jealous of Rainer. In the days after he disappeared, she wrote that she wondered whether it was you who had attacked him in the courtyard. And she implies that there *was* an attack."

"Me jealous of Rainer?" said Maria. "Because of Amy? If that's what she thought then she was mistaken. She and I had one intimate moment, that was all. I have a lover. But that doesn't mean that after what happened between us that I didn't still like Amy. As a friend. If she mistook my friendship for something else, then she was very wrong."

Hill picked up the diary and placed it in front of himself.

"So it's a matter of interpretation," he said. "But I still want to know what happened in that courtyard, Maria. Amy mentions an attack. And you both lied to me about what happened out there."

Maria's lips remained shut.

"Very well then," Hill said. "We'll come back to that. Let's move then to Dennis Fortthompson's murder, as I said I would. And I'll be frank with all of you." He looked around the table, his eyes tinged in red. "This upsets me, perhaps even more than Rainer Gräss's death. While murder is not condonable under any circumstances, it is, I suppose, understandable. I've come to learn that Dr. Gräss may not have been the most pleasant of men. And there was animosity between him and some of you. But Dennis Fortthompson was murdered for one reason only. Because he happened to be on Garret Hostel Lane Bridge at twelve thirty-five Monday night and had the fortitude to come forward. He was a family man who didn't deserve his fate."

Hill paused, taking a sip of his now-warm coffee.

"So where were we all last night just before midnight?" he said. "Professor Frontis?"

"I was at home reading. With the cat. Guess I should consider getting a lover if I'm going to keep turning up as a murder suspect."

"Gaines, how about you?"

"I was at my college. In and out of my room, and the graduate common room."

"Dr. Beggs?"

"I was at home too. Cheerfully asleep."

"And Maria, we've already spoken," said Hill. "We know you were at Smithson, and you say you left right before Fortthompson was killed. Any change to that story?"

"No."

"Which leaves you, Mr. Boye."

Boye sat forward, fiddling with one of his rings.

"Where were you?"

"I was at Ghislaine's."

"Ah. Were you there the whole night?"

"No. I returned a little after midnight. I had an eight o'clock class this morning."

"Do you know how Mr. Fortthompson was killed, George?"

Boye shook his large head.

"He was suffocated. Or strangled and suffocated. By plastic bubble wrap."

Boye's tongue thrust through his lips, swiping across them.

"I had nothing to do with that."

"And you're sure you were with Ghislaine until after midnight? You couldn't have left earlier?"

"I don't know. Maybe a bit earlier. But not early enough to have gone to Smithson."

"We telephoned Mrs. Gräss last night, George. After Fortthompson's death we couldn't find you. She told us that you had been there, but that she had been asleep from about eleven o'clock on. So she can't say with certainty what time you left."

"Okay," Boye said. Sweat was building on his forehead and his fingers fidgeted. "So I did leave earlier. But I didn't go to Smithson like you say. I went back to Darwin."

"And what about Monday night?" Hill said. "Why didn't you tell me that you had left the Old Hall?"

"Because it didn't mean anything. I didn't see anything."

"Did I say there was something to see?" said Hill. "Or did Amy's diary jog your memory? Look, George, I know that you think Dr. Gräss was a bastard, but Fortthompson wasn't. If you know something, you'd better tell me. What happened in the courtyard Monday night? How long were you out of the hall?"

Boye slid back in his chair and stared up at the ceiling.

He took several long breaths.

"I really should have done something," he said softly.

"Do it now," DCI Hill said.

Boye brought his palms together, then rocked his head around with his eyes closed.

"Okay," he said. His head stopped rocking, and he looked toward Maria Lendtmayer. "She attacked him. Rainer and Amy were arguing in Cloister Court and Maria came out of nowhere and pulled him him away. Amy ran back inside. Maria then just sort of dragged him across the courtyard."

"To where?"

"To the corner of Cloister Court. I retreated south, so I wouldn't be seen. Then I think Maria left him on the grass, and went back toward the Old Hall. It was just a minute later that I saw Gaines Simpson."

Every eye in the room turned to Simpson. His head cocked back, and his jaw began to move again.

"What then?" asked Hill. Silence enveloped the room.

"He came across the courtyard," said Boye. "He and Rainer had words."

Boye paused, his big brown eyes now moving around the table.

"I then heard footsteps. At first I thought it was Gaines going back toward the Old Hall, but then I realized the sound was coming from

he was back in the hall at twelve thirty-five, which was exactly the time Dennis Fortthompson saw the punt pass beneath Garret Hostel Lane Bridge. So it couldn't have been him."

"But if you believe George," said Simpson, "then you know that I was back in the hall not five minutes later."

"Correct," said Hill. "And though one would think it would be impossible for someone to have gotten from Garret Hostel Lane Bridge to Trinity and back in five minutes, if anyone could have done it, it would have been you, Gaines."

"But how about what George said happened in the courtyard? He said that I was not the person whose footsteps he heard."

"He did. But he didn't actually *see* that person. He could have been mistaken."

"Well, for my defense," said Beggs, "I have alibis for both the phone call about the wallet and about the fax."

"You don't have an alibi for the fax," said Simpson.

"If I was out front locking up my bicycle," said Beggs, "then how could I have been in the office?"

There was a knock on the door, and a short woman whom Ramsgill recognized as the department's librarian stuck her head in. Detler followed her out of the room. He returned a moment later and said, "That was the coxswain from Pembroke. She did see Mr. Simpson Tuesday morning. Said she would never forget his tongue."

Simpson gave himself a self-satisfied smile.

"Which leaves us with two," said Hill. He looked to Beggs, then to Maria Lendtmayer, who was sitting across from the history professor. She had still not touched her tea.

"Dr. Beggs," said Hill. "Why were there no corrections to the last chapter of your manuscript?"

"Like I said," replied Beggs, "I have no idea."

"I am reminded of the fact that you took Dr. Gräss's briefcase home with you after the party. You didn't perhaps swap Dr. Gräss's edited version of your last chapter for a clean one, did you?"

"Why?" said Beggs. "Give me a good reason."

"How long were you out of the hall?" said Hill. "George has already testified that you didn't return until twelve forty-five."

Beggs shrugged, then adjusted his eyeglasses.

"Oh, fifteen minutes, I suppose," he said.

"That's a lie," snapped Maria, her voice enraged. "I saw him up near the loos just after twelve twenty."

"Inspector," said Beggs calmly. "You don't believe her, do you? We already know that she attacked Rainer. It's only a matter of time before she admits it."

Hill looked over to Maria.

"Maria?"

She didn't speak.

"Maria, did you lie to me last night?" said Hill. "About Fort-thompson, and about Amy not having shown up at your house yesterday morning?"

"Of course she did," said Beggs.

"I did not. Amy told me Wednesday night that she was owed money by someone, enough money to have her abortion performed privately. Who among us has that kind of money?"

She stared laserlike at Beggs. Hill did too, momentarily, before returning his gaze to Maria.

"Interesting idea," Hill said. "But other issues contradict that assertion. Once again he reached into the briefcase. This time he pulled out a large gray envelope. He set it before him, and placed his hands on top of it. Maria's eyes glanced down at the envelope. Hill then spoke:

"Forensics found hairs on Rainer's body. Blond hairs about your length, Maria. As well as blood and tissue beneath Dr. Gräss's fingernails. Now, we don't know whose hair and whose tissue at this point, but we will. And with the proper documents, we will solicit samples. I keep wondering, though, as I sit here, why you are wearing that turtleneck sweater. I myself think that it is rather warm in this room. It isn't to hide something, is it? Scratch marks, perhaps, like the ones Christina Appleford saw on your neck Tuesday night at her life-drawing class?"

Maria turned her head toward Hill, evading the sinister smile planted on Beggs's lips.

"I *did not* kill Rainer," she said emphatically. "I did attack him, but only to protect Amy. Afterwards I followed Amy back toward the hall. But I ran into Iain up near the portal. He was obviously heading into Cloister Court, and I did not want him to see what I had done. That's why I told him Rainer had returned to the hall. The only reason."

"And what did you do then? Truthfully? Because you weren't out of the Hall for thirty minutes like you told me on Wednesday. You were out from midnight until twelve forty-five."

"I went to the loo, like I said. I wondered if I were bleeding, so I wanted to take a look at my neck. That's when I saw Cheverton."

"And did you stay at the loo for twenty-five minutes? That's an awfully long time."

"No. I went into Old Court and smoked several cigarettes. I didn't know what to do. I knew that my career would be over when Rainer realized that it was me. Attacking him was a stupid thing to have done, but at the time I felt I had no choice. He was going to beat Amy."

Hill tapped a finger on the envelope.

"If you were worried about your career," he said, "wouldn't another solution be to get rid of Dr. Gräss? Once and for all?"

"No."

"Didn't you go back to Cloister Court?"

"No."

"Didn't you knock him unconscious, then take him across the river and up to Trinity?"

"Absolutely not. I'll tell you a hundred times, Inspector, no."

"Where is Amy now, Maria?"

"For God's sake, Inspector," said Beggs. "Show her the photograph."

All eyes turned to Hill as he looked down to the envelope. Ramsgill rose from his chair and moved to Hill's end of the table.

"Dennis Fortthompson never got the chance to see any of you in an identity parade," Hill said, now pulling back the envelope's flap. "And he wasn't exactly sharp on detail. But he did remember one particular detail about the second person in the punt that night."

Hill pulled several large photos from the envelope.

"He remembered pale hands. And pale, I think you can see, are just the way I would characterize yours, Maria."

Ramsgill nudged forward, looking down at the pictures. There were several copies of the same shot. The picture was of the six people left at the party at 1 A.M., after Rainer had been taken away in the punt. The four men—Beggs, Frontis, Simpson, and Boye—sat in chairs before the Old Hall fireplace. Behind them stood the two young women, Maria to the left and Amy to the right. It was not a particularly good photograph, most of the light coming from the camera's flash unit. Several of the subjects suffered from red eyes, the result of the flash.

Behind the group, Ramsgill could see the four candlesticks on the mantel. One of them was slightly out of place.

The thing that first struck Ramsgill was Maria's clothes. She was dressed in a long black sweater, and tight burgundy pants. Her blond hair and white face stood out against the dark tile behind her, but her hair was tucked into the shawl of her sweater. And she wore a black beret.

But Hill's comment was not directed at the clothes. Maria's hands could be seen at her side, hanging naturally, one just to the side of Beggs's right shoulder and the other between Beggs's left shoulder and that of Frontis. The sleeves of her sweater ended just above her wrists, with a small area of flesh below. It was only a small area of flesh, though, and not her whole hand. For one simple reason. In the photograph, she was wearing white gloves.

Sixteen

*M*aria Lendtmayer remained motionless, her breathing so shallow that she hardly seemed alive. Lyndsay Hill gestured to Chris Detler, and Detler walked over to Lendtmayer, touching her lightly on the padded shoulders of her smart tweed jacket. Without emotion she got up from the table. Detler led her out of the room. She walked with the long, cool stride of a runway model.

In her wake she left a room of silence. Ramsgill couldn't tell if the quiet was a reflection of relief, of sympathy, or of bewilderment, but it seemed to stamp a finality on their meeting and on the investigation of Rainer Gräss's death.

"Poor girl," said Cheverton Beggs finally, without sarcasm. He tugged at the sleeves of his suit jacket and folded his hands neatly before him.

"Hardly," said Gaines Simpson. "I hope you fry her, Inspector. And she'd better give up Amy."

"You'll take her to Parkside?" said Ramsgill to Lyndsay Hill.

Hill rose. His face hardly showed relief at having Lendtmayer in custody. He nodded.

"We'll question her straightaway and search her house. Hopefully we'll find Amy there."

Hill reached forward for the candlestick and wrapped it in cloth, then placed it carefully in his briefcase. He then picked up the photographs, put a couple of them in the envelope, leaving the rest on the table.

"I won't need these," he said. "You folks might as well keep them, as Amy had originally intended. And thank you for your cooperation."

He then turned and, in silence, left.

Iain Frontis picked up a photograph. Boye did likewise, then the others, then one by one they exited the room.

When Ramsgill and Fiona were the only ones remaining, she got up from her chair and walked over to the end of the table where Hill had sat. She picked up the last of the photographs and looked at it. She was crying.

"It's funny," she said, wiping a thick tear from her cheek. "When Rainer told me he was going to retire, I briefly considered quitting also. It was a ridiculous notion, but I thought to myself that the school would never be the same once he left. That I didn't want to outlive my memories. But now, God, look at how different it will be."

Ramsgill reached over and put a hand on her shoulder.

"You were fond of him," he said. "Despite yourself and the kind of person he was."

Fiona nodded.

"You can't quit, Fi. You know that. Who would hold this place together?"

She tried to laugh. "They do need help, don't they?"

Ramsgill took the photograph from her hand.

"They do indeed," he said. "Look, why don't we get out of here. Go get a bite to eat or something."

She looked up at him, her face only inches from his. They stood motionless, each staring into the other's eyes. Ramsgill could feel the warmth of her breath, and he could see the network of tiny lines that shaped her face. She was a beautiful woman who didn't deserve what life and Dick Mallow had given her. Someone needed to make her happy. He was sorry that it couldn't be him.

He squeezed her hand.

"I loved you, Jamie," she said.

"And I you."

She unexpectedly pulled him closer.

"I still love you," she said.

Ramsgill tried to smile. Her eyes, full and rich, drew his attention like a magnet. Her lips parted, but when they approached his, he turned his head to the side, holding her in an embrace.

Later, he wouldn't remember how long they had held each other. He would just remember the feeling. The discrete pleasure of being back in her arms, coupled with heavy guilt.

He squeezed her one final time, then stepped back.

"It's too late," she said. "Isn't it?"

"I'm afraid so. Timing has never been our strong suit, Fiona."

She gave him a smile.

"Now, how about something to eat?" he repeated.

"I wish I could," she said. "But I have work to do."

She started to walk away. He put his hand on her wrist.

"Fiona?"

"What?"

"I'm glad I came over. And that we had our chance to talk. Thank you for that."

She nodded, her eyes reddening. She left the room.

He followed her down the hall to her office. She went immediately to her desk and began shuffling through the pile of papers that lay on top of it. Ramsgill pretended to read notices on the faculty announcement board, but he noticed that the tears had come again. He didn't know what to say, but he didn't want to leave her, either.

Finally, she stopped crying.

"By the way," she said, after regaining composure, "Ghislaine telephoned. Rainer's funeral is going to be at two on Sunday. She wants to know if you would be a pallbearer."

"Of course," Ramsgill said. He began to search his pockets for a scrap of paper on which to write the funeral time.

"Where's the funeral going to be?" he asked.

Fiona started to answer, but as she caught the look on Ramsgill's face, she hesitated. He was staring down at a small yellow slip of paper, a look of consternation on his face.

"What's the matter?" she said.

He didn't answer. His mind was racing over the week's events, his body beginning to shudder. He felt nauseous.

Fiona walked over to him.

"What is it?"

He handed her the slip of paper and she read it. It was a phone message to Ramsgill from the previous day. The message had been taken by a Darwin College porter at 11:30 in the morning. It stated that Cheverton Beggs had telephoned, and that he would be have to cancel their appointment for Ramsgill to come to Purdington End, because Beggs had to take his mother to Peterborough to the doctor.

"So?" said Fiona.

"Take his mother to *Peterborough?* He told Lyndsay Hill that they had gone to Newmarket to the doctor."

"Think he was mistaken?"

"Hell no. You don't watch horses parade around the heath in Peterborough."

Fiona looked off for a second, then back to Ramsgill.

"Jamie, I didn't say anything earlier, but something struck me as odd when you were talking about Cheverton's manuscript."

"What?"

"That last chapter. The one Inspector Hill said might have been swapped."

"You mean that it was so different from the others? So original?"

She shook her head from side to side.

"No. Actually the opposite. I could have sworn that I've read it before. Or heard about it."

"When? How?"

Fiona's brow tightened into a funnel of converging lines. She sighed.

"I don't remember."

"Think," said Ramsgill. "Please."

Suddenly, her face looked as though she had been slapped. Her eyes shot open and her head snapped back, her thick auburn hair bouncing over her shoulder.

"I remember," she said. She stepped away from the counter and walked to a bank of file cabinets on the opposite wall of the room. Ramsgill quickly followed.

"What?" he said.

She didn't answer. She opened up a file drawer labeled *Graduate Admissions.* The files were divided by year. She went straight to two years prior and pulled out a folder.

The name on the folder was *Amy Denster.*

She set the file on top of the file cabinet and opened it. Inside were application forms, letters of recommendation, grant applications, and examples of her undergraduate work. Fiona disregarded everything but one bound item. She pulled it out of the file such that she and Ramsgill could see it. It was Denster's Diploma thesis from the University of Saint Andrews, Scotland.

Ramsgill read the title: *Towards the Dissolution of Tradition— The Cult of Ruins during the Enlightenment.*

Ramsgill hurriedly flipped through it. It was divided into several chapters on themes not unlike Beggs's own book-in-progress. There was background on picturesque theory, a full chapter devoted to ecclesiastical ruins left from Henry VIII's dissolution of England's monasteries, a long section on the gentleman architect and gardener Batty Langley, and a final chapter entitled "The Notion of Fragment," which was a comparison of Robert Wood and Constantin Volney's books. Ramsgill scanned it and realized, almost immediately, that it was Beggs's final chapter almost verbatim.

"Son of a bitch," he said.

He closed the thesis and looked at the cover. Denster had received a first for the work, including a letter of highest recommendation from her professor.

"So Cheverton plagiarized this from Amy?" said Fiona.

"Not in the traditional sense," said Ramsgill. "He paid her for it. Remember? Maria said that someone owed Amy money. And she was to have gotten it before she went to London Thursday morning. Perhaps she went to Beggs's estate."

"Are you saying what I think you are?" said Fiona. "But it doesn't make sense. Remember, Beggs had an alibi for the phone call about the wallet, and about the fax."

"Or so it seemed," said Ramsgill. "I don't know about the phone call, but as far as the fax goes, he could have already been in your office, sent it, then returned outside to make it look like he had just arrived. You said yourself that you go to Greenway's almost every morning. Beggs would know that, wouldn't he?"

"I suppose," said Fiona. "But surely Rainer or Frontis knew about Amy's undergraduate thesis. It takes two faculty members to approve a candidate for admission. How in the world would Beggs think he could get away with it?"

Ramsgill set down the thesis and rifled through the other papers in the file. When he came to Amy's application, a memo was attached from Renny Heard-Matthews, head of the school. It stated that Amy was being admitted having been reviewed by only one faculty member, because at the time of her application, Rainer Gräss was out of the country and Iain Frontis was on a six-month sabbatical. The signature of the approving faculty member was at the bottom of the application. Cheverton Beggs.

"There it is," said Ramsgill.

"But what about the fax?" said Fiona. "And Beggs couldn't have made that phone call when he was in the same room with me. And the photograph, for heaven's sake. There is no denying that Maria was wearing gloves."

Ramsgill thought for a moment, then clutched Fiona's shoulder.

"Come on," he said, pushing her forward.

He followed her up to the second floor and down a long hall to the area of his and Beggs's offices. Beggs's door was closed. Ramsgill rapped loudly on the wood several times, confirming that Beggs wasn't there. He then tried the knob, but it was locked. Just then, three doors down, Iain Frontis came out of his office, carrying a load of books.

"Have you seen Beggs?" asked Ramsgill.

Frontis was wary of Ramsgill's turbulent eyes.

"He's gone for the day," said Frontis.

"Did he say where he was going?"

"He said he had a meeting down in London."

Ramsgill looked to Fiona and shrugged.

"What's the matter?" said Frontis.

"Nothing. Thanks, Iain."

Frontis loped off. When he was out of earshot, Ramsgill said, "Do you have the key to Cheverton's office?"

"What? Jamie we can't . . ."

He grabbed her arm.

"Well, I have the master."

She unlocked the door. Once inside, they closed the door behind them, and he booted up Beggs's computer. A small green light on the front of the computer's CPU flashed like a strobe, then the hard drive spun up.

"What are you looking for?" Fiona said, now at his side, seated in Beggs's desk chair.

"I remember telling Hill about the photograph that was taken at the party. At the time, I was wondering what everyone at the party was wearing, because Fortthompson said that he thought the second person in the punt was wearing dark clothes. I told Lyndsay to look at the photograph, because photographs don't lie."

"So?"

"So maybe I was wrong. Photographs can lie. When you think about it, Maria would have been crazy to have worn gloves in the photo if she had really killed Rainer. It was a dead giveaway. And then I remembered that when I was in here the other day, I saw that Beggs had photographic manipulation software, the kind graphic designers and artists use to create special effects."

He pointed to a software box on Beggs's desk. The hard-disk window came up on the computer screen, and immediately Ramsgill found the icon on the computer. He opened the icon folder and searched for a file that might have something to do with the photograph taken at the party. He opened several files, most of which were manipulated images of early Renaissance paintings, nothing in the way of a group photograph. He then searched through a plastic disk storage unit on Beggs's desk, which was filled with floppy disks. He found a couple of unlabeled diskettes, and he put them into the computer's floppy drive. But they were empty. He searched the "trash bin" icon on the computer's desktop, but it too was empty.

"Damn," he said.

"You still haven't told me what you're looking for."

"Just a minute."

He rose and left the room, returning a moment later with his notebook computer from his office next door. He set it on the desk and booted it up, and while the screen came up, he said, "I want to see if his trash is really empty. Beggs's computer doesn't have wiping utility software on it, so there's a chance that any files he's gotten rid of are still in the background of his hard disk."

"What does that mean?"

"It means that when you have a file that you want to get rid of, you usually just drag the file to the computer's trash icon. That frees up space on the disk for new files, but it doesn't exactly destroy the old file. Not, at least, until a new file is written over it. To totally get rid of it, you have to use a wipe disk or reinitialization software. My notebook has a data-recovery program. If a file was trashed, it's possible I can bring it back."

She watched him as he copied his recovery program to one of Beggs's blank diskettes. He then popped the disk into Beggs's computer, and copied the software to the desktop. He opened the utility, something called "File Recover." He instructed the software to recover any files that had been previously trashed. Surprisingly, the software found some 126 of them. A PICT file entitled "Rainer's Party" had been trashed that very morning. Its chances of recovery, according to the software, were good. Ramsgill instructed the software to recover the file, and within five seconds the file appeared on the computer's desktop.

"Beautiful," he said.

He then went into the photographic manipulation program and opened "Rainer's Party." The group photograph from the party appeared on the screen, filling most of the monitor as a muted color image. To the left of the photograph was a "toolbox," a number of tool icons that were available for manipulation. Ramsgill selected an icon of a magnifying glass and brought it into the area of Maria's hands. Holding down one of the buttons on the computer's mouse, he then dragged the magnifying glass across the hands, and immediately the screen zoomed in. The hands, now greatly enlarged, looked like a mosaic of beige, taupe, and yellow boxes. The boxes were individual pixels, each one a tiny digitized portion of the photograph.

"There," said Ramsgill.

He pointed to an area where the white gloves met the skin of Maria's wrist.

"See how the line representing the top of the glove is absolutely straight? In reality, in true perspective, it wouldn't be like that. It would be slightly curved.

Fiona nodded.

"But I still don't understand how Beggs made the gloves," she said.

"Watch."

Ramsgill used the mouse to pick the pen tool from the toolbox. He returned to the digitized image of Maria's hands on the screen, and moved the pen tool around them, tracing the perimeter and stopping to click the pen every half-inch or so. When he had made a complete circuit of the glove, it was as if he had connected the dots in a coloring-book exercise. He then chose a command called "Brightness/Contrast." By moving a slide bar from light to dark, he could manipulate the glove to whatever tone he wanted. Ramsgill slid the bar to the left, making the glove darker, such that its value was the same as her skin. Suddenly, Maria was wearing no glove at all.

"I see," said Fiona. "Smoke and mirrors."

"And digitized photographs."

"But how do you make a photograph from a computer file?"

"Most labs can produce photographs from disks. In fact, you can buy cameras that don't even use film. They digitize information directly to disk. What must have happened was that Beggs had the film developed on Tuesday, got the prints back on Wednesday, then scanned one of them into his computer to be manipulated. He then sent a disk back and the doctored prints were delivered Wednesday night."

"But certainly the photo lab would be able to tell the police that the second time they made prints it was from a disk. It would tip them off."

"Why? All they knew was that they were doing a job. And the prints went to Beggs, not the police. Chris Detler talked to the lab. They told him they were making prints from a disk, but Beggs told Detler that the disk-generated prints were completely unrelated to the party photograph."

"But how about the phone call regarding the wallet?"

Ramsgill closed the file containing the photograph and returned to the computer's desktop. He knew, of course, that if Beggs had been in the office with Fiona when the call came, then he was incapable of having made the call. Ventriloquism doesn't work through phone lines.

But digitized voice activation does.

He again searched the roster of deleted files on Beggs's hard disk. Nothing seemed to jump out at him, so he reordered the file names by date. The computer responded by placing the most recent files at the top of the screen. There was a file created on Monday in a program called Cardstack. The title of the file was "Earl of Pembroke." Ramsgill instructed the software to recover the file.

A moment later he opened the file in Cardstack, which he knew was a fairly simple programming utility. By manipulating graphic images of cards, Cardstack allows creation of an interactive multimedia environment on a computer. Each card contains either text, sound, or video. Or all three. And each card can reference other cards in the stack by means of user-definable buttons, such that an entire string of film clips, for instance, can be put together, depending on how the user guides the program. In considering how to make a phone call using this technique, Ramsgill figured that first Beggs would have to record individual loops of dialogue, feeding them into the computer by means of a microphone, each loop on a separate card. He would then have to anticipate Fiona's response to the supposed policeman's questions. Somehow—and this was over his head—Fiona's response must have prompted the next card to come on line, in essence, moving the conversation forward.

Once it was recovered, Ramsgill opened the "Earl of Pembroke" file. It was made up of several cards. He pushed the Play button of the top card in the stack and heard a deep voice, possibly Beggs disguised by sound-editing software, say, "Hello, this is Parkside Police." He dragged the first card to the side, then pressed the Play button on the second: "Is Rainer Gräss a member of your faculty?" Then the third card: "Is he there now?"

Fiona clutched Ramsgill's arm.

"That's eerie," she said. "You know, now that I think about it, the call was rather strange. I remember telling the caller that Rainer wasn't in, then just after that, he asked if Rainer was there. I thought he was an idiot."

"You must have thrown the loop sequence off by not answering the questions the way Beggs had thought you would."

"I suppose. But how was the call actually placed?"

"My guess is via modem. Perhaps from Beggs's estate. And you can program the computer to do it without your even being around."

"So what do we do now?" said Fiona.

"Phone Lyndsay."

Ramsgill picked up the phone and dialed Parkside Station. He was put on hold. While he waited, he shut down the computer. A moment later, a female voice came back on the line.

"Inspector Hill is unavailable," she said.

"I *have* to speak to him," said Ramsgill.

"I'm sorry," said the voice. "I was specifically told that he was unavailable. To anyone."

Ramsgill hung up.

"What?" said Fiona.

"They won't put me through. He's probably interrogating Maria."

"Why don't we just go to the station, then?"

"Yes. No, on second thought . . ."

"What?"

"You go to the station," said Ramsgill. "I'm going to Purdington End."

"Why?"

"Where would you hide a hostage, if you were him?"

"But Jamie, let's just get Hill and . . ."

"No. Look, Amy's been gone for two days. And you heard Iain. Beggs is down in London. I'll be fine."

"How are you going to get there?"

"Where's your car?"

"In the car park."

"Then I'll take it. Do whatever you have to do to get Hill out of interrogation. Tell him where I've gone."

"Be careful, Jamie."

"Believe me, I will."

Seventeen

The car turned through mammoth iron gates, engaging the long gravel driveway that led up to Purdington End. The January sun was low on the horizon, and even though it was almost midday, very little of its light penetrated the deep woods that led up to the house. An allée of stout plane trees fronted the woods and embraced the drive, casting long shadows over the straight line of gray.

Passing in and out of shadows like a shark making its way through a school of fish, the yellow Ford approached the house. The house itself stood at the end of the drive, as if it had always been there, as if it would always remain. Ramsgill parked and stepped slowly out of the car. He gently closed the car door, and listened as the sound it made reverberated across the formal forecourt, returning to his ears from the old stables to the right of the main house, and from the orangery to the left.

The front of the house faced north, a fortress of brown brick and gray limestone, obscured by the patina of shadow. It was a grand collage of bays, turrets, crenellations, and chimneys, all held together by pockmarked brick, and softened by clinging ivy. It was difficult to tell if lights were burning behind the large traceried windows, and the entrance itself was set within an even darker covered porch.

Ramsgill cautiously made his way across the gravel to the front door. He rang the bell. When he didn't get an answer he rang again, three times in succession, pausing between each ring. He then left the porch and walked around the house, stopping at each low window to look inside, but uncovering no sign of activity.

He had been thinking during his drive to Grantchester how it came to be that someone at Beggs's station in life could indeed commit murder, not once, but twice, or perhaps even three times. He had recalled Rainer's statement at the retirement party, the one that Ramsgill had repeated over and over again for the last four days until it had almost become a mantra.

"For the sake of the department," Rainer had said that night, "for the sake of the department" he wasn't resigning. By resigning, he would have given Iain Frontis a spot on the faculty, and his change of heart therefore seemed like a condemnation of Frontis, and a strong motive for Frontis to have killed him. That was what everyone, including Ramsgill, had originally thought. It was now clear, however, that Rainer had meant something entirely different, something more honorable, and something that pointed directly to Beggs as the murderer. It was true that Beggs wouldn't have killed Rainer because of jealousy alone. Gräss must have threatened to reveal Beggs's plagiarism to the Proctors, which undoubtedly would have gotten Beggs fired. And once sacked, Rainer would need to stay on, "for the sake of the department," otherwise the faculty would have been short by one member and the department's reputation would have suffered. Gräss's remaining presence on the faculty would equate to credibility, during what would surely be a difficult time.

Ramsgill turned the corner at the right rear of the house, which offered a vista of the gardens and grounds. In the far distance the ruins of Purdington Abbey rose out of a line of leafless, black trees, its soft orange stone bathed in the winter light. A low wall of gray-white clouds formed a backdrop for the ruins, with a broad dome of blue sky above. To his left, a marble stair rose to an upper terrace, its steps spilling down onto the rear lawn like a cascading brook. Ramsgill bounded up the shallow steps three risers at a time, and within seconds he was at a group of French doors that opened onto the terrace from the house. Through the glass he could see a grand room filled with antiques. But the room was empty.

He turned and walked out to a stone balustrade that bounded the terrace. Looking out over the property, it was just then that he realized where Amy would be, if she was alive and Beggs was holding her at the estate.

He hurried back down the stairs and out onto the lawn. The grass was still wet from the morning's dew, and a few patches of frost remained in shadowed sections. He walked a good half mile away from the house, past the Jekyll borders and winding watercourses and clumps of beech. Finally, he reached a small plateau and there the ruins of Purdington Abbey rose before him like an architectural ghost. The ruins were nestled into a crook at a wood's edge, lying perfectly flat on a table of green lawn. The great pendentive arches of the church spanned over the ruins like long-ago-abandoned suspension bridges, with no evidence of a former roof, the arches now holding up only sky. The tops of the pendentives were overgrown with vines and tendrils of ivy, and even small trees were gaining foothold into the crumbling stone. The church walls for the most part still stood, great side-aisle arches cut out of stone, the mortar between individual building blocks long since eroded. At the top of the wall smaller pointed clerestory windows punched through, but none of the windows contained glass, and several of the embrasure jambs had tumbled to the earth. Pieces of the building were scattered about the site, protruding out of the lawn like icebergs floating in a calm green sea. At the far end of the nave the remains of a winding stair could be seen.

He made his way to the central tower of the church, where the nave intersected the transept. The floor of the church was now formed of grass, and intermittently, slabs of carved stone marked ancient tombs. In the area of the chancel, he paused to look around him, then in one corner of the south transept, he saw what he was looking for. Several long slabs of stone formed a rectangle against the outer walls of the church. He approached and saw that one of the slabs was smaller and thinner than the rest, no larger than a bath towel. It was covered by several boulders each small enough to be removed by one man.

He knelt beside the slab and began to roll away the smaller stones. As he was removing the third of the stones, he paused and listened, as he thought he heard singing. He then continued, and once he had removed all of the boulders, he stood, and with one great heave, he slid the slab to one side.

Immediately, a pungent air rose like ether from the dark hole that had been uncovered. He again pushed the slab to one side, peering down into what had once been the church's crypt. A set of steep stone steps led into the darkness, and beyond, he no longer heard singing, just the sound of water dripping, and the surreal echo it made as the sound bounded through the underground chamber.

"Amy?"

He listened for a response, but heard nothing.

"Amy? It's Jamie Ramsgill. Are you in there?"

Again, nothing.

"If you're down there, please, give me a signal."

Ramsgill had no flashlight. If she were in the crypt, and unconscious, it would be impossible to locate her. He wondered if Fiona had a light in her car.

"Amy, please. If you can hear me, say something. It's not Cheverton. It's Jamie Ramsgill. I'm here to help you."

He thought that he heard a slight sound, but followed only by silence. He then rose, determined to go back to Fiona's car. Just as he was about to leave, he heard another sound, hardly communication, but unmistakeably human. He stepped down into the hole.

Cheverton Beggs's heart skipped a beat as he pulled the Bentley in front of his house and saw the yellow Ford. He had purposefully told Iain Frontis at school that he had to go down to London, in order that he could remove Amy Denster from the estate's property. If she was still alive, he would kill her and dump her body in the fens up near Wisbech along with several incriminating items.

Like most students at Scroope Terrace, Maria Lendtmayer kept personal effects at her desk. It had been no problem then for Beggs to get several fibers from a discarded sweater, and cigarette butts left in her ashtray. When the police finally found Amy's body, the sweater fibers on her clothing and a cigarette butt several hundred feet away would link Maria to the crime.

Killing Amy would be simple, considering what he had already been through. But he knew that he had to hurry, with Maria already in custody. The body would have to be in the fens long enough to make it appear as if Amy had been killed before Maria had been arrested.

Now there was the matter of the car in his driveway. It was Fiona's, that much Beggs knew. He could see that no one was at the front door, and as Cox had taken his mother to Ely for the afternoon, he knew that whoever was driving Fiona's car had not been let into the house.

He walked to the front door, assuring himself that the door was locked, then went around to the side and let himself in by the scullery door. At the foyer there, Beggs unlocked a case, taking out a twelve-gauge pump-action shotgun and a box of shells.

After assuring himself that no one was in the house, Beggs made his way into the library, and opened one of the French doors that led out to the terrace.

Once back outside, he surveyed the property. He neither saw nor heard anyone on the grounds. That left one possibility.

Whoever was here was at the ruins.

Fiona Mallow sat impatiently, staring across the detective pool to the door of the interview room. A group of men stood just outside the door, which was closed, the glass to either side curtained. She had been here five minutes, but still the detective she had spoken to had refused to interrupt the interview. Finally, Chris Detler emerged from the room, and the detective spoke to him.

Detler walked across the room with purpose, not bothering to say hello.

"How can I help you, Ms. Mallow?"

"You've got the wrong person in that room," she said.

Detler started to smile, but restrained himself.

"And why is that?"

"Cheverton Beggs lied about where he was yesterday. And the last chapter of his manuscript was lifted from Amy Denster's undergraduate thesis. He paid her for it and Rainer Gräss must have found out about it. That's why he was killed. And Amy went to Beggs's estate to collect her money, possibly just before she disappeared."

"What are you saying? That Beggs killed Gräss?"

"Yes."

"But what about the photograph? And Beggs's alibis."

"The photograph was manipulated by Beggs on a computer to frame Maria. And the phone call about the wallet was rigged up by computer too. To give Beggs his alibi."

Detler rubbed the back of his neck. His eyes were brilliant pink, the lids dark from lack of sleep.

"The next thing you're going to tell me is that a computer punted Gräss downriver and dumped his body into those footings."

"I want to see Inspector Hill," she said.

"The inspector is tied up," said Detler. "Look, Ms. Mallow, not to be difficult, but we've got a young woman in that room who has admitted attacking Dr. Gräss in the courtyard that night, and a witness who saw her do it. She has wounds to her neck which according to the forensic scientist match the blood and flesh under the deceased's fingernails. Several of her hairs were found on the body. And given all of this evidence, we're supposed to disregard it and go arrest Professor Beggs? Don't answer that . . . because we're not doing it anyway. I'm going back into that room. We've got about ten more minutes with the girl, and if you want to talk about it with the inspector after that, we can."

He turned and entered the interview room once again, and shut the door behind him.

Ramsgill hobbled down the steep, slick stairs, and when he reached the bottom, he paused and tried to get his bearings. It was pitch dark in the space, blackness filling the full frame of his vision. A damp cold seemed to accost him. His ears could sense that the ceiling of the crypt was just above his head, and his nose was filled with the bitter smell of decay and mold.

"Amy?"

The sound moved through the crypt like a beacon, reflecting off of unseen walls and returning to him in a flutter of echo.

"Amy?" he called again.

There was no reply, but suddenly a sound came from some distance away, and in the dim light provided by the stair opening he thought he sensed a figure.

The figure was humming an unrecognizable tune, like a child lost in a world of play. Ramsgill moved forward, careful of his step, and walked toward the figure, which he now realized was hunkered up against a wall, wedged into a corner of the crypt. He approached her cautiously, kneeling down in front of her, listening to her drunken song. He then reached out for her and said, "Amy. It's Jamie Ramsgill. I'm not going to hurt you."

He touched the sleeve of her wool coat and she recoiled, but he touched it again, and this time she let him hold her. He brought her head over to his shoulder, and tried to give her some comfort. He then lifted her chin and looked at her face.

"It's over," he said. "I'm going to take you out of here. Do you understand?"

Just then, from behind him, Ramsgill heard a sound that made him flinch. He turned, and in the dim light of the stair opening he could see the silhouette of a man hurrying down the stairs. The figure passed in and out of the light in an instant, but long enough for Ramsgill to realize it was Cheverton Beggs. And he had a gun.

Amy Denster heaved a deep breath, and was about to scream when Ramsgill thrust his hand over her mouth. He huddled closer to her, wrapping her in his arms, trying to keep her still.

Beggs froze near the bottom of the stair, just out of the light.

"Anybody home?" he said. His voice was crackly, eerie as it snaked its way through the chamber.

"Have company, do you, Amy?"

Ramsgill tried to think of a way to get to him without being heard. Beggs was still a good fifty feet away, though, and the slightest movement on Ramsgill's part would be instantaneously detected.

Beggs started in their direction. It was too dark for him to see, but he must have sensed that there were figures here in the corner.

"Come out, come out, wherever you are," he said, his voice a mix of delirium and trepidation.

He kept moving forward, each slow step signaled by the crack of debris underfoot.

Ramsgill released Amy's mouth and turned back in Beggs's direction. He could just make out the outline of Beggs's left shoulder against the light at the far end of the chamber. Ramsgill remained frozen, his legs bundled beneath him, his arms at his side. Beggs was but fifteen feet away.

Suddenly, Ramsgill was blinded as a sweep of light caught him in the face. And as quickly as the light had come, so too did Beggs have the barrel of a shotgun pointed at Ramsgill's head.

"Jamie," Beggs said. "What a surprise. I wanted you to see the ruins, but I didn't think it would be under these circumstances. And how is poor Amy?"

Amy's breathing intensified, and Ramsgill reached back to try to calm her. She buried her frigid fingers into the palm of his hand.

"Gallant, aren't we?" Beggs said. "But terribly stupid. Are you glad now that you figured out how I got the final chapter of my book?"

Ramsgill didn't reply. He tried to think of some way to disarm Beggs but Beggs held the gun with authority, his eyes full of frenzy.

"Get up," Beggs said.

Ramsgill did as he was told.

"Amy too."

Amy was incapable of following Beggs's instructions. Ramsgill helped her to her feet. She was unsteady, and leaned against his back.

"What are you going to do with us?" said Ramsgill.

"I'm going to kill you, Jamie. I have no choice."

"You'll be heard."

"There's no one on the grounds. Cox has taken Mother up to the antiquarian book fair in Ely, and the neighbors will only think I'm hunting."

"The police know I'm here," said Ramsgill.

A hint of fear showed on Beggs's face. He exhaled, his breath a fine stream of mist against the blackness.

"Don't try to scare me, Jamie."

"It's true," Ramsgill said. "Fiona went there straight from school. And she's told them everything. How you doctored the photograph and rigged your computer to make the phone call about the wallet. How you appropriated Amy's thesis. It must have come as a complete shock to you when Amy and Rainer began their affair."

Beggs's lip quivered.

"I never thought that he'd have anything to do with her," Beggs said. "She's so . . . so . . . "

"Beneath him?" Ramsgill said.

"You could put it that way. It never occurred to me that Rainer might find out about her thesis. It had taken some hard convincing to get her to go along with it in the first place, even though she was in the worst sort of financial shape. Didn't it, Amy? Do you know that her father is an unemployed ironworker, Jamie? Her mother a charwoman?"

Ramsgill listened with disdain. He could feel the trembling of Amy's body.

"After I had incorporated her work," Beggs continued, "I gave the manuscript to Rainer to proofread. That was three months ago. I don't know when he and Amy began to see one another but I knew he didn't know about her thesis. I was the only reader of her admission application. But once they became intimate, she told him about it. Isn't that right, Amy?"

Amy had begun to cry, half singing to herself again in between the sobs.

"But after you killed him," Ramsgill said, "why didn't you just destroy the manuscript? That way I would never have found those discrepancies."

"That was my intention. I had convinced Amy to let me take Rainer's briefcase from the party. But when I gave her a lift home, she looked into it, thinking she had left some papers there. And she saw the manuscript, so I couldn't very well destroy it then. She might have mentioned the fact that it was missing to the police."

"Why did you do it, Cheverton?"

Beggs stared at him without emotion.

"I didn't plan to kill anyone," he said. "All I wanted was to gain some respect. And don't tell me I'm the first historian who ever made use of someone else's work. I just got caught at it. It was the wrong choice, but once discovered I couldn't let the truth come out. So I had to kill Rainer, and the decision was easier than I thought. How often have you said to yourself that you'd like to kill somebody—the chap who cuts in front of you on the motorway, or the thug who lifts your wallet on the underground? On the one hand you absolutely mean it, and yet decorum tells you that you can't. But what if you were convinced the fellow deserved it, and that if planned perfectly you wouldn't get caught? That's what I thought about Rainer. I hated the bastard, and thought that I had devised a faultless way to get rid of him. But if it is so well planned that you're the only one who can appreciate the genius behind it, then it has no meaning. So I dreamed up the phone call about his wallet. Then I served up another, the note with the Cole Porter line. Do you know what I felt like walking up to that construction site with the note in my pocket, with you and the police just beyond the construction fence? I felt like an exhibitionist, on the one hand completely titillated, and yet at the same time terrified that I would get caught."

Ramsgill's eyes were fixed on the gun barrel. He wondered whether he could reach it before Beggs could get off a shot.

"And what about Fortthompson?" Ramsgill said, trying to keep Beggs talking.

"Who? Oh, the Smithson porter. Yes. Well, what can I say about that, Jamie—that I'm sorry? It's unfortunate, but it had to be done. Don't you understand? I had no choice."

Had no choice, thought Ramsgill. He was seething. He started forward, but Beggs pumped a live shell into the firing chamber of the gun.

"Turn around," Beggs said, his voice now solemn. "Against the wall."

Ramsgill reluctantly did as he was told. The barrel of the shotgun dug into the small of his back.

"Should I do you first, Jamie?" Beggs said. "Or should a lady have the honor?"

Amy's crying intensified, resounding through the crypt.

"Quiet!" said Beggs.

Which only made her cry louder.

Beggs pulled the gun away from Ramsgill's back. Out of the corner of his eye, Ramsgill could see the barrel move to the rear of Amy's head. He was about to close his eyes when in the distance, from beyond the stair opening, they could hear a voice.

Beggs hesitated for only a second, but it was a second too long.

Ramsgill grabbed the gun barrel, pulling it away from Amy's head. Beggs realized what was happening, and slapped the barrel back in Ramsgill's direction. The flashlight fell to the ground and the light bounced wildly around them. The cold iron of the barrel caught Ramsgill in the face and he was knocked backwards off his feet. Beggs came at him with the gun. Ramsgill again grabbed the barrel, and the two men struggled for control. Then a flash of blue-white light ignited the chamber, followed by a deafening explosion.

The sting of shot seemed to hit him all at once in all parts of his body. But he still had the barrel of the gun, and Beggs was just above him. Amy was screaming frantically now, a mind-numbing pitch that was everywhere simultaneously. Beggs jabbed the gun down into

Ramsgill's chest, and again pumped the rifle's stock. Just as he was about to fire, Ramsgill thrust his feet upwards, sending Beggs reeling.

Beggs landed five feet away and let go of the gun. It clattered to the ground beside him with a live shell in the firing chamber. Beggs sat up, and before Ramsgill could get to him, made a grab for the gun.

But he didn't reach it.

Out of nowhere, Amy Denster kicked it away from Beggs, then picked it up herself. Beggs stood slowly and started in her direction. She said nothing, but began to shake her head, still sobbing. Ramsgill was frozen in his tracks. Beggs kept coming, and she kept shaking, until all at once, a silhouette filled the stair cavity.

"Easy," said Lyndsay Hill, now coming down the stairs.

Beggs looked from Amy to Hill and back again. She now had the gun pointed at his head.

"No, Amy," said Hill. "Let's put that down."

But Denster didn't hear him. She was on her own plane now, still shaking her head, humming again.

"Do as he says," Beggs said. "Please, Amy. Do as the inspector says."

Hill slowly came toward her, and the head-shaking became more furious.

"Amy," he pleaded. "No!"

And then the explosion erased Cheverton Beggs's head.

Eighteen

"*D*oes that hurt?" asked Robin Mallow, looking at Jamie Ramsgill. Ramsgill was seated on a sofa in Fiona Mallow's parlor, the five-year-old boy across from him, one knee propped on top of a leather ottoman. Ramsgill's face had a long purple bruise on the right cheek, and was peppered with small scabs—vestiges of his shotgun wound.

"Robin!" barked Margaret Mallow, seated beside Ramsgill. "That's cheeky!"

"It's okay," said Ramsgill.

The boy made a face at his older sister.

He then stepped away from the ottoman, held his hands out like he was an airplane, and zoomed out of the room.

"Mum says you are responsible for catching Cheverton Beggs," said Margaret, once they were alone. This was the first time Ramsgill had seen her since Fiona had told him he was Margaret's biological father. He found himself staring at her, trying to pick up small details that might connect her to him.

"That's stretching things," he replied. "Lyndsay Hill, the police inspector, had a lot to do with it, as did your mom."

"Did that girl really shoot him in the head point blank?"

Ramsgill smiled. He could see that Margaret was uninhibited, a trait he was sure he had contributed to.

"Yes."

"Will charges be brought against her?"

"It's doubtful. She was in a bad state of duress. I don't believe she knew what she was doing."

"Mum's been pretty down about the whole thing," said Margaret. "She says you might stay over here, to help out with the department."

"I'm afraid not," said Ramsgill. "In fact, I return to America in the morning."

Margaret's eyes fell to the soft fabric of her green skirt.

"You and Mum were close once, weren't you, Mr. Ramsgill?"

"Yes. Very close."

"What happened?"

"Well, your mom had to leave school, and soon after, I had to leave England."

Margaret looked up at him. Ramsgill saw the reflection of his nose, and the shape of his cheek in her tender face. Her blue eyes fluttered from side to side in a beguiling spasm, then locked onto him like question marks.

"Do you ever wonder what would have happened had you stayed?" she said.

"Sometimes."

"Mum thinks about you, that much I know for sure. I can see it on her face, when she mentions your name."

Ramsgill's lips eased into a smile.

"I know it's not fair," continued Margaret, "but I really don't want Mum to get remarried."

"Is that what you think?" said Ramsgill. "That your mother and I . . . ?"

Margaret shrugged.

"Margaret, I'm leaving tomorrow. I have someone back home whom I care for very much."

A visible sense of relief came over her.

"But there's nothing wrong with your mother's wanting to have a relationship. You know, even adults need love."

"But *we* love her."

"Of course you do. But not in the way that a man could."

"But . . . my father . . ."

She paused, biting her lip.

"You would like your mother and father to get back together."
She nodded.

"That would be nice," said Ramsgill. "But it probably won't happen."

Fiona Mallow came out of the kitchen and crossed the dining room, followed by Robin. She was carrying a tray of coffee. She placed the tray on an end table and handed Ramsgill a cup.

"And what are you two talking about?" said Fiona.

"Your love life," said Ramsgill.

Margaret nodded, her face slightly red.

"I can think of more interesting subjects," said Fiona.

"Yes," said Robin. "Like murder and gunfights."

"Robin, please."

Ramsgill took a sip of coffee, laughing softly.

"But Mum, you said yourself that that Beggs man deserved it."

"I know I did. But I'm sure it's a subject Mr. Ramsgill is tired of. And besides, it's your bedtime, young man."

Robin collapsed on the ottoman, clinging to its sides.

"I should really be going too," said Ramsgill, setting down his cup. "I've got to leave for London early."

Fiona looked at Ramsgill. "Do you really have to go? You haven't had your coffee. And I'm warming some bread."

"Thanks, Fi, but I'm afraid so. And this will only keep me awake." He turned and looked at Margaret, who was still studying him, then rose. Margaret stood and lifted her little brother.

"I'll take him up," she said.

"Thank you, dear." Fiona patted her daughter's cheek.

"Good-bye," said Margaret, shifting her brother's body so she could shake Ramsgill's hand. Ramsgill held her hand for a moment longer than a stranger normally would. He then let it go.

"Remember what I said," Ramsgill told her.

Margaret nodded.

"And good luck at university next year."

"Thank you."

She then carried Robin out of the room. A moment later Fiona's other son Colin came down to tell Ramsgill good-bye. Ramsgill and Fiona then walked to the front door. They stepped out into the dark night, which was charged with cold. Panton Street was redolent with the smell of wood smoke.

"Thank you for dinner," Ramsgill said, pulling up the collar of his jacket.

"You're welcome."

"And good luck with the department. Don't worry, things will work out. They always do."

She nodded.

"Have a safe trip," she said. "And tell Elena hello for me. I do want to meet her, Jamie."

He smiled and touched her shoulder. He knew that whatever he and Fiona once had was now a memory. But he was glad that she had told him the secret she had kept for almost two decades, and glad too that they were still friends.

"Oh, I almost forgot," she said. "I have something for you."

She went back inside. She returned a moment later with a small leather photograph wallet.

"Pictures of Margaret," she said. "I couldn't give them to you earlier."

He took the wallet and unsnapped the catch, fanning through them slowly before shutting it again.

"Thanks," he said.

"What's the matter? Don't you want them?"

"Yes. Yes. It's just that . . ."

"What?"

"Nothing. She's a wonderful young woman, Fiona. Let me know how it goes with her in school."

"I will."

She crossed her arms, then cocked her head slightly.

"By the way," she said, "what did you tell Margaret to remember in there?"

"That's our secret," he said. "Which reminds me. I have something for you too."

He dug into his pocket and pulled out a folded scrap of paper. He handed it to her.

"What's this?"

"It's Lyndsay Hill's home telephone number."

"What do I need this for?"

"Because he's expecting your call."

She gave him a dubious look.

"What did you do, Jamie?"

"I just told him a little white lie."

"What little white lie?"

"That you had told me you wanted to invite him over for dinner."

"Thanks very much." She frowned. "That's embarrassing."

"It's all I could do," he said snickering.

"Why?"

"Because I suggested he call you, and he said that he would, but there's no telling how long that would take. He'll find excuses. Just like you would find excuses, if I didn't make up the story about your wanting to have him over."

She smiled.

"You're devious, Mr. Ramsgill."

"Aren't I though?"

She reached out her hand. He pulled her to him and they embraced.

"So good night, Ms. Mallow."

"Good night."

Ramsgill slowly turned away from her, stuffing the picture wallet into his coat pocket. The leather heels of his loafers met the sidewalk and he gazed northward, resisting the desire to look back. A stiff wind curled in between the tight houses of Panton Street, and a few fat flakes of snow had begun to sift out of the blackness above. As he reached the streetlit corner he thought of being on tomorrow morning's plane. In his mind he could now see Elena's face cutting through the darkness, beckoning him. His lips edged up into an almost imperceptible smile. For the first time in almost two weeks he felt good about himself, and good about the prospect of returning home.